ZODIAC TACTICAL
RESCUE UNIT

CODE NAME:

VIRGO

D1519413

USA TODAY BESTSELLING AUTHOR

JANIE CROUCH

Cover created by Deranged Doctor Designs.

A Calamittie Jane Publishing Book

CODE NAME: VIRGO - ZODIAC TACTICAL

To Chasidy.
If you liked the back you ought to get a huge kick out of the front.
Thank you for all your help and encouragement.

Chapter 1

Harrison "Sarge" McEwan
   Five Years Ago

The Navy SEALs trained you to within an inch of your life.

Almost everyone had heard of the twenty-four-week BUD/S—Basic Underwater Demolition and SEAL—training and the infamous Hell Week SEAL candidates went through to weed out anyone who couldn't hack it.

But that was really only the beginning.

You still had months of training ahead of you before you officially earned your Trident: training in combat diving, land warfare, weapons, maritime operations, small unit tactics, demolitions, cold weather survival, parachute operations, and medical skills.

Only after that, oh yeah, and another full year of making sure you had all that information locked tightly in your head—training until all of it became muscle memory —did you become a SEAL.

I'd been in the Navy for the past seventeen years and a SEAL the past eleven. There wasn't much someone could throw at me that I hadn't been trained to handle.

But today's circumstances were one of those things.

Standing down.

Any trained soldier, anyone with a warrior mindset, would tell you that the most difficult missions weren't necessarily the ones where you looked death in the eye. The hardest ones were where you geared yourself up to do whatever needed to be done only for the mission to be canceled at the last minute.

That's what had happened to my team today here in the middle of the Czech Republic.

We'd been seconds away from infiltrating a building—fully armed, prepared to kill—when we'd been told to stop. The hostage situation had been resolved through more diplomatic means.

We'd immediately backed out silently, no one aware we'd been there, especially since we weren't officially supposed to be in the area at all. No lives lost, but the sudden reverse had left a shit-ton of adrenaline pumping through our systems.

After we'd debriefed, my team and I had been given some downtime to make up for the powers-that-be jerking our chains. Most of the guys had hit the bars. The liquor was cheap in Eastern Europe, and so were the women. They would spend their time drinking and fucking the frustration out of their systems.

Normally, I'd join the guys at the bar if only to babysit more than anything else. I was older than the majority of the team. Less rowdy. I made sure no one went too far off the deep end.

But today, I needed to be away from people, a chance

to get out of my own head. No one was surprised by me going off on my own. I wasn't exactly a people person.

We were in Prague, the canceled mission having been about a hundred miles south of here. The Navy had sent me all over the world, but this was a new location for me. I spent a few hours walking around the tourist trap areas of the city, then as the sun set, I found myself off the beaten path. The buildings weren't quite as clean here, the electricity a little more sketchy.

Another good thing about being a Navy SEAL was your training gave you confidence to go where most tourists wouldn't want to venture. I was pretty far from Pražský hrad—Prague's famous castle—or the Charles Bridge, another favorite of travelers.

And while I wasn't worried about handling any trouble if it came my way, I wasn't trying to attract it either. I kept my head down so it looked as if my eyes were on the ground, although I still took in everything going on around me.

And that was when I saw her.

A girl, she had to be a teenager, sitting on the lowest windowsill of an old house, reading a ratty paperback as night fell on the city. The book was falling apart in her hands, kept together only by her grasp on it. I would have walked by without giving her much thought if it weren't for that book.

I wondered what she was reading the way only someone who loved books could do. I didn't see a lot of young people reading paperbacks anymore—which made me feel so fucking old—they tended to be too plugged into electronic devices. So seeing her gave me a little hope that I wasn't completely over the hill yet.

I had barely passed by on the other side of the street when I heard her cry out. I spun out of instinct to find two men had joined her—one older, one younger. One of them had thrown her to the ground from her perch.

She got back up, pieces of paperback clutched in her hands, and said something to the men I couldn't hear. The younger guy, maybe in his mid-twenties, backhanded her.

All the adrenaline I had spent the past few hours attempting to get rid of came rushing back as her face jerked to the side.

This was not my problem, not my business. I knew that going over to help her could make the situation worse in the long run.

I had learned that growing up on our farm in Iowa when I'd found a butterfly attempting to make it out of its chrysalis. It had been struggling so hard I'd decided to help it and cut the outer shell just a little with my pocketknife.

But in the end, my help meant the butterfly didn't develop the muscles needed to survive once it was out. The butterfly had died because its wings were too weak to fly.

Helping this girl now might save her from a beating, but could very likely cause bigger problems for her now or in the future, which was the last thing I wanted to do.

But when the young man hit her again and she fell to the ground, paperback flying, my legs started moving on their own, walking toward the trouble. I could take out both men, permanently, but that would cause more problems also—international problems.

I knew the second they saw me. All three of them froze.

It was my size. I knew how to downplay both my status as an American and my size at six foot three and two hundred twenty pounds of muscle. But right now, I wasn't trying to downplay anything.

By the time I crossed the street, the two men had turned and walked away, the young one giving the girl one last glare. I stopped before I reached her, watching as she got off the ground and picked up the pieces of her book.

Her eyes, the clearest fucking blue I'd ever seen, met mine. Her brown hair fell around her shoulder as she wiped a little bit of blood from the corner of her mouth.

I didn't say anything. I doubted she spoke English. I just nodded and then turned back the way I'd come, hoping I hadn't made her life worse.

"Thank you."

I could have sworn I heard the words as I turned away, but I didn't look back. It was better for her if I left her completely alone.

I forced myself to walk back toward the touristy part of town and grab a bite to eat. That was better than the plan I wanted to pursue—tracking down those assholes and teaching them what it was like to get a hit by someone bigger than them.

Not my problem. I had to say it almost as a mantra as I walked.

I nursed a watered-down beer as I read my own paperback at an outdoor table facing the Charles Bridge a couple hours later when I blinked and did a double take.

It was the girl again.

She looked different. Her brown hair was pulled to the side over her face, covering those distinctive blue eyes. Her makeup and posture were different too—she was making sure not to draw attention to herself.

I took a sip of beer and watched.

She almost seemed to be lost, walking a little bit in one direction, then turning in the other, not making eye contact with anyone or trying to interact with them. But when she passed by one couple a little too closely, I realized what she was doing.

She was pickpocketing them. I chuckled to myself.

I watched over the next hour, switching from beer to coffee, as she found three different marks. There was no better place to find tourists not paying attention and caught up in the romance of the Vltava River than here.

And she was good at what she did. Small, quick, unmemorable…as long as she kept those blue eyes downcast.

Then he showed up—the younger asshole from earlier. He waited in the near darkness of one corner of the bridge. As soon as the girl saw him, she ran her earnings over to him.

By the look on his face, it wasn't enough. He grabbed her arm with enough force to leave bruises, jerked her closer, and whispered something. She nodded and pulled away quickly.

Whatever he'd said put her into a near-panic. Twice in the next twenty minutes, she tried to lift another wallet but was almost caught. Her movements were too jerky. Plus, it was getting later, the shops were closing, and people were more scarce and naturally more suspicious.

I kept my head down and my book in front of me so it didn't look like I was watching as the guy signaled for her to come back over to him. An overweight, balding man stood next to him.

I knew by her hesitant steps and the sly smile he gave the overweight guy, that the asshole had just become the girl's pimp for the night.

God fucking damn it.

Once again, I told myself not to go over there—literally or figuratively. This was a situation I couldn't do anything about in the very limited time I had in Prague. But still, I found myself paying for my meal, ready to move.

The girl wasn't interested in spending time with the fat

man; that was obvious. It was also obvious that she wasn't going to have a choice in the situation.

I scrubbed a hand down my face as Asshole pushed her closer to the fat man. She didn't pull away, but she hunched her shoulders like she was hoping she could disappear into the medieval-aged bricks.

Once again, I found myself rushing somewhere I had no business going.

Asshole saw me first, his eyes narrowing. This time, he wasn't going to walk away.

"This has nothing to do with you," he said in surprisingly good English when I got within earshot. "Go back to your business."

The girl's head flew up at his words, those striking eyes growing wide as she saw me. But then she went right back into her hunch, not pulling away from the fat man now holding her arm.

"How much for her for the whole night?" I didn't know any other way of getting her away from here without this ending in a beating for her.

That fucker who'd hit her earlier smirked. "Five hundred."

I kept my cool. "We both know that's not going to happen." Not that I wouldn't have paid five hundred to get her out of this situation, but I knew that would only cause more trouble in the long run. "I'll give you a hundred."

He crossed his arms over his scrawny chest. "For a hundred, you take her back behind the alley, and she'll make you very happy."

"Nikolai," the girl gasped, face flying up again, despair blanketing her features. This obviously wasn't usual business for her.

I wanted to beat Nikolai into the ground.

He smirked. "How about for one hundred and fifty,

7

you both can split her. $75 for each. Yeah? She can take it."

The fat man licked his lips as the girl blanched, breathing so rapidly I thought she might pass out. Fat guy obviously spoke English, looking excited because he was getting a bargain.

I was done with this shit.

I crossed my arms over my own chest, mimicking Nikolai's posture, but I had at least fifty pounds of muscle on him. "How about I pay you one hundred and fifty, I get her the whole night in my hotel room, and I don't beat the shit out of you?" I looked over at the fat man. "Out of either of you. My final offer."

The fat man turned and left. Good. Fucking pervert.

Nikolai didn't like my solution. He obviously wanted the girl to be as humiliated as possible.

"What are you going to do with her all night?"

"That's between her and me." I grabbed the cash out of my wallet and slammed it against his chest. "Don't look for her again until the morning."

Nikolai folded the money slowly. "You like my feisty girl? Fine, you have her all night. But I'll escort you to the hotel to make sure you get there safely."

So much for my plan of sending her on her way as soon as Nikolai was gone. I wanted to beat this little shit until he dragged his ass home crying for his mama.

"Fine by me," I said.

The girl was silent, all but dragged her feet as we walked the few blocks to my hotel. She sure as hell didn't look very feisty right now. There wasn't anything I could say to reassure her, so I didn't try.

Nikolai had the nerve to walk us all the way to the door of the lobby. "I'll see you in the morning, Bronya. I'm sure you'll have a big tip from your American. Be safe, sister."

Bronya.

I didn't know whether to hope that she was really his sister or not. If she was, maybe she wouldn't be subject to any of Nikolai's own advances. But if he was selling his own sister against her will…what a clusterfuck.

We left him and went inside.

"Do you speak English?" I asked her. I spoke a couple of other languages conversationally, but I didn't necessarily want to make that information public.

"A little," she whispered with no trace of an accent.

"Will Nikolai be waiting to see if you actually go up into the room with me?"

She nodded. "He will wait here at least a couple hours. If I come out early, he will want…"

She faded off. He would want her to give him any money? Obviously. He would want her to find a second John for the night? Probably. He'd want to slap her around some more because he was a dick, and I'd spoiled his humiliation plans? Maybe.

I had no idea what I was going to do with her once I got her in my room.

I had absolutely no interest whatsoever in having sex with a traumatized teenager being forced into something she didn't want to do. I had zero people skills, so talking to her to make her feel comfortable wasn't going to happen either.

As usual, all I wanted was to be left alone. But that didn't seem like an option. Not tonight. Not with her.

"I know my word doesn't mean anything to you, but if I promise not to hurt you, not to touch you at all, would you agree to come up to the room with me?"

9

Chapter 2

Bronya
  Five Years Ago

The big man was right—his word didn't mean anything to me.

But I followed him silently into the elevator anyway. I hadn't been lying about Nikolai waiting outside for the next couple of hours. By now, he would've called another member of his crew so that someone was watching both the hotel's front and rear exits.

If he caught me sneaking out of here before morning, I would definitely spend the rest of the night on my knees servicing anyone he could find who would pay. He'd probably offer my body for free to get back at me for turning him down last week.

His father had made it very clear that Nikolai wasn't to touch me unless I wanted it. And Gregory's word was law in our neighborhood. It had kept me out of Nikolai's bed for the past two years. I'd been sixteen when he'd noticed I had breasts and started a haphazard pursuit of me.

Until recently, making my life hell had merely been a random pastime for him. I hadn't crossed his mind often, so he hadn't made trouble for me.

But when I'd turned eighteen a few months ago, I'd publicly shunned him in front of some of his crew. It was then Nikolai had decided to put more effort into making me miserable.

Gregory had always been content with the money my pickpocketing put into his coffers. I'd been doing it since I was little, and I was quite proficient at it. Gregory had also used me for some larger burglaries from time to time.

I was good. I knew how to make myself unnoticed and work it to my advantage. That skill had kept me fed and relatively safe in the seven years since my parents died.

Until Nikolai had decided he wanted me.

I should've slept with him. Pretended to be in love with him. That would've bored him and sent him running.

The moment I said no, Nikolai became obsessed. When he realized I meant my no, that decision backed up by his father's edict, he became vicious.

There had been no leeway anymore if I couldn't bring in enough through my stealing. Suddenly, I was expected to use whatever means I had available—including my body— to bring in the required amount to stay within Gregory's protection. And without Gregory's protection, I wouldn't last long on the streets on my own.

I'd learned to live through it—even when Nikolai went out of his way to pick the least attractive men to sell me to —and I would live through whatever the big man walking down the hall in front of me had planned.

But no, I didn't believe him for a second when he said he wouldn't touch me. Not hurt me? Maybe. He'd seemed upset both times today when Nikolai had been exerting his power over me.

But no one spent one hundred and fifty American dollars for a woman and expected nothing in return.

I glanced at his face as he used the key to open the door. He was a lot more handsome than most of the men I was around—dark hair cut short. A strong jaw with a full day's worth of beard. But mostly, he was just big with wide shoulders—twice the width of mine.

I lowered my gaze when his brown eyes met mine, and I slowly walked into the room. It didn't matter that he didn't repulse me. I still didn't have any choice about being here.

I flinched at the click of the door closing. I was at his mercy. No one was going to help me, not even if I screamed. I'd never been sold to someone for a full night.

I knew what a man could want when he only had fifteen minutes. The thought of the things that could happen when he had a full night… I grabbed the strap of my rucksack across my shoulder, rubbing it between my fingers. Maybe I could use it to…

Then I let it go, dropping my hands to my sides. The bag wouldn't offer much protection against him even if I swung it as hard as I could. All it would do was make him mad, and then I'd still be at his mercy.

With every second he didn't say anything, terror spread further throughout my body. I stood in the corner of the room, afraid to look at him, afraid to run, almost afraid to breathe.

The room was plain but clean. The big bed took up most of it except for a dresser and a small refrigerator. My gaze dropped to the floor, and I saw his booted feet walk by then heard the creak of the bed as he sat down.

He still didn't say a word, but I knew what sitting at the

edge of the bed meant—what he wanted. Maybe he would still keep his promise and not touch me, but it looked as if I would be touching him.

There was no point postponing the inevitable. I swallowed and walked toward him, dropping down on my knees between his feet, reaching for the buckle of his pants.

"Wait, what? No." He stood up so fast I fell backward, blinking up at him.

"That's not what I want," he continued. "There wasn't anywhere else for me to sit, so…"

He was so much bigger standing over me with me lying on the ground, so I scrambled to get back on my feet. "You want me in the bed?"

He rubbed a hand down his face. "I would like for you to sit on the bed, and I will sit on the other side. So we can talk."

I stared at the giant bed then looked back at him. "Talk?"

"Yes, talk."

I sat down on the corner of the bed and looked at him, hoping this was what he wanted, afraid that at any moment, the rather polite American would disappear and a monster would take his place.

He sat down on the opposite side and held out a hand as if to make sure I didn't come over and kneel in front of him again. I wasn't going to do that unless he told me to.

"Your name is Bronya?" he asked. I nodded. "Do you have a last name, a family name?"

"Roch," I responded, surprised enough by the question to tell him the truth.

He nodded. "How old are you?"

I swallowed the bitter ball of despair. That was what the questions were about. The big man didn't want to have sex with a child. I thought about lying, telling him I was younger than I was. Maybe that would save me from his plans.

But all that would accomplish was getting me sent back downstairs to Nikolai. "I'm eighteen."

"Really?"

"Yes. Truly." I closed my eyes, back stiff, ready for a command, for me to resume what I'd started on my knees.

Or maybe he wouldn't speak. Maybe he would snap and point to himself like Nikolai had to the woman he'd forced to suck him off in front of me and his friends.

But the man didn't move. Once again, he didn't say anything at all.

So I sat there, watching him out of the corner of my eye, without looking like I was watching him.

"How do you speak English so well?" he finally asked.

I wasn't sure why he cared, but the longer he talked, the less time we had for...other things.

"My parents spoke English," I whispered. We'd spoken English almost exclusively for the first few years of my life.

"Spoke? Past tense?"

I nodded. "Yes, they died."

"How long ago?"

"I was almost eleven."

He reached up and rubbed the back of his neck. "You've been...working on the streets since you were eleven?"

I shook my head quickly. "No, not like this. Not..." I waved my arm around me. "Not with men. That has just been in the past few months."

I glanced over at him. He nodded, relief evident in his brown eyes. "You pickpocket."

"Yes. Usually. Only the other"—I waved my arm toward the bed again— "when Nikolai makes me."

His eyes narrowed, and he fell silent again. It still made me nervous. Should I try to say something?

"How did your parents die?" The question came suddenly.

"A car accident." I didn't know why he was asking, and I didn't know why I was telling him the truth, but somehow, I wanted to. "We moved to Czech Republic from Ukraine. My parents were professor and student, but after the civil unrest, we couldn't stay. And there weren't many jobs for a university professor of American literature."

"Your father was a college literature professor and your mother his student?"

I shook my head. "No, Mother was the professor. Father was her student."

For the first time, the man smiled.

"That goes against type. I like it."

I wasn't sure what that meant, so I just nodded.

"Their love of American literature explains a lot about you—your excellent English, and probably the fact that I saw you reading earlier today. Do you have the book you were reading in your bag?"

I swallowed. "No, I don't have it with me." I didn't want him to take it. I'd rather he take my body than my books.

His eyes narrowed. "You're lying. You need to be better at lying if you're going to survive."

He stood up, and fear shut down everything inside me. Now I would get a beating as well as being forced to do whatever he wanted.

"I'm sorry," I whispered.

I flinched as he walked past me, but he didn't stop, didn't grab me, didn't pull me my hair. Instead, he walked over to the fridge in the corner of the room and opened it. He took out a bottle of water and handed it to me.

"Don't be sorry. Be better at lying." I still waited for the blow, but nothing came. "Drink it." A moment later, a chocolate bar fell in my lap. "And eat that."

I tore open the wrapper immediately. It might end up costing me later, but I didn't care. When was the last time I'd had something like candy? I only got treats like that if I stole them, and usually, they weren't worth the risk.

I had barely finished the last bite when a package of peanuts dropped next to my leg. "Eat that too."

I wasn't going to argue. I hadn't eaten anything since this morning, and the money I would normally set aside to buy food I had given to Nikolai in hopes that I wouldn't be in the position I was currently in.

The man took his seat back on the other side of the bed, and I relaxed a little bit.

"The book you were reading earlier, was it in English?"

I nodded, taking another handful of the nuts.

"I like to read too. Will you tell me what book it is? Maybe I've heard of it. I promise I'm not going to take your book. Let me guess. It was one you got from your parents?"

I slowly lowered my arm and looked over at him. He was the only one who had ever figured out why my book was so precious to me even though it was falling apart.

"Yes. My parents brought their favorite book when we had to flee Ukraine. But the book is for children. Teenagers. That is what Mother taught—adolescent litera-ture. Not books a man would read."

"Try me."

"It is called *The Outsiders*."

He smiled.

Everything about his face changed when he smiled. He was still dangerous and big—someone who could hurt me

Chapter 3

Sarge
Two Years Ago

I touched the small scar that ran along my left eyebrow as I crossed the Charles Bridge. I hadn't returned to Prague for three years. I wasn't sure what I was doing back here now.

That wasn't true; I knew why I was here. I had just finished an operation for the security company I now worked for, Zodiac Tactical. My new boss and former SEAL teammate, Ian DeRose, had sent me to head up a kidnap and rescue mission, ironically not far from the village where our SEAL team had been told to stand down in a similar situation three years ago.

The day I'd met Bronya.

This time, there had been no standing down, no resolution via diplomatic measures. This mission, like most Zodiac Tactical handled, didn't involve governments or military. My team and I had been sent in to ensure the recovery and safety of a billionaire's kidnapped nine-year-old son.

Everything had gone according to plan if you didn't count the two dead bad guys. The kid had been reunited with his parents. No one on my team had been hurt.

These were the types of missions we handled as part of the company Ian had started last year. I'd been with him from the beginning and was part of his inner circle. I loved the work we did.

I'd always thought I'd be a lifer in the Navy, but fucking up my knee during a routine training exercise had ended my special forces career. It wasn't so bad that it affected me too much in everyday life, but it was enough that I couldn't be a SEAL anymore. Deciding not to re-up hadn't been hard. I'd been in twenty years, so I got out.

Zodiac Tactical had given me a job and a purpose. Ian trusted me to handle things for him—things like this mission—and I did. I liked being part of a team that got things done when normal routes or law enforcement couldn't.

In short, Zodiac Tactical kicked ass.

And while I'd participated in a number of Zodiac missions in the past year, Ian had also sent me on this one because he knew about my obsession with Prague, although he didn't know why.

He thought it was because of the beating I'd taken three years ago, the one that had given me the scar at the edge of my eyebrow. He thought I still had unfinished business here.

I touched the scar again, faded to the point where it could hardly be seen. I did still have unfinished business here, although not revenge on some thugs like Ian thought.

I had thought about my business here every day for the past three years. Had read *The Outsiders* way more times than any grown man should, and I wondered what other books her parents had taught her about.

To Kill a Mockingbird? Little Women? The Lion, the Witch and the Wardrobe?

I'd read them all. A grown-ass man reading *Are You There God? It's Me, Margaret* probably seemed strange to damned near everyone. There'd definitely been too much adolescent literature in my life these past three years, that was for sure.

Especially since after what had happened, I could only be called a fool for thinking of her at all. Or the damned books she loved so much.

Definitely a fool after she'd led Nikolai and his buddies right to me that morning. A fool for taking a beating I had the training and skill to stop because she would've been the one to pay the price.

And looking for her now in every possible person who could be her size? That made me a complete dumbass.

Yet, here I was.

I spotted her near sundown, still casing potential marks like she had been three years ago. Her hair was a little longer, pulled back into an inconspicuous braid, wisps hanging out to hide her face and those striking eyes. She was dressed like everyone around her—jeans, light-weight dark jacket, shoes that allowed her to move quickly.

I had no doubt if she was caught and had to run she'd shed the jacket and let down her hair, giving herself a different appearance in a few mere seconds.

She would run from me when she eventually saw me. She had too much self-preservation, too much intelligence, not to. Not that it would make any difference.

I'd still catch her.

I watched her for two solid hours. She wasn't the only

one who knew how to blend in and make themselves less noticeable.

She'd gotten better at pickpocketing, and she'd already been good when I'd studied her before. She chose her marks well, kept her body relaxed and nonthreatening, and used her petite stature to her advantage.

Nobody ever suspected a thing. She knew exactly when to crouch down to tie her shoe to keep out of a line of sight. Knew what people to bypass and what people to concentrate on.

Properly trained and off the street, she could be a huge asset for a business like Zodiac Tactical. Some of what our company handled needed someone with a deft touch who could disappear into a crowd. And we had an office in Paris.

Offering a beautiful thief a job was not why I was here.

Why the fuck was I here?

I was about to turn away, about to walk away from Bronya for good, when she made a face from where she was standing at the edge of the bridge and pressed a hand to her side.

She was hurt.

I watched her now, mindful of that, and could see the slightest stiffness in her posture when she was resting. She ignored it when casing a mark, but I could tell she was in pain.

I was so intent on studying her, figuring out how badly she'd been hurt that I forgot to make sure she didn't notice me. I knew the exact second she did.

She'd turned to follow a well-off couple so wrapped up in each other that they would never notice her, then froze as she spotted me, letting a prime mark get away. Her eyes narrowed, then grew large as she recognized me. Then she turned, smart enough not to run, but knowing she needed to get out of here.

I'd been watching her long enough to know which way she'd be going and turned the opposite direction so I could double back to cut her off. She would look behind her and think she'd lost me.

Using my long legs to my advantage, I walked quickly along the side of the bridge, careful not to draw undue attention to myself. I ducked into an alley—the same alley where Nikolai had offered to sell me Bronya. Once I was in the dimness, I ran, getting to the other end moments before she did.

She'd already ditched her jacket and let down her hair like I'd expected. She was looking over her other shoulder, in the direction from which I should've been coming, when I grabbed her arm and pulled her into the alley, trapping her between the wall and my body.

"Hello, Bronya."

Those striking baby blues blinked up at me. "What? How…?"

"You need to vary your routine more. I've been watching you the past couple hours. This is where you go when you want a break."

"I'll scream."

"Will you?" I kept my arms on either side of her, pinning her in, but didn't press up against her. I didn't know how bad her injuries were. "Do you want to bring the police here? Have them take us both in for statements? Make sure they know what you look like?"

Her mouth popped shut. We both knew she wasn't going to scream.

"How badly are you hurt?" I asked her. "I saw you flinch at certain movements."

She turned her face away. "I'm not hurt."

"I see you still haven't gotten much better at lying."

She glared up at me. "I'm not hurt enough for it to be any of your business."

That fire in her eyes sent me shifting back a little even though I wanted to press closer. It was way too alluring for someone who was a decade and a half younger than me. She may not be a teenager anymore, but that didn't mean I was going to be one of the men who used her.

"But you're hurt enough for it to bother you. What happened?"

She shrugged. "I was running and needed to jump over a banister. I hit it wrong and bruised my ribs."

I wanted to ask for more info. Who had she been running from? Police? Nikolai?

I wanted to ask if her life had gotten any better since I'd seen her last. She looked okay. Intelligence and wariness simmered in her eyes, not defeat or blankness. But she was obviously still in a shitty situation.

"What do you want, Sarge?"

She remembered my name. Why the fuck that mattered to me, I had no idea. But it did.

"I want a repeat of three years ago."

I didn't know who was more surprised by my words, me or her. They definitely hadn't been what I expected to say.

"Minus the part where you bring your boss and his goons to kick the shit out of me," I added.

She stiffened. "Do you want revenge? To beat them? To beat me?"

The hell of it all was that she looked prepared to take the beating if that's what she had to do. Maybe that was part of her life now.

"What if I told you that I could have stopped what

Nikolai's men did? That I was trained to do exactly that, even at five-to-one odds?"

"Then why didn't you?"

I eased a little forward. "Because I knew who he was going to take it out on if I fought back. I have a couple of brothers who I scuffled with all the time growing up. I know how to take a beating." Much better than someone of her size would.

"Why would you do that for me?" she whispered.

That was the question, wasn't it? I didn't have an answer.

"Where I come from, men protect women," I finally said. "My father always protected my mother, my brothers protect those who need it too."

She looked down then back up at me. "I didn't lead Nikolai to you that day. He tricked me. But I'm sorry. I should've done more to stop it."

"No harm done."

She reached up and touched the small scar above my eyebrow. "Some harm done."

I stepped back farther at the touch of her fingers on my face. Damn it, why was she affecting me so much more today? For three years, I'd thought about her, and not one bit of it had been sexual.

But now...everything about her was affecting me differently.

Sex wasn't why I was here. But at least now I was figuring out what had brought me to this particular area of Prague. My subconscious had known all along.

I dropped my arms from either side of her, a little surprised when she didn't bolt immediately.

"Will Nikolai be coming by for his daily take soon?"

She shook her head. "Probably not him, but someone, yes."

"Do you have enough?" The thought of someone forcing her to sell her body again sent rage coursing through me.

"Yes."

"Do you want to make more? Like I said, I'd like a repeat of three years ago. I'll pay one hundred fifty dollars if you come up to my room for the whole night, and I promise not to touch you."

"Why?" she whispered, still right in front of me as if my arms still had her caged. "Last time, you were trying to save me from Nikolai. Why this time?"

"I want to offer you a job."

Chapter 4

Bronwyn Rourke
Present Day

S arge was in trouble, and I was finally going to have the chance to rescue him for once. I didn't think this day would ever come.

Not that a Paris bar with two women hitting on him was much of a dangerous situation. Still, he looked... panicked. Which was pretty hilarious, given that the bar where we'd all gotten together held at least a dozen Zodiac Tactical employees. All trained to handle multiple sorts of dangerous situations with deadly force.

So was Sarge himself.

Sarge was quite safe, not that you could tell by the look on his face as the two women, both with American accents, fawned all over him.

I hadn't known he was going to show up today at the Paris Zodiac office. He hadn't visited once in the entire year I'd been working there. Ian DeRose, the owner of

Zodiac, had been around a few times, plus a number of people high up in the company. But not Sarge.

I hadn't known what to expect when I'd finally made it to Paris six months after Sarge found me in Prague for the second time. I'd walked into a nice office on the outskirts of the city, the card he'd given me clutched in my bloody hand. I'd handed it to the lady sitting at the desk and expected to be laughed at and turned away. Instead, she'd asked me to wait while she punched the code written on the card into her computer.

Within a few minutes, I'd been shown into the back, then subsequently hired, fed, clothed, and trained.

Bronya Roch had died. Bronwyn Rourke had been born.

I watched Sarge now as he smiled awkwardly when one of the women slid a little closer, laughing at something he said that couldn't possibly be that funny. He turned to face the bar, and both women turned with him.

He had no idea what I'd done, the risk I had taken by trusting him. I could never return to Prague. Ever. I'd die a horrible death as soon as Nikolai got word I was back. And he would. He would look for me forever.

But he wouldn't find me. I became more confident of that each day that passed. Became more confident in myself with each day of training Zodiac provided.

I would never be under Nikolai's control again.

Granted, I had spent the first few months in Paris looking over my shoulder every second, even knowing that Nikolai and Gregory didn't have ties here.

If the job with Zodiac hadn't existed, if Sarge had been tricking me, I wouldn't have made it. I knew that without a doubt. I owed Sarge everything I had become in the past year.

This life where I lived with the freedom to answer only

to myself, never forced to do things I didn't want to do? I owed that to him.

And I guess I could start my repayment with this rescue.

From two beautiful women.

The woman on the left side of him touched his wrist, and I narrowed my eyes as I picked up speed, crossing toward them from my table near the door.

I didn't like to see any other woman touching Sarge, which was ridiculous, of course. Our relationship wasn't like that. Our relationship didn't exist at all.

He'd always been handsome to me. Even when I was eighteen and terrified, I'd been able to recognize the good looks of his dark hair, strong jaw, and deep eyes. Meeting him again at twenty-one, I'd been even more aware of his appeal. And now, at almost twenty-three and no longer living in constant survival mode, I could see what was obvious to the two American women flanking him.

Even with his back turned to me, I knew his eyes were the shade of melted honey, clear with intelligence. His big body was formidable—long legs, broad shoulders—but not something he used to make others feel smaller unless he deliberately decided to. The stubble on his jaw did nothing to hide his handsome features. If anything, it accentuated them.

But that handsomeness was rugged, honed, like the man himself. There was nothing pretty about him.

Given that he had paid for two full nights with me in a hotel, Sarge had never shown any sort of physical interest in me whatsoever. But I still didn't like that woman's fingers on his arm.

My training at Zodiac Tactical had taught me multiple ways I could break her hand, multiple ways that I could do much worse than merely break a bone. I'd actually excelled

31

at it over the past few months. It ended up that my dexterity when it came to picking pockets also translated into close-quarter fighting. I now knew multiple ways to take down men twice my size.

Too bad I couldn't use it to take out these women.

I walked up behind Sarge and placed a possessive hand on his shoulder. I had to remind myself that this was an act as I felt the firm muscles under my fingers. "Sweetheart, I leave you alone for a few minutes and you make all sorts of… friends."

Insecurity hit me as he spun in my direction. Did he want to be rescued? Worse, did he remember me? So much about me had changed since he'd seen me eighteen months ago, including my name.

But all that melted away when he gave me a smile. A real smile.

"Hey, Pony Girl."

That nickname combined with his deep voice did something to my insides that I wasn't sure I'd ever feel. The women on either side of him who'd also turned around, scoffed.

"Pony Girl? What kind of nickname is that?" the laughing one asked.

"Must be because she looks like a horse," the one now closer to receiving a broken hand replied. They both giggled.

I looked them over. They were everything I was never going to be. Feminine with ample breasts almost falling out of their tops, makeup skillfully applied to draw attention to their best features.

I'd lived my entire life trying to ensure I didn't draw the attention of others. I wouldn't know how to draw attention if I tried. And no amount of makeup was going to give me their figures.

But Sarge wasn't responding to them at all. He was only looking at me. Waiting to see what I would do.

So I said the first thing that came to mind. "Do you want to dance?"

"With you? Absolutely."

The women sulked as he set his beer down and didn't say another word to them, taking my hand and leading me out to the dance floor.

The area wasn't very big, and a number of couples were already on it. The song playing was an upbeat pop song that I'd heard before but had no idea how to dance to.

What had I been thinking? I could feel the women staring at us as I glanced over at the dancing couples, hoping I could copy some of their moves. That's what I had done my whole life—mimic others.

But I had no experience dancing whatsoever. Sarge might decide he was better off with the bimbos at the bar when he saw me try. They'd know how to dance.

I'd only made one small awkward swing of my hips when his arm came around my waist, and he pulled me up against his body, his other hand reaching out and grabbing mine.

"Slow is the only way I know how to dance, so it'll have to do." We began an unhurried sway that somehow worked with the song's upbeat tempo.

One of his hands cupped mine, and my other landed on his shoulder. My nose barely came up to the middle of his chest, and I found myself wanting to burrow in against him.

But, of course, that would make things a lot more awkward.

"Yeah, this is good," I said. "I'm not much of a dancer."

"Thanks for the assist with the double trouble over there. I wasn't sure if I was supposed to pick one or if they were going to double-team me."

I couldn't help but laugh a little. "I think most guys would consider both acceptable alternatives."

"Maybe. But those women aren't my type. I don't do casual sex."

Neither did I, although probably for very different reasons.

He swayed us back and forth. I could feel his big hand on my waist. "I didn't know you were in Paris until I saw you as everyone was leaving the Zodiac facility this afternoon."

"I came in yesterday. I watched you doing some training, but I wasn't sure if you would want to talk to me. Bronwyn."

I grimaced. "Yeah. I changed my name when I first got here. Thought it might be a little bit more common than Bronya. And Roch got changed to Rourke."

To my surprise, he nodded. "Those are both good choices. With your lack of an accent, the name won't label you as Eastern European."

I looked up at him. "You're not mad at me for lying to the place where you got me the job?"

We kept swaying. "All I did was approve the employment code that got you in the door. You making your way up the chain and proving your skills are valuable and that you could handle it? That was all on you."

I forced myself not to focus on his fingers making small circles on my waist. "I never really understood how that code worked. I wasn't sure that the job was real until I got to the Paris office."

He shrugged. "All the core team members of Zodiac Tactical have a code that we can give contacts, people who might be useful to the company on a contractor or employment basis. So we're all able to connect people to the business if we feel it's appropriate."

After a year with Zodiac, understanding how the company worked, the business they did, I could understand the policy. More than one person I worked with here in Paris had been recruited by a core member.

On paper, Zodiac Tactical was labeled security contractors, a private military company. It had been started by billionaire Ian DeRose three years ago, and thanks to his own military background and the team he'd surrounded himself with—people like Sarge—it had grown into one of the largest and most respected security organizations.

Zodiac did a little bit of everything: risk consulting, intelligence gathering, private and corporate guarding, international hostage negotiation and rescue. But not just for the rich who could afford it. Zodiac helped those in need whether they could pay or not.

And I was part of this organization. It meant everything to me.

"Thank you," I whispered up at Sarge. "Thank you for giving me a chance."

"Thank you for rescuing me tonight. I'm not good with people, even ones like them." He nodded toward the two women who were still glaring at us. "Especially ones like them."

"If they bother you any more, I can take them out in the parking lot and teach them a lesson. I've got the training for it now."

He smiled, and little dimples appeared on either side of his jaw that I wanted to reach up and touch. "I've heard you've become one of the most skilled full-time employees we have in this office. And I saw you sparring. It was pretty damn impressive, and I already knew how quick you were."

My fingers smoothed out the material of his shirt on his shoulder. "It ends up what I knew about fighting was wrong. I thought the strongest and biggest person would always win. But that's not the case."

"No, it's not," he said. "The smartest person wins the fight. You use what you have to your advantage. And you have a lot of advantages."

His words sent a heat through me. He admired me. It was almost inconceivable. "I haven't had to use any of those skills on a mission yet."

I wished I'd had them when I'd lived in Prague. It would've made my life a lot easier.

"Good," he said, "I hope you never have to."

"It turns out I like stealing from bad guys." I smiled up at him. "Rather than tourists who aren't paying attention."

"Your supervisor showed me your file today. It looks like you've been doing some good work. Important work."

I was never going to be a bodyguard like many of the people on the Paris team—I didn't have the size or patience for it. But my ability to get in and out of places unnoticed and to liberate or retrieve needed items had been put to good use the past couple of months after my supervisors had made sure I was trained properly and trustworthy. I'd done my best to prove that.

The music changed, but we kept dancing. "I'm going to Marrakesh next month."

Was it my imagination or did he pull me slightly closer? "I know. I was on the conference call when the mission got approved. You be careful."

I would be breaking in to the office of a museum to retrieve stolen data. It would be the first mission where I was the lead.

"So you already knew I was going? You already knew for sure I was an employee here, even with the name change?"

He nodded. "The inner team discusses all important missions. So yes. And yes, I've known you were here since that code was first entered."

"I'm surprised I haven't seen you before now. I expected to." I shrugged. "I thought you worked here."

"No. You needed a chance to make a fresh start on your own. To make your own decisions without anybody else around. I hope you've been able to do that."

I had, and it was because of him. But…I'd thought he'd be a part of the process more and been strangely disappointed when he wasn't.

"I have eight hundred dollars for you," I blurted out. It had been the first thing I'd saved and it was sitting in a drawer in my kitchen.

"Eight hundred dollars?" he said with a laugh. "What for?"

"For the two nights at one hundred and fifty dollars and for the five hundred dollars you gave me to help get me out of Prague that second night."

It hadn't been enough, and I had paid the price with blood and terror, but he didn't need to know that.

"I never expected you to pay back that money. There's no need."

"I want to," I said. "Please. I don't know how to explain it, but it's important to me."

"You don't want to be in anyone's debt again."

Relief flowed through me. He understood. "Yes."

"Then yes, I'll accept it."

We danced the same way through a couple more songs, and soon the Zodiac team members were all heading home after enjoying an evening together. Sarge and I found ourselves outside in the cool Paris night air.

"Can I walk you home?" he asked.

I wanted him to walk me home. I wanted to show him the tiny flat I lived in. I wanted to show him all the books I had on my shelves and my own kitchen with dishes and even my own bathroom. I wanted Sarge to see what my life had become.

And…I wanted him to stay with me tonight.

I knew my fellow employees at Zodiac thought I was distant and maybe conceited. I kept to myself and never dated. I wasn't interested in anyone romantically, only in making myself the best Zodiac employee I could and in carving out a future for myself. Sex, romance… They had no place in my life.

But for the first time in years, maybe ever, I wanted a man.

This man.

"Yes, walking me home would be great. I'm not far from here."

We talked about literature on the way, not my parents' books, but current favorites of our own. In the past few months, I'd spent all my free time reading. Evidently, he had too.

He climbed silently behind me up the four flights of stairs to my flat. I smiled as I let him inside and showed him all my private treasures—candles, a collection of sunglasses, my beloved books, including the ragged copy of *The Outsiders* sitting proudly on the shelf.

If he thought it all ridiculous, he never let me know.

I gave him the eight hundred dollars in cash. He respected me enough to take it without argument and put it in his pocket.

The studio apartment was tiny, and I didn't have

anywhere for us to sit comfortably. I had just one chair at my small table; the only other option was the bed on the other side of the room.

I gestured toward it. "Want to sit?"

"I should probably go."

"You don't have to go." The words came out in a rush. "I mean, I'd like you to stay. Here. With me. Tonight."

He closed his eyes and let out a breath. "I can't."

"Can't or not interested?" It took all my nerve to ask that, but I needed to know.

He opened his eyes. "Actually, neither option."

I tilted my head as I studied him. "Doesn't that mean you can and you are interested?"

He crossed the few feet between us more silently than someone his size should be able to. He cupped my cheeks. "Yes, it means both those things. But I'm wheels up in a couple hours, and some rushed quickie wouldn't be right for either of us. You deserve more, Pony Girl. Better."

He knew that the rushed quickies I hadn't wanted were all I'd ever had. I hated that he knew it almost as much as I hated that it was the truth.

I nodded, keeping my eyes down. "I understand."

He stepped back, letting go of my face. "In a few months, there're going to be some transfer opportunities into the Denver office. Maybe you'd consider trying out the United States for a while. I'd like that."

That would mean seeing him on a regular basis. I smiled. "I've always wanted to see the USA. I'll definitely look into it."

"Good." He smiled too. Those dimples. "Good luck on the Marrakesh mission. They're not going to know what hit them. You'll be perfect."

"I've been training every day to make sure of it."

He nodded, and we stood there looking at each other for a long minute.

"Close your eyes," he whispered.

I did, amazed that there wasn't a single bit of hesitation or fear in the action. This was Sarge. He'd gone out of his way to never hurt me.

His lips brushed against mine. Softly, gently. Not quite a full kiss, but a promise of more to come.

My first real kiss ever. He couldn't possibly know that.

"It was nice to meet you tonight, Bronwyn Rourke. I hope to get to know you better in the future."

With one more brush of his lips against mine, he was gone.

Chapter 5

Bronwyn

I was in Africa.

Morocco was in North Africa, so it wasn't the Africa most people thought of. No rhinos or elephants here. But a lot of desert.

Still, I was in Africa.

A couple of months from now, I'd be in America if everything went as planned. Transferring to the Denver office.

At that point, I would have been to three out of seven continents. Maybe I should make it a goal to get to all seven sometime in my life. A bucket-list item. I'd learned that term pretty recently.

Maybe Sarge would visit a couple continents with me. Asia. South America.

I hadn't heard anything from him since he'd left Paris three weeks ago, but I hadn't expected to. He knew I'd be spending every spare minute preparing for this mission. A lot of pieces had to fall into place perfectly in order for this to work.

"How you liking Africa so far?" The voice of Jenna Franklin, tech support for the mission, came through the earpiece I was wearing.

"Currently, it's a little underwhelming," I whispered.

Jenna and I had become almost friends over the past month as we prepared for this operation. She was also based in Denver. Yet another reason to go there.

Not that I needed another one.

"Hanging out in that tiny section of closet for hours can't be fun. Glad you're not claustrophobic."

Being cramped in here for three hours to wait for the small museum on the first floor to close was more uncomfortable than anything else. But I didn't mind. Uncomfortable I could do.

"Boring but manageable. I'll have to come back to Morocco sometime and take in more sights. Have you ever been here?"

"No. I don't really travel."

"You mean outside of the USA?"

"I don't travel anywhere. Zodiac lets me work from a computer command center in my house. It's why I took the job, because I wouldn't have to go into an office. I...I don't like to go outside. It's complicated."

"Oh." There was obviously so much more to the story than she was saying, but I didn't want to push. I knew what it was like to have things you didn't want to discuss.

"Yeah."

"Do you mind that everyone calls your team the nerds?" I wanted to change the subject, but as soon as the words were out of my mouth, I realized this new topic might be just as bad.

But Jenna laughed. "No. It's a badge of honor—

nobody means it with any disrespect. Plus, we actually gave ourselves the nickname. Everyone else merely makes sure it never dies."

We fell into silence, and I took turns tightening and loosening different muscle groups in my cramped space.

"Did you have any problem switching the key card with Omar Zeroual?" Jenna asked.

That was why this mission had been deemed perfect for me. It required someone who could pickpocket a key card without being caught, hide in a tiny section of a storage closet, not get spotted by any security cameras or guards, and get the data that had been stolen via corporate espionage out of the safe. Make it out then hand it off.

All skills I'd already had that Zodiac had honed in the past year.

"Not at all. I would've thought he would've been more on edge, given that he stole the drive to begin with."

"Overconfident. That's brought down a lot of people."

We fell into silence again, and I waited, keeping my mind focused on what I needed to do next.

I would not mess this up. I would prove myself a valuable member of this team. When Sarge read the report of this mission, and I knew he would, he would see that he'd been right to recruit me.

It was another hour before Jenna spoke again. "Okay, Bronwyn, you're clear to go."

"Roger that."

I eased out of my tiny hiding place, stretching to get the blood flowing correctly to my body parts. Jenna and her team were electronically hijacking the cameras, so I wouldn't be spotted. They were also using infrared to let me know where the guards were.

I had studied the blueprint of this building so I could make my way around in the dark, which I did. I couldn't use any sort of light that might be visible through the windows.

I made my way down multiple hallways, stopping when Jenna told me to, sometimes rerouting in a different direction. A very close call with a guard forced me to hide in a stairwell and got my heart racing, but he didn't notice me.

I was dressed from head to foot in black, my hair tucked under a beanie. If anyone caught sight of me, they wouldn't be able to tell my gender or age. Given the sociopolitical climate of this area—part of what I'd studied to prepare for the mission—the average person who might catch a glimpse of me would assume I was male. Another reason I'd been chosen.

Because I could be mistaken for a boy. Sigh. But not something to think about now.

I made it to the office and used the key card—plus a code a different member of Zodiac had accessed last week —to open the safe.

I stared at the contents of the safe a little longer than I should have. Stacks of cash, some jewelry, and various papers filled up the space around what I was here for. More wealth than I had ever seen or thought would ever be kept in one place.

If I grabbed the necklace—diamonds—and money, I would never have to worry about being poor again. I could do whatever I wanted. Go wherever I wanted.

Except Denver.

If I grabbed anything but the computer drive out of this safe, my time with Zodiac would be over. My time with Sarge would never start.

"You good, Bron?" Jenna asked in my ear. "Is it there? You seem frozen."

I switched out the small computer drive and shut the safe. "I've got it. I'm on my way out."

"Roger that."

She directed me back through the hallways to avoid the guards. A tiny window in the staff breakroom on the first floor was my way out. Another Zodiac team member had changed the hinges a couple weeks ago so that it opened much wider than it should've. But it was still too narrow for almost anyone to fit through.

Almost anyone. I climbed onto the table and shimmied my way through, catching myself with my arms and rolling into the alley on the outside. A moment later, I was on my feet and walking away from the building.

"I'm out."

"Roger. You're still clear. Change appearance at next block."

I removed the beanie and wrapped a scarf around my head. I turned my jacket inside out, so I wasn't in all black. I never stopped walking the whole time.

"Outlaw is standing by at the rendezvous spot. Great job, Bronwyn," Jenna said. Mark Outlawson—everyone called him Outlaw—worked for Zodiac as a contractor. He would've been my backup if I'd gotten into trouble in the building.

But I hadn't gotten into trouble. I'd done the job they'd given me. I couldn't stop smiling. "Thanks. That was actually fun. You missed out."

She chuckled. "I'll leave the adventuring to you adventurous types. I'm quite happy here with my computers."

She stayed in my ear until I met Outlaw in the lobby of my hotel a few blocks from the museum. I handed off the computer drive without making any eye contact with him at all. If anyone saw us, they wouldn't have noticed a thing.

Outlaw would get the drive out of the country and back into the correct hands. If someone had caught sight of me in the museum, they definitely wouldn't be looking for anyone his size, and now I wouldn't have any incriminating evidence on me.

"Outlaw reports he has possession. You're done, Bronwyn."

"Thanks for guiding me, Jenna."

"My pleasure. Congrats on a successful mission. We'll talk more at debriefing tomorrow."

The earpiece clicked off. I was still smiling as I rode up the elevator to my room. I would fly out tomorrow, back to Paris, but tonight, I was on my own.

I would call Sarge. I would let him know how it went. I knew I couldn't use any specifics over an unsecure line, but maybe I could talk through the temptation I'd run up against when I'd opened that safe.

Sarge would understand. I'd always hated that he knew my past, but that would come in handy now.

I opened my fancy hotel room door with the key card, still smiling. I wasn't sure I'd ever think of a hotel room without them reminding me of Sarge. This was the only one I'd ever been in without him.

I flipped on the light switch, but the light didn't turn on. I went over to the smaller lamp by the desk.

It didn't turn on either.

I was a second too slow, too complacent, too secure in my own newfound skills.

That one second cost me everything.

I hit the wall of the hotel room with a force that stunned me. I fought back, but there were at least two attackers, both equally as trained as me. One caught my kick, the other pushed me back up against the wall, restraining my arms behind my back so I couldn't move.

I must have been spotted. Maybe earlier today? Omar Zeroual was a millionaire. Maybe he had sources we didn't know about. At least I didn't still have the drive on me.

I felt a sharp pinch in my bicep. I threw my head back-ward to try to catch the one holding me, but that just got me slammed harder against the coolness of the wallpaper.

"No bruises," another man said from the other side of the room. "I have a message that needs to be delivered to your boss."

The guy holding me spun me around to face the man who had spoken. I couldn't make out any of his features in the darkness where he sat on my bed.

"Telephones work better for messages," I spat out at him.

"I was informed you were feisty. Obviously true."

What the hell was going on? If these weren't Omar Zeroual's men, who were they?

And why was the room spinning?

"I'm not interested in passing along any messages." I struggled not to show my dizziness.

The man shifted on the bed. "We don't need you to pass on a message. You will be the message."

"I don't understand."

My words came out funny. The spinning increased. They'd given me something. That sharp pinch on my arm had been some sort of injection. I fought harder against the man holding me, but it didn't do any good.

The man spoke again. "I need Ian DeRose to start looking for ghosts. Until I make him one."

"What are you talking about?" If the big man hadn't been holding me upright, I would've slumped to the floor. "I've only met Ian a couple of times. He doesn't really know me. Who are you anyway?"

"My name is Erick Huen. I'm an old friend of Ian's. But who I am doesn't matter right now. Only you. You're young and pretty, and you work for him. You'll do just fine."

He stood up and walked closer. He was much smaller than the man holding me, but that didn't make me any less afraid.

"Unfortunately, this process is going to be…uncomfortable for you." He was close enough now that I could see him; I didn't recognize him at all. I understood less and less as whatever they'd given me made me feel as if I was living outside my own body. He reached to brush a strand of hair away from my face. I didn't attempt to move from him.

"You're prettier than I thought. Younger. Such a shame you won't be either by the time we're done."

He nodded to the man holding me, and he let go.

I should run. I should fight. I should do something.

But I couldn't.

My body didn't seem to be mine anymore.

Chapter 6

Sarge

I didn't let Bronwyn know I was listening in on the feed between her and Jenna during the mission. I didn't want to make her nervous or put undue pressure on her.

But I wanted to be available if anything went wrong, to be able to lend immediate assistance from half a world away. If Bronwyn panicked, I wanted to be in her ear to provide support.

Hell, I wanted to be in Marrakesh ready to step in if needed. I had almost inserted myself into the mission. But that would've brought up way too many questions. Not only from the Paris office, but from my own friends here in Denver.

I was high up enough that I wouldn't have needed to explain myself, but my silence would've raised more questions.

I never wanted anyone at Zodiac—especially Bronwyn

—to think she hadn't made it on her own. Truly, all I'd done was get her in the door.

And check up on her nearly daily since. That was one of the advantages of my position in the company. Access to all forms, reports, and footage.

But she had been the one to succeed since she'd arrived in Paris. She'd worked hard, constantly learning and improving. Every single supervisor had been impressed by her work ethic, intelligence, and, of course, nimble little fingers that could take whatever she wanted without anyone noticing.

I listened silently in my office as the mission in Marrakesh unfolded perfectly. Bronwyn had kept her wits about her even when a guard came way too close. She'd gotten into and out of the safe and made the transfer to Outlaw like she'd been doing this sort of thing for years.

I was so fucking proud of her. It was almost a fatherly pride, except despite the more than a fifteen-year age gap between us, there was nothing fatherly about the way I felt toward her.

I'd known it the second our lips had touched in the apartment. Hell, I'd known it for a long time before that.

My nickname in the Navy may have been Sarge, which had started as a joke since the Navy didn't have a sergeant ranking, but my code name at Zodiac was Virgo. I did happen to be born in September under that star sign, but that wasn't why I'd been given Virgo as my moniker.

Virgos were known for being practical, honest, and people who took their commitments seriously. I could've been the Virgo poster child.

The Zodiac Tactical code names might have been haphazardly created by Ian DeRose's housekeeper/mother figure, but the one she'd chosen for me fit me well. And she hadn't known my birth date.

Virgos were also stubborn. I hadn't escaped that trait either. But my stubbornness when it came to Bronwyn was to give her all the time she needed. I could wait. I could wait until Bronwyn was ready. See if she and I fit together the way I hoped we would.

I heard Jenna's congratulations to Bronwyn for a successful mission and shut down my computer with a smile on my face. Bronwyn had done it. Not that I'd had any doubts she would.

I was still smiling as I fell asleep with eyes as blue as the sky filling my vision.

~

My smile was gone eighteen hours later.

"Why am I just hearing about this now?" Ian barked into the phone at his ear.

I was only halfway listening, waiting with coffee mug in hand to see how I needed to be involved. I'd stayed up half the night listening in on Bronwyn's mission then had put in a full day and evening at work. I'd been about to go home when Landon Black, another one of Ian's right-hand men, and I had been called to the conference room by one of Ian's assistants.

I made a beeline for the coffeepot. Zodiac had offices all over the world, and there was always something that needed to be handled. It was like being back in the SEALs —we had to be prepared for anything.

"Do we have people still there?" Ian continued.

I took a sip of my black brew. Ian was worried. He scrubbed a hand across his forehead as Landon and I looked at each other. For once, Landon didn't have a half smile on his face. Whatever was going down wasn't good.

"Send everything you have on Rourke. And the transcript of the Marrakesh mission. Have Outlaw report in on the hour and get more boots on the ground immediately."

I set down my coffee at his words, caffeine no longer needed to get me firing on all cylinders. Adrenaline coursed through my veins at the sound of Bronwyn's name and the details of her mission.

Something had happened in the hours since I'd stopped listening.

"What's up, boss?" Landon asked when Ian dropped his cell phone down onto the table in front of him.

"The mission in Marrakesh went south."

I had to stop myself from contradicting him. If that mission had gone any further north, it would've been knocking on Santa Claus's door. It had not gone south.

But I shouldn't know that, should I?

"What happened? Is someone down?" Landon asked.

Is someone down?

That was the important question. Was Bronwyn down?

Ian touched a button, and screens silently slid up in front of each of us from the conference table. A few moments later, electronic files appeared on the screen... details of the Marrakesh mission, the transcripts Ian had demanded that I'd already heard, and a large picture of Bronwyn with those blue eyes.

"Bronwyn Rourke didn't show up at her exit point from Marrakesh six hours ago."

I blew out a silent breath. There wasn't a dead body. That was the most important thing.

"Rourke." Landon sped through her file. I didn't need to look at it. I was already aware of the contents of everything on the screen in front of me. "I remember us approving the mission last month. Rookie but with exceptionally high marks. Mission success probability was high."

"Looking over this transcript, mission was a success. She did her job perfectly."

Damned right she did.

"The drive was handed off without any problem in the hotel lobby," I interjected. Both my friends nodded.

"From there, she should've been fine. Gone up to her room and laid low until time to leave," Landon said.

Ian nodded. "Jenna and the tech team are working their angles. There was no footage in the hotel lobby, which is one of the reasons that hotel was chosen for use, so that's a dead end. The nerds are checking to make sure she wasn't spotted in the building she robbed. Outlaw is there too, poking around in person. So far, nothing unusual."

"She's a complete noob," Landon said as he flipped through one of the files. "Are we sure she didn't get lost or lose track of time or something? Marrakesh is a maze."

I didn't say anything. As a leader at Zodiac, I'd be pissed if that were the case, but as a man, I'd be nothing but thrilled if she'd just gotten caught up in the moment.

"She's yours, right, Sarge?" Ian asked. "Got any insight?"

Mine. I grimaced. "I knew she'd be useful based on observation of her pickpocketing skills and ability to blend into a crowd when I saw her in Europe. I gave her the Paris office address eighteen months ago and didn't have much contact after that."

All true, but not the whole truth.

Ian looked up from his screen. "Any concerns we should be aware of?"

"No. Except for maybe she's young." Way too young for me to have kissed her or to be thinking about anything else. Maybe I needed to put a halt on her transfer to

Denver. Having her on the same continent was a mistake. This situation might prove it.

"Roger that," Ian responded. "The team is going to run the normal drills—check hospitals, keep trying her cell, focus to make sure she wasn't caught after the handoff. Let's hope this was a rookie mistake and we have her back in pocket in a few hours."

A few hours later, we had no new data. But we did have a shit-ton more questions, and I didn't like any of them.

Both Jenna and Outlaw were on video conference with us.

"She seemed fine at the handoff." There was the slight delay in Outlaw's words since he was on the other side of the world. "Didn't give any duress signal."

"The drive was legit." Jenna looked into the camera. "Team has already cracked it. And there's been no sign that the bad guys are aware it's missing yet."

"How do you know?"

"The replacement drive has a virus that will put them back to the stone ages." Jenna's smile was vicious for such a small and generally nice woman. "If they connect it to any computer linked to their network, they're going to feel it hard. But there's been no sign of that all day."

Landon leaned back in his chair. "We're way past the point where she could've gotten lost or spent too much time in the shops."

I didn't say anything, but nobody expected me to. I'd never been the most talkative person in a room.

"I've been going over her file." Ian looked at me. "I know you recruited her based on her unusual skill set. Those skills are also the reason she was chosen to lead this mission. A thief who can blend in without trying."

"Yes." True, although I'd recruited her to get her out

of that hellhole of a situation, not necessarily because of her skills.

"She didn't give us much info for her file. Name. Date of birth. That's about it. She didn't have an address, no known kin, no tax ID number. We were paying her under the table until Jenna built her IDs."

Jenna ran a hand through her shoulder-length black hair. "And, full disclosure, there was no record of a Bronwyn Rourke when I built her ID. I wanted to make sure I wasn't linking into further problems, so I did an extensive search of that name in most of Western Europe."

She hadn't been looking in Eastern Europe, although it wouldn't have mattered. Jenna wouldn't have found a Bronwyn Rourke even if she'd gone farther east.

I shrugged. "She's not the first Zodiac contractor to use an alias."

Everyone murmured agreement. The entire rogue subsection of the company consisted of team members who had pasts that needed to stay buried. Granted, most of them weren't used for normal missions, but Zodiac had never shied away from people with secrets.

Hell, Ian had his own secrets.

"Was there anything about the mission that struck anyone as odd?" Ian asked. "I've read the transcripts. Bronwyn was in that closet a long fucking time."

"She seemed to handle it okay," Jenna responded. "No claustrophobia or any indication she was under duress. The only time I wondered if—never mind."

"What?" Ian, Landon, and I all said at the same time.

"I'm not trying to say this is what I think happened," Jenna prefaced. "I've gotten to know Bronwyn over the past couple weeks, and I like her a lot."

Ian looked at her on the screen. "It's okay, Jenna. Speak your mind."

She blew out a breath. "At the safe, Bronwyn paused. It was the only time when I was concerned we might have a problem."

"What do you think that means?" I asked.

She got quieter. "Probably nothing. Forget I said anything."

I saw the slight tic in Ian's eye, but he didn't let any of his impatience show with Jenna. The woman wasn't open about her past, but we all knew it involved enough trauma that she never left her house. I'd only met her in person once, and that was because I'd gone to her.

I took over for Ian. I wasn't the best with people, but this was important. "Jenna, tell us, even if it looks bad. Nothing is off the table at this point."

"It was Omar Zeroual's safe. He's a criminal, but he's also one of the wealthiest men in Morocco. There had to have been a lot more in that safe than just the drive. Cash, almost definitely. Jewelry, probably. Bonds. All sorts of valuable stuff. Maybe the temptation was too much for her."

I wanted to deny it outright, but I couldn't. The truth was, I wasn't sure I could blame Bronwyn if she'd done exactly what Jenna was insinuating.

Ian looked over at me. "You got an opinion about this theory?"

I kept my eyes steady on his. Ian and I had been friends and teammates too long for me to be anything but honest. "It's possible. Like everyone has pointed out, Bronwyn is young and has a history we're not familiar with."

I was familiar with it more than anyone else, and knowing it didn't make the situation less feasible.

Ian nodded. "If she stole from Zeroual, then she's in the wind, and I don't want to waste time and resources looking for her. What does your gut tell you?"

I looked down for a moment to really let myself process the question.

What did my gut tell me? Not what I wanted to be true, but what did I really think was going on here?

Ian didn't rush me for an answer.

I thought about Bronwyn's sincerity in Paris when she'd thanked me for getting her the job at Zodiac. The light in her eye when she'd told me about her training. The feel of her sweet lips against mine when I'd kissed her.

But mostly, I thought about the eight hundred dollars sitting in a drawer in my bedroom. She hadn't had to give that to me—I definitely hadn't expected it or wanted it. But it had meant so much to her to pay off her debt.

Without any words at all, that spoke volumes about her honor.

"My gut says she's in trouble. I don't think she took anything out of that safe she hadn't been sent there for. It might have been a temptation, but she resisted."

Ian nodded. "Then we keep looking."

Chapter 7

Bronwyn

I sat in a dark cell. I didn't remember how I'd gotten here. There was no furniture, no toilet. Only a cold floor, cold walls, and a cold metal door.

The slit in the door opened as it had multiple times before. I blinked at the light, which felt garishly bright against the darkness even though I knew it wasn't.

"Say it."

A male voice. I didn't know who. Not Erick Huen, the man from the hotel. Someone else.

My answer was the same as it had been each time. "No."

I wouldn't say it. They couldn't force me.

They could keep me here, covered in my own filth, no food, and barely enough water to stay alive, but I would not say it.

The slit in the door slammed closed.

The light was gone. My bravado went with it. The

temptation to call out, to ask the man to come back, to say what they wanted me to say almost overwhelmed me.

I knew what was coming next. It didn't change. It wouldn't change, not until these people got what they wanted. Whatever that was.

I exist only to obey orders. My final mission is to go home. I exist only to obey orders. My final mission is to go home. I exist only to obey orders. My final mission is to go home.

I gritted my teeth as the recording played from speakers I couldn't see, high in the corners of the room I couldn't reach.

Over and over and over.

It only stopped when they came in to give me the injections or to demand I say the words myself.

Injections happened every two hours. I had forced myself to count the seconds after my third shot, doing my best to ignore the words droning on around me. Seven thousand two hundred seconds. It had taken me nearly as long to figure out exactly how many minutes that was.

Three men came in each time to give me the injection. Two to hold me down, one with the needle.

Four days' worth of shots and the words that never stopped.

I tried to walk around in the darkness, to dilute whatever they were putting into my system, but by day two, I was too weak.

I exist only to obey orders. My final mission is to go home.

I was close to breaking.

Maybe I could've withstood the darkness, or lack of food or sleep, or the constant phrases. Maybe I could've withstood whatever it was they were injecting into me that alternated between making my mind feel fuzzy and separated from itself and making my skin itch until I was sure there were bugs all over me.

But I couldn't withstand it all.

I tried. I tried to remember anything from my Zodiac training that would help. I tried to think of what Sarge would do in a situation like this. He would remain strong. He would refuse to say the words. He would keep himself quiet and calm.

I wasn't as strong as him. I was weak. I'd always been weak.

I wrapped my arms around myself, covered my ears, and tried to hang on to something. To find something to hope for.

The only thing I had worth hoping for was that Sarge and the rest of the Zodiac team would come rescue me. I'd been gone for four days. By now, they would know I was missing. They would be looking for me.

They wouldn't leave me here.

Sarge wouldn't leave me here.

I exist only to obey orders. My final mission is to go home.

I tried to count the seconds as the words continued. Tried not to cry, but my body was on the verge of severe dehydration, so there were no tears available.

I failed at both, rocking myself on the cold, hard floor. I wished I were anywhere else. Even back on the streets with Nikolai. Anything was better than this.

When the three men came back in, I didn't fight. Fighting them had never accomplished anything. I didn't even feel the sting of the injection.

They went away; the words continued. This time, whatever they'd put into my body didn't hurt so much. Or maybe I was getting used to the pain.

Something about the recording changed. The words

seemed less jarring, more…something. Easier to listen to. Melodic.

Maybe my mind had completely cracked.

I stopped rocking, laying my head on my knees. At least I wasn't hurting anymore.

Nothing hurt.

There was nothing at all.

Nothing.

I breathed in and out to the sound of the words from the speakers. They relaxed me.

Everything inside my brain turned off. I couldn't feel anything. That was good. So much better. Why had I been fighting this?

Eventually, the recording shut off, and the slit in the door opened again.

"Say it." The same male voice. "Say your words."

This time, I didn't hesitate. I didn't fight. I didn't remember why I had been fighting.

"I exist only to obey orders. My final mission is to go home."

When my mind floated back into my body, I was strapped in a medical chair. This wasn't the first time I'd been in this chair. I'd been here months ago.

No, days ago, not months. Or maybe only hours. Keeping track of time had become impossible.

Everything hurt. Sometimes it did, and sometimes it didn't, but right now, there was pain. Dull throbs radiated through my body as if the blood in my veins was beginning to overheat. I knew it would get worse.

I knew I would scream.

But right now, I focused solely on breathing in then

back out, keeping myself still. They didn't know I was awake. I was at the point where the pain hadn't overwhelmed me and the drugs hadn't shut down my mind again.

This was the only time I was me. It wouldn't last long.

"Is she awake?" That was the man from the hotel. Erick Huen.

I didn't open my eyes to look. I needed to learn, see if there was any way to escape.

At least I wasn't still in the darkness.

Why had I hated the darkness? I couldn't remember.

I couldn't remember specifics of anything.

"No," another man responded. Doctor. I heard his voice often. Medical stuff I didn't understand.

"We need her awake," Erick whined.

"We're dealing with a complex mix of gene editing and chemical subjugation. It can't be rushed. If she were conscious right now, she'd be in a lot of pain. There's no need to make our subjects suffer unnecessarily."

Suffer. Doctor had no idea.

Breathe in. Breathe out.

"We need to get the message to DeRose. I want him looking over his shoulder, trying to figure out what's happening. I want him confused and scared."

"I would like to remind you that this project is more than your personal vendetta for someone in your past. This is groundbreaking scientific work."

Erick scoffed. "Groundbreaking work in mind control that you would never get approval for legally. My partner and I are what is allowing you to conduct your research. Don't forget that."

There was a long pause. The fire in my blood was getting worse, making it almost impossible to keep silent. But I had to.

"I haven't forgotten," Doctor said. "Just like I haven't forgotten that until we learn more, parts of this experimentation are akin to torture. Don't lose sight of that."

"As long as it's Ian DeRose's people being tortured, I'm pretty sure I don't care."

"I do. We're rushing the process with Bronwyn. We're destroying parts of her memory, and unless I give her this daily drug regimen, the gene editing will be agonizing for her. Look at her blood pressure and pulse rising. If she were awake right now, she'd be screaming."

Almost. It was taking more and more effort not to.

The pain burned through me, scorching me, but it was the only time my mind was clear. The only time my mind was mine. Once he gave me the daily drugs, I wouldn't hurt anymore…but I also wouldn't be me.

"Will she be ready for London?" Erick asked.

A sigh. "Did you hear anything I just said?"

"Tippens, do what you're paid to do and get me my results. My partner is going to be very upset if you can't come through with what you've promised."

I swallowed a moan as the pain spiked. I could feel Dr. Tippens moving around me.

"It will work. And yes, she'll be ready for London. Every skill set she has under our control."

"Good." The glee was clear in Erick's tone. "And once she's outlived her usefulness professionally, we ship her back. She won't be our problem anymore."

The moan I'd been forcing down escaped my lips. I couldn't help it. Something Erick said triggered a memory, but I couldn't focus in on it. But it was bad. So bad.

I needed to get out of here. I began pulling at the wrist restraints.

"She's waking up. Let me give her the medication for the pain."

"It won't affect her abilities? London is important. She has to fool them all. DeRose has to think she's working for us."

No. No, I didn't want to trick Ian DeRose. Because that meant tricking Sarge too. I didn't want them to think I'd betrayed them.

I fought harder. Pulling at the wrist restraints that kept me strapped to the medical chair. I yanked as hard as I could, thrashing. I had to get out of here. I had to—

"You'll have your perfect thief, don't worry, Erick. Now, let me do my job. She's obviously in pain."

They thought I was pulling because I was in pain. I was and the pulling was making it worse, but it wasn't enough to make me stop. I had to get out.

I pulled at my wrists again, even when I felt the straps bite into my skin. Even when I felt the tiny pinch of the injection.

If I could get out of this chair, I could use my training, take down the doctor. Tippens, Erick had called him. Dr. Tippens. I could take him down. I didn't know if there were other guards, but I could get past them too.

I would fight.

But I had to go now. Now. I had to go now before...

Before what?

Before...

I stopped pulling.

"That's right," Dr. Tippens whispered. "It's already better, isn't it? The drugs work quickly."

The pain was subsiding, manageable. I opened my eyes and looked down at my wrists. One of them was bleeding.

That was important. My bleeding wrist. I needed to do something with it, but I couldn't remember what.

"Feeling better?" the man next to me asked. He was in

a doctor's coat. Was he a doctor? Who was he? Did I know him?

Where was I?

Who was I?

I couldn't seem to answer his question or ask any of my own. My voice didn't work.

"Say your words, Bronwyn."

The invisible fist that had been around my throat released. I could talk. Nothing hurt. Nothing was confusing. Everything was clear.

"I exist only to obey orders. My final mission is to go home."

Chapter 8

Sarge

"Sarge, we've got something on Bronwyn."

My head jerked up to meet Landon's eyes where he was standing at my office door. Something on Bronwyn would be either very good or very bad. It had been nine days with no word of anything having to do with her.

"A body?" Please, God...

"No." Relief coursed through my veins as he continued. "Ian received some sort of video concerning her. Nerds took it to make sure it wasn't some sort of virus and just gave the all clear. He's waiting on you to watch it."

I left everything at my desk and immediately walked out the door, jaw clenched to the point of pain. A video sent deliberately to Ian concerning Bronwyn couldn't be good.

"What's the word on Omar Zeroual?" I asked as we sped down the hall toward the conference room.

"Nothing new. We have eyes on him twenty-four seven, and there's been nothing to lead us to believe he has Bronwyn. He's busy trying to figure out what the hell happened to his entire computer system when he accessed that drive."

I gave a curt nod. Zeroual had the most reason to want to hurt Bronwyn. If he didn't have her, and they hadn't found her body floating in the Mediterranean, that was a good sign.

Ian was talking to Jenna via one of the conference table screens when we walked in. His lips were tight. "Good. Let's do this."

I knew it was a sign of utmost respect that Ian had waited for me to watch this footage. Zodiac Tactical was his company, built with his money. He hadn't needed to afford me this courtesy, even as a friend.

"Thanks for waiting," I told him.

He gave a curt nod. "Jenna, go ahead."

Jenna didn't look any happier than Ian as we sat around the table, each of us looking at our own screens.

"We received this video via email at zero seven hundred Denver time. We checked it for possible viruses first, but it came back clean. Subject line: A message for Ian DeRose."

"Play it," Ian muttered.

I gripped the table until my knuckles turned white as Jenna became smaller on the screen, making room for the video footage.

Please God, do not let this be a snuff film. Do not let me be looking into those beautiful blue eyes…lifeless.

The video was almost ridiculous, made to be deliberately jarring and annoying. Like something from MTV thirty years ago—logos and colors flashing, discordant sounds on top of music.

"What the fuck?" Ian muttered exactly what I was thinking.

After a few seconds, the obnoxious colors and audio subsided. I sat up straighter in my seat as a video image faded in.

Bronwyn walking on a sidewalk with three men.

She wore a sharp black blazer and pantsuit with heels, her brown hair pulled back in a business ponytail, sunglasses covering her eyes. She looked more mature than I'd ever seen her, for once not trying to blend into the environment around her. The woman on the screen didn't care if people noticed her.

The men walking with her, also dressed in sharp suits and sunglasses, weren't doing anything to keep a low profile either. They all walked with a purpose, although that purpose wasn't explained.

Bronwyn was alive. Right now, that was all I cared about.

A voice, disguised by a modulator, spoke.

"You destroyed what was ours. Now we will take what is yours, piece by piece. We will destroy."

The image of Bronwyn and the men faded to black and was replaced by one word and silence.

Mosaic.

The footage ended, looping to play again.

I looked over at Ian, expecting anger or confusion. Definitely not expecting to see most of the color drained from my friend's tanned cheeks and rage burning in his eyes.

He looked over at Landon, who seemed every bit as disturbed by the footage.

"What the fuck just happened?" I asked when neither Ian nor Landon said a word. "Play it again, Jenna."

Ian nodded, and we watched the clip again. This time,

I looked for any sign of…anything from Bronwyn. Distress, anger, tapping Morse code with her fingers. But there was nothing. Nothing more than an emotionless face—Bronwyn's emotionless face—as she walked with purpose toward some unknown goal.

As soon as the footage faded out, I wanted Jenna to play it again so I could look for more nuances, but Ian stopped everything.

"Mosaic," he whispered. "That can't be right. They're done. I ended them more than two years ago."

He looked over at Landon again, this time as if he needed reassurance of the accuracy of his facts.

"Mosaic was that organization you went undercover with law enforcement to stop, right?" I asked.

He nodded. "Yes. I took down the leader personally. Mosaic was destroyed."

I remembered vaguely. Ian had gotten out of the Navy before me. I knew he was doing some undercover work but hadn't known the details. All I'd known was by the time Ian hired me at Zodiac Tactical a few months after that, he was different from the man I'd known in the SEALs.

He'd had demons in his eyes. The same ones he had now.

"What exactly is Mosaic, and what do they have to do with Bronwyn?" Right now, it didn't matter if Ian had been incorrect in his assumption that Mosaic had been destroyed the first time or if they'd decided to rebuild and weren't clever enough to come up with a new name.

What mattered was that they were using words like take and destroy while zooming in on footage of Bronwyn.

Ian sat back in his chair, still looking stunned. It was Landon who answered. "Mosaic is a pretty name for a group of ugly people. They were a well-funded domestic terrorist organization into all sorts of criminal activity—

drugs, money laundering, weapons sales, information sales. Basically providing bad guys with whatever they needed."

Ian leaned forward, resting his elbows on his knees, combing his fingers through his hair. "It can't be them. It can't be."

He looked like he had seen a ghost. I wasn't sure I'd ever observed him this shaken.

"Ian killed the leader of Mosaic with his own hands," Landon explained when Ian stopped talking. "After that, the organization crumbled."

"Evidently, somebody decided to take the crumbles and rebuild," I said with a shrug. "Otherwise, what the fuck are we looking at here? And why did they involve Bronwyn?"

"Jenna, what do we know for sure about this footage?" Ian asked, sitting up a little straighter in his seat, finally looking more like the man who'd been our SEAL team leader and owner of a million-dollar security company.

Jenna enlarged herself on the screen. "The email it came from is untraceable. They made sure we wouldn't be able to get any sort of useful data concerning that. But the footage is real. That is definitely Bronwyn walking with those three men. It wasn't doctored."

"How about a timeline?" I asked. "Could this have been in Paris during some of her training and this Mosaic group got hold of it?"

Jenna shook her head on the screen, looking down at something else. "The footage is from London. We have the team working on specifics, but I can tell you that the shadows from the footage match the weather pattern in London over the past three days."

I scrubbed a hand down my face. "What exactly does that mean?"

"Mostly, it means that we're pretty sure she was in

London walking with those three dudes sometime in the past seventy-two hours."

"How sure?" Landon asked.

Jenna was typing as she spoke. "If I was going to put a number on it, I would say ninety percent."

We all let out curses under our breaths. We'd run entire missions based on lower-percentage surety from the nerds than that.

"Okay," I said. "What else do we know besides the fact that she's been in London with three guys recently?"

Jenna bit at the corner of her lip. "I'd prefer if you would give us more time to be sure before we make any accusations."

Accusations.

Landon's eyes met mine. Accusations meant once again Jenna was afraid Bronwyn was making bad choices.

"Speak your mind, Jenna. We work better knowing all the facts," Landon said, his eyes still on mine.

I gave a nod. He was right; knowing all the facts—even the ugly ones—was always better.

"In the hour since this email was received and cleared for potential electronic threats, I've had the whole tech team on it." Jenna straightened. "Figuring out they were in London was simple. There's a reflection for a couple of seconds in a car that goes by. Paused and zoomed in, you can see the wrought-iron fence and one of the shell-covered huts found in Grosvenor Gardens unique to London."

I nodded. "Okay, fair enough." She hadn't gotten to the accusations part.

"And like I said, based on weather patterns, it holds that this footage was in the past three days."

None of this was her point. "Continue."

"There was an office heist in South London twenty-four hours ago. One that would match Bronwyn's skill set. From what we can see from the police report, two people were caught on a security camera from the rear—a large man and smaller woman—both in suits. The woman had a brown ponytail. Not enough details to give the police anything. No arrests were made."

Two caught on camera, not four. But the other two men could've been acting as lookout and driver, not in the building.

"So you think she's working with them?" I asked, doing my best to keep my voice neutral.

Jenna shrugged and shook her head slowly. "This is why I wanted more time before saying anything. When I first heard the voice-over, taking piece by piece and destroying" —her voice deepened to mimic the melodramatic tone on the footage— "my first thought was that Bronwyn was in trouble. That she was being forced to do something against her will."

"Given what I know about the original Mosaic, if this new group is similar, that assumption would probably be accurate," Ian said.

Jenna let out a sigh. "The problem is I ran both of our nonverbal communication software programs on the images of Bronwyn, and nothing about her body language, posture, or movements suggests that she is being coerced in any way. Everything our programs could tell us suggested she wanted to be there."

"Those programs aren't always accurate," I muttered.

Landon raised an eyebrow. "They're accurate more often than they're not."

I threw a hand up. "You heard big bad voice-over guy say they were going to take and destroy. Doesn't that concern anyone but me?"

Jenna pushed her glasses up onto her head. "My

thoughts too, but then I wondered if it meant recruitment. That Mosaic was going to take whatever Zodiac employees they could flip and would therefore destroy the company."

I gritted my teeth and remained silent. Jenna had a valid point.

"I'm not taking anything at face value." Ian stood up. "None of it. Not that Mosaic is back, not that Bronwyn is working against us, and definitely not that we have all the facts."

Landon nodded. "This could definitely be someone trying to spook you. You have a lot of enemies "

Ian's face remained neutral. "Handle this," he told Landon. "I need to dig into my other contacts and see what I can find."

He walked out of the room without another word.

Landon looked back at Jenna. "Run everything again. All of it. We continue to assume that Bronwyn is in trouble, even if it doesn't readily appear that way. Report back as soon as you have anything."

She nodded. "Roger that. I'll get everyone on it."

I continued staring at the screen after it went dark.

"What the hell is going on with Ian?" I felt as if there were big chunks of info I was missing. "If Mosaic has formed a two-point-oh version, why does that have him shitting his pants?"

Landon was silent for so long I thought he might not answer.

"Ian paid a high personal price to shut Mosaic down the first time. I don't blame him for not wanting to face them again."

"The claustrophobia?"

Landon crossed his arms over his chest. "You know about that?"

"I know he's the first one out of an elevator and dislikes

being in the back seat of a car. He wasn't like that in the SEALs."

"It's Ian's story to tell if he chooses, but yeah, shit got bad for him when he was undercover. Real bad. So if he's a little jumpy at the mention of Mosaic, he has reason to be."

"Whatever this is, it feels personal against him. Somebody wants to spook him." And it looked like they had succeeded.

Landon nodded. "Agreed."

"My big question is, if they're trying to get to Ian, why use Bronwyn?" I asked, clicking so I could watch the footage again. "He doesn't really know her at all. She has no personal ties to him."

"Maybe low-hanging fruit." Landon shrugged. "She's a newer employee, might need money, easier to pick off. Plus, young with those big eyes. She has a fragile look to her sometimes when she doesn't realize it. Pokes all of us where it hurts to think of her being abused in some way."

I was very fucking aware of Bronwyn's fragility. She hid it well most of the time. She was smart and capable, but pieces of her were still the lost and broken teenager I'd met in Prague.

I watched the footage of her walking with the men. Nothing about that woman on the screen seemed fragile or lost in those moments.

Landon stood. "Look, I know I feel some sort of bond with Bronwyn, but you need to prep yourself for the fact that she may not be one of us anymore. Hell, she may not ever have been one of us. She could've been working an inside angle from the beginning."

I watched her walk with such purpose in her suit and heels. I had to admit, this was not the Bronwyn I knew.

"If I have to take her down, I will."

Chapter 9

Sarge

I watched the footage of Bronwyn at least a hundred times in the next twenty-four hours. I watched it in slow motion and at double speed. I watch it backward, in black and white, every way I could think of that might help me see something I'd missed watching it the time before.

I watched it until I knew every second of it from memory. The entire time, hoping Bronwyn would speak to me in some way. Anything to show she was in trouble rather than working for the enemy.

I watched until my eyes turned gritty, then I watched some more. But I never found what I was hoping to see.

As the hours went by, the news didn't get better. Every test the nerds ran on the footage of Bronwyn's body language made it look more like she was guilty. Details that trickled in from London painted a dark picture. The office burglary had been custom made for her abilities. A phone lifted off a businessman then used to gain access to his office and accounts.

Twelve million dollars had been stolen from electronic accounts. Even worse? The accounts hadn't been criminals or businesses. They'd been individuals' savings and retirement accounts. Bronwyn hadn't been stealing from bad guys this time. She'd stolen from people who would get hit hard by the loss.

And every single trail we followed pointed to her doing it willingly.

Shit.

I hadn't seen Ian since he'd left the conference room after we'd watched the video the first time. He was too busy digging into discovering if Mosaic was really back in business to care much about Bronwyn at the moment. He'd shut everyone out of his office, including Landon and me.

I stayed in the office all night the first night, but I knew I would be doing more harm than good if I tried to stay a second night. I was about to walk out of the building and head to my property on the outskirts of the city when I got a message from Jenna.

Might have something on B.

I spun and headed back into the conference room, video calling Jenna on the way. "What have you got?"

"I found something that might be something in the footage." Her words weren't as concise as they normally were, and she looked as exhausted as I felt. "To be honest, I'm not sure if it's legitimate or not."

"Tech stuff or about Bronwyn herself?" At this point, I would take either.

"Bronwyn." I sat down at the table so I could have a bigger screen. Jenna brought up the footage that I now knew by heart and stopped a few seconds in, zooming in on Bronwyn's arm.

"There." A red circle appeared on the screen to show me where to look. "It's some sort of bruise, I think. Here on her right wrist—an abrasion, like she may have been restrained."

I'd been so busy looking at Bronwyn's face or in how she held herself when walking with the men that I hadn't caught sight of what Jenna had noticed. "How did I miss that?"

"I don't think you can see it in the version of footage you have. I only saw it when I was looking in a reflection when they walked by that shop. I enhanced that."

I studied the zoomed-in reflection. Calling the quality grainy would be generous. But at one distinct moment, the sun peeked out from behind the clouds at just the right angle, casting a light on Bronwyn's wrist.

I sat up straighter at my desk when I saw the red mark on her skin—as if she'd been tied or handcuffed but had fought against it.

The blemish only lasted for a split second before the bracelet on her wrist slid and covered it.

It was enough for me. If Bronwyn had been restrained to the point of damaging the skin on her wrist, then there was more to all of this than met the eye.

Relief crashed over me. This was enough for me to fight for her. To demand that no one give up.

Jenna showed me the split second of footage again. This time, I was even more convinced.

"I think you're right. This is proof that there is fuckery going on, and we don't have all the facts."

Jenna enlarged herself on the screen. "I agree. And not because of the markings on her skin, but because I don't think Bronwyn would do this. I never should've said anything to make it sound like I thought she was guilty."

I shook my head. "Your job is to present the facts as they are, not as what we want them to be. Regardless of whether she was forced or not, the fact was Bronwyn was in London, and she almost definitely was part of that burglary."

Jenna let out a sigh. "The worst thing is I don't think this is enough to convince anybody else she's innocent. There are too many ways the data can be interpreted."

The markings were too indistinct. And even if they were conclusive as bruises or abrasions, that didn't mean Bronwyn was being forced against her will.

But it was enough for me. And as long as I was in her corner, I could help manage what people at Zodiac thought. "You're probably right. But it's enough to stop any sort of witch hunt."

"What are you going to do?" Jenna asked.

"I'm not going to give up on her."

I didn't give up. There wasn't a single day that I let my faith in Bronwyn slip.

But a month went by with no word from or about her.

I hadn't sat in the Denver office waiting for information to fall into my lap. I'd traveled to Marrakesh to make sure nothing had been missed. I'd gone to London and stood on the very street Bronwyn had walked with those men. I'd looked into the shop window that had provided the reflection that had let us know something wasn't right with Bronwyn's situation.

Neither London nor Marrakesh had yielded much

extra info. The scenes were too cold. I talked to multiple people, but no one remembered anything.

Both Landon and Ian were convinced that Bronwyn had flipped. Out of respect for me, they hadn't said so outright, but they were both too logical and tactically minded not to take what was so clearly in front of them at face value. Even the marking on her wrist hadn't convinced them.

I went to Paris on my own dime, taking vacation days. I wanted to see her apartment myself.

It told me everything I needed to know.

Nearly everything in it was gone. All her clothes, all the cash, everything of value. The empty apartment was meant to reaffirm that she had jumped ship and was indeed working for Mosaic.

But standing inside her door after having picked the lock, I knew with one look that she hadn't left this apartment of her own will. Someone had taken her.

Someone who didn't know her well enough to know that she never would have left the copy of *The Outsiders* her parents had given her.

All the other books, she might've left behind, especially if she'd had to travel light or was in a hurry, but not that one. Not under any circumstances.

I grabbed the book. It was coming with me.

"You hang on," I told Bronwyn, as if the pages in my hand were some sort of conduit to her. "You're not alone. I'm coming for you."

That book was never far from my sight as the weeks passed.

Landon and Ian were focused on figuring out what Mosaic 2.0 was up to. There were no more videos or direct threats, no more kidnapped employees, but evidently, this new Mosaic was real and back in business.

Ian no longer had demons in his eyes. Instead, he had determination. Whatever version of Mosaic was coming back, he was committed to defeating it.

And since Mosaic was the only link I had to Bronwyn —they had her, they'd bruised her—I'd been doing everything I could to help Ian.

Plus, we had all the regular aspects of Zodiac Tactical to run. People still needed guarding, international hostage situations needed negotiating, intelligence needed gathering. Our services were still vital, despite where our focus was right now.

But I still spent every spare second looking for any clues I could find about Bronwyn.

There was nothing.

When Ian got a message from some colleagues in Wyoming with information about Mosaic, he and Landon took off to hunt down the details. I didn't go with them since there was no mention of Bronwyn, and Wyoming seemed like the wrong direction to find anything about her.

Whatever info Ian brought back about Mosaic, I would sort through for any angles everyone else missed. Any angles particularly to do with her.

She'd lost everyone important in her life, had been used by the ones she'd been left with. I wasn't going to give up on her. I would keep searching.

I expected Ian and Landon to be back in a day or two —how much intel could they really get from a tiny town in Wyoming from a bunch of guys who taught civilians self-defense and weapon safety, for Christ's sake? But when they'd been there three days and Ian had already nearly gotten himself killed by Mosaic soldiers, I decided it might be time for me to join the party.

I was packing, about to head for the airport, when my computer started making an annoying beeping sound at me. I growled at it. I was shit with computers for the most part, much preferring to have a weapon in my hand than a keyboard. I'd rather be out in the action than at a desk.

I clicked on the mouse to get it to shut the hell up, then stared at the screen as it woke up and showed me why it was making all the commotion.

Because I had told it to.

Because Bronwyn had been spotted.

Chapter 10

Sarge

B ronwyn was in New York.

The nerds had had every facial ID software on the market—and some they'd developed themselves—running from cameras all over the world since Bronwyn had disappeared.

Even with full nerd genius behind it, we always knew spotting Bronwyn would be a long shot. There was no way to run the footage from every camera we could access. We'd just gotten very fucking lucky.

I would take it.

The footage had caught Bronwyn in Midtown Manhattan walking alone down a busy sidewalk. She wore a navy blue dress and heels, no sunglasses this time, which had undoubtedly aided in her being identified. Once again, she didn't remind me of the Bronwyn I knew. Nothing about her was trying to blend in or remain invisible.

Of course, it was New York, so there were a lot of businesspeople who looked quite similar. She definitely didn't stick out.

"What do we do?" Jenna asked via phone as I drove to the airport.

"Home in on every camera you have in this area. See if we can pinpoint where she goes."

"We need to tell Ian."

"I will. Can you get someone to find me the quickest flight to New York and text me the boarding pass? I'll call you again when I'm on the ground to get any new updates."

Jenna hung up without another word. I didn't take offense. She wasn't good with people either, and she had a mission.

I immediately called Ian.

"Sarge. What's going on?"

"One of our facial recognition software programs pinged Bronwyn a few hours ago."

"Where?"

"New York. I'm going after her."

He was silent for a long moment.

"I know the chances of finding her are slim," I continued. She could be long gone before I got out of Colorado. "But I also know the chances of me sitting in the office without going fucking crazy are even lower. So I'm going. I'll take personal time if I have to."

Ian let out a sigh. "You don't have to take personal time. Just…watch your back. We found out that Erick Huen is part of Mosaic, which means this is more personal than we first figured."

I muttered a curse under my breath. Erick had been Ian's brother's best friend—and was a psycho bastard. We'd all thought he was dead, but evidently no such luck.

Erick's involvement meant exactly what Ian said: this was personal in the worst possible way. Erick wanted revenge for Ian taking down Mosaic the first time.

"Take somebody with you to New York if you want backup," Ian said. "Report immediately if you have any info."

"Roger."

But that wasn't going to happen. I didn't want anyone with me if I found Bronwyn. I wanted to be able to talk to her alone and find out what the hell was going on and how I could help.

And if she was making some bad choices, I was going to…help her figure out better ones. Even if that meant kidnapping her for a while.

I disconnected the call without another word. I was on my own. That was how I liked it.

~

Bronwyn was casing the situation for an upcoming heist.

By the time I made it into the city, the nerds had narrowed down her location to a high-end hotel in Midtown Manhattan. Once we knew where to focus, we were able to find out more details.

Bronwyn had been here at least forty-eight hours. The nerds had found all sorts of footage of her in different wigs and outfits, on different floors of the hotel, as well as the lobby. Jenna had sent me the snippets of footage she'd found.

Bronwyn didn't look like the girl I'd known in any of the footage, but I recognized her mannerisms—the way she kept her eyes averted, her body language subtle and unassuming. Now she was blending in the way she'd done in Prague.

She was definitely casing for a heist.

When the nerds cracked the guest list and we saw Peter Kerpar on it, we knew we'd found out whom she was targeting. He was a mid-level criminal from Boston who ran with the Bollini family. Mostly involved with their money laundering and cybersecurity. There were any number of things Bronwyn could want to steal from him. The nerds were digging deeper.

Normally, I wouldn't give a shit if someone like Kerpar got robbed. Zodiac wasn't in the business of protecting criminals. But Kerpar had a lot of security—four guys with him damned near everywhere he went—and if they caught Bronwyn, she'd be in trouble. Dead sort of trouble.

She had to realize that. What could she be about to steal that was worth her life? Was she being blackmailed?

When Kerpar and three-quarters of his entourage sat down at the bar in the hotel lobby, I parked myself in a corner booth and waited for Bronwyn to arrive. This was when she would make her move.

I didn't have to wait long. I forced myself to stay casual, barely looking up from the beer I wasn't drinking as she entered.

Just like old times. Me watching her while she did something dangerous.

She was dressed damned near perfectly. A flirty dress designed to draw attention but not look so risqué that anyone would mistake her for a working girl. Her hair was pulled back and makeup artfully applied to make her blue eyes seem bigger—if that was humanly possible—and to draw attention to her lips. A choker-style necklace adorned her neck, a bracelet on her wrist.

It took every ounce of self-control I had not to march

up to her, throw her over my shoulder, and carry her out of here. Get her somewhere safe then work out whatever shit was going on with Mosaic.

But I had no guarantees she didn't have someone else watching her to make sure she did whatever she was being forced to do to Kerpar. The nerds hadn't spotted anyone who fit those parameters, but that didn't mean the person didn't exist.

So I kept my ass in the booth and watched.

Bronwyn was smart, sitting at the opposite end of the bar, waiting for Kerpar to come to her. They chatted for a few minutes, her smiling, him moving closer. I saw the instant when her fingers slipped into his blazer and got his room key. He never noticed a thing. Neither did his shit guards.

She stayed with him long enough at the bar to keep him from getting too suspicious and then stood with a smile, his key card somewhere in that flirty dress.

Had she replaced the key card with an identical fake one? If not, he was definitely going to remember and suspect her when he couldn't find it. She was playing with fire.

As she turned from Kerpar with a smile, she looked in my direction. There was no way she didn't see me. I didn't duck. Didn't move. Our eyes met, held.

Nothing. There was nothing. Not a hint of recognition in her features as she looked at me. She may have become a good liar, but there was no way she was that good of one. A moment later, our gazes unlocked, and she turned toward the exit.

I immediately sent Jenna a text, standing once Bronwyn was out of the bar, walking in that direction.

I need to know what floor Kerpar's room is on.

I had a reply before I made it to the door.

1708

I knew where Bronwyn was heading. She would take the elevator, so I took the stairs. Seventeen floors wasn't an easy task, but I didn't let it slow me down. By floor twelve, I was fucking glad that we trained every single day at Zodiac to keep in battle-ready shape. You never knew when the battle would find you.

I spotted her as soon as I entered the hallway. She was almost to Kerpar's door. I needed to stop her. I threw my key card down the hall in front of me.

"Excuse me, miss?" I called out. "I think you dropped your key. Is this yours?"

At my voice, she stiffened and turned to me. Again, no recognition in her blank eyes.

"No, I have my key right here." She held up the key she'd stolen from Peter Kerpar.

"My mistake. Enjoy your evening."

I continued walking toward her. She gave me a smile that was as blank as the look in her eyes. She watched me as I traveled toward her, as if she didn't want to turn her back on me. Not necessarily unusual for a woman faced with a strange man in an otherwise deserted hallway.

But I knew the truth. She didn't want there to be anything that identified her as entering this room.

I walked past, breathing in perfume that smelled expensive and not at all the scent I placed with Bronwyn.

What should I do? I couldn't exactly knock her unconscious, throw her over my shoulder, and carry her out of the building. That would draw too much attention.

My phone buzzed in my hand, and I looked down at it.

911. Kerpar is on his way up to his room.

Shit. I needed to get Bronwyn out of there now. She was still standing at the door, and I turned and took a few steps back toward her. "Look, I know you don't know me and this seems weird, but I was wondering if you were interested in having a drink down at the bar."

Her expression didn't change. "Now's not a good time. But maybe tomorrow night? Around nine?"

She was completely blowing me off. This wasn't working, and we were out of time. I needed to try something different.

I stepped closer, into her space, and she stiffened. "Don't have time for an old friend, Pony Girl?"

My words changed something in her. She stiffened further, but not in the same way—not in a need to fight, but something else.

She was in there. Whatever was keeping her from recognizing me wasn't permanent. It didn't have total control.

"I… I…" She couldn't seem to get words out.

"That's right, Pony Girl," I murmured again. "Fight it. Whatever this is. Come back to me."

Those big blue eyes blinked. Then blinked again.

"Sarge?"

She was with me.

"Bronwyn. What the hell is going on? Come on. We've got to get out of here. Peter Kerpar is on his way up to the room. If you go in there now, you're busted."

And by busted, I meant that she was going to take a bullet to the head. Her hand was still on the door handle.

"I… I…" She shook her head back and forth, like she couldn't make a decision.

My phone buzzed again.

Stalled by holding the elevator. ETA 15 seconds

I had to get her out of there. I cupped the back of her neck and brought my forehead against hers. "You have to run, Pony Girl. Save your mission for another time. You can't do it right now. Kerpar is on his way up in the elevator. Run."

She did.

She dashed down the hallway, away from the elevators. I snatched the key card out of her hand and threw it back toward the door. Hopefully, when Kerpar figured out his key was missing and saw the one on the floor, it would alleviate suspicion from her.

I didn't wait to see if the plan would work. I ran behind her. We were barely into the stairwell before I heard Kerpar's obnoxious laughter behind us. So far, so good.

We both bolted down the stairs. She didn't try to say anything else to me. Didn't look at me or acknowledge I was with her in any way. By the time we reached the seventh floor, I was sure no one was following us. The plan had worked.

"Bronwyn, wait."

She kept going.

We made it down another half flight before I grabbed her arm and pressed her up against the wall, trapping her there with my body.

Just like old times.

"What the hell are you doing, mister?"

Those blue eyes were blank again. She didn't recognize me. Jesus. What the fuck was going on?

I pressed up farther against her. "Do you know who I am, Bronwyn?"

She obviously didn't. Her eyes darted around the stairwell.

"Pony Girl, it's me. Sarge. Do you know where you are? Do you know who you are?"

Those eyes flew back to mine. "Pony Girl."

"That's right. Do you remember?" I eased back from her slightly.

Once again, I saw recognition in her eyes. I smiled at her.

"That's right. I'm here to help. We'll get you whatever you need. I'm here to take you home."

She stiffened. "Home?"

"Wherever. We'll work out the details later. Zodiac can get you situated wherever will help you most."

"Zodiac." She blinked slowly, and when she opened her eyes, they were dead again.

Shit.

Her hand came up and touched her necklace, then her entire body stiffened. I waited for her to argue.

Instead, she kneed me in the balls at the same time her arm flew out with a punch meant to knock me to the floor. I forced myself to react through the pain, not to double over, protecting myself as she came at me in a series of punches and kicks that were designed to not just take me down, but to make sure I stayed down.

"Bronwyn, stop." I spun to the side then blocked her as she moved around for another attack.

She didn't respond. I grunted as I caught a side kick to the chest followed by a combination punch to the same area.

Fuck. That cracked a rib.

She was fighting as dirty and as strong as she could. I didn't mind a dirty fight, but it was much more difficult to win when I was trying not to hurt my opponent. Eventually, I would lose. That was inevitable.

"Pony Girl. Listen to me." The nickname had been the only thing that had gotten through to her thus far, but it didn't do anything now. She still attacked me with blazing speed and all the skill she'd learned from her Zodiac instructors over the past year.

She came down slightly off-balance from a roundhouse kick, and I seized my chance, locking her in my arms from behind, hoping my strength and size would be a determining factor. I got a headbutt that I was pretty sure broke my nose for my efforts, and she slipped out of my grip.

She followed that up with a right hook to the jaw. The left uppercut, I was able to block, but a kick to the kidneys that would have me pissing blood for a week dropped me to my knees.

She was trying to kill me.

If she had had a weapon, I had no doubt she would have used it already. I was going to have to really fight her if I wanted to survive. I jumped back up and threw out an uppercut of my own, catching her on the jaw and spinning her to the side.

"I don't want to fight you, Pony Girl."

"I exist only to obey orders. My final mission is to go home."

What the hell was that? The words themselves were scary enough, but that monotonous tone to her voice was spooky-clown scary.

We fought some more. Her doing her best to hurt me, and me doing my best not to hurt her but also not get killed in the process.

I wrapped my arms around her again, careful to keep my distance from that headbutting little skull this time then pushed her body face-first up against the wall, using my size against her. She had a lot of skill and a lot of speed, but when it came to size and strength, I had her beat. I still had to pin both her legs and her arms to keep her trapped against the wall.

"Bronwyn, stop fighting. Let me help you," I murmured against her ear, then quickly dodged another headbutt.

Her breathing was ragged. "No. I have to complete my mission. I must or…"

She threw her neck to the side, and from this close up, I was able to get a better look at the necklace around her neck.

What the fuck? It wasn't a necklace at all, at least not jewelry. It had some sort of small spikes that were pointing into her throat.

"Bronwyn, what is that thing? Is it hurting you? I don't understand."

"I have to complete my mission," she said again.

"Bronwyn. Goddammit, hold still." She started struggling against me once more, and I pushed her up harder against the wall. "If they're listening, if they're coming after you, I can get you out. I promise. Please, Pony Girl, I want to take you home."

She stopped struggling at that word—home.

"No. My final mission is to go home. This is not my final mission."

I didn't know what she was talking about. I didn't know how to help her. We both stood there against the wall, breathing hard.

"You have to let me go," she finally said. "It's the only way. I have to complete this mission."

She started repeating *the only way, the only way, the only way* under her breath.

I stepped back and let her go.

She was right. I didn't have the backup that I needed to help her. And if Mosaic was waiting right outside, I was going to do nothing but get us both killed.

And that necklace, I didn't know what the fuck that was, but it was obviously something being used to control her. Best-case scenario was that I knocked her unconscious, but then I'd have to carry her out through the lobby which was going to do nothing but get me arrested.

It took everything I had to stay still as she turned and fled down the stairs. I didn't want her out of my sight, but she was right.

This was the only way. At least for right now.

Chapter 11

Bronwyn

I sat in front of the mirror, sweat pouring down my face. I stared at my hand that hovered on the outside of my necklace on the left side.

I fought not to press the injector hidden in the piece of jewelry. Not because of the slight pain I would feel as the needle punctured my skin, but because of what I knew came next.

The emptiness, losing myself.

Pony Girl.

I closed my eyes as I heard Sarge's voice in my head. For a moment, the throbbing stabs in my brain and fire scorching along my skin eased.

I had been programmed to resist anyone saying my name. But Pony Girl was different—not me, but still me. The words had drawn me out of the depth of my mission-induced haze.

Sarge. It had been him. But the rest I could only

remember in jagged flashback. Had we run? Had we fought? I couldn't remember.

Pony Girl.

When I gritted my teeth and focused, I could still hear his deep voice in my ear.

That was what was stopping me from pressing the medication into my neck like I'd been trained to do. Like I'd been programmed to do. Like I wanted to do.

The pain would get worse until I pressed it again. I knew that. I knew it would eventually overcome me. But for the first time, I had a reason to endure the pain.

Sarge was here in New York.

Right? Was he here?

He would help me.

If he was really here.

I looked at myself in the mirror again. Was this another trick my mind was playing on me? Was I back in the dark cell? Was my mind cracking once again? Maybe Sarge wasn't nearby at all.

The phone on the vanity in front of me buzzed, and I lowered my hand from my neck to pick it up.

"Report," a male voice said. I didn't know whose.

"Plan A failed. Switching to Plan B tonight."

My eyes burned, and my stomach heaved at not providing all the information. Again, I was trained, programmed, to give all pertinent data concerning the mission.

But if I did, I would be putting Sarge in danger. So I fought, knowing if the voice on the phone asked for specifics, I wouldn't be able to hold them back.

I swallowed a shaky sob when he didn't.

"Will you be able to complete the mission?"

"Yes." I tried to keep my voice as cold and calm as

possible. Any emotion would give away that my conditioning was failing.

"Good. Complete your mission. Press your regimen now."

I couldn't disobey a direct order. I brought my hand up to the side of my neck and pressed the button in my necklace, feeling the pinch of the needle entering my skin.

"Finish and report," the man said.

"Yes." My voice was already steadier. Blanker.

"Say your words," the voice on the phone commanded.

"I exist only to obey orders. My final mission is to go home."

He ended the call, and I replaced the phone on the dresser in front of me.

I tried to keep Sarge's face in my mind, the sound of his voice in my ears. But with every second, it faded until it was gone for good. I stared at the face in the mirror until the person staring back at me was no longer familiar either.

•••

Sarge

There wasn't enough time to get the people I would trust most with this situation to New York. Especially since Ian and Landon were up to their necks with Mosaic shit in Wyoming.

I was still on my own. But I knew what Bronwyn's mission was and that she'd make another attempt at robbing Kerpar soon. That gave me at least a slight advantage.

Where I distinctly did not have an advantage was with

the woman herself. I had no idea what was going on with her. And I certainly didn't know what that scary-as-fuck necklace was she wore. When I described it to the nerds, they all agreed that it could be some sort of kill switch— something she couldn't control that could end her life if she didn't do what was being required of her.

That would explain a lot. But it wouldn't explain why I should probably be getting looked at by medical professionals right now. Why not tell me her life was in danger rather than do her best to make sure I didn't make it out of that stairwell alive?

Why had there been no recognition whatsoever when she'd first seen me? Then once she had recognized me, it had been as if she came in and out of her own consciousness.

This had been more than Mosaic holding her life in their hands. More than some sort of blackmail.

I wanted to know what the fuck was going on.

So the plan had changed. I wasn't going to stop her from robbing Peter Kerpar. The guy was scum anyway. I was going to help her. At the same time, I was going to put a tracker on her so we could figure out a game plan.

Ian wasn't going to be thrilled that I had commandeered his private jet to fly out a four-centimeter tracking device a couple hours ago, but he would have to bill me.

Now, I needed to get the tracker on Bronwyn. We knew her mission had to do with Kerpar, so we made sure we had eyes all over the hotel and especially on him. Jenna and her crew were able to hack his phone so that we could know his whereabouts.

I basically spent the next few hours lying around in the hotel, icing my various aches, waiting for Bronwyn to strike. As soon as the nerds got visual confirmation of her breaking in to Kerpar's room again, I would make my move. He'd been gone for a few hours, so I knew she'd be making her attempt soon.

Jenna had been nice enough to load a communication headset in with the tracker I'd be putting on Bronwyn. That way, I could communicate with the nerds, but it wasn't her talking with me now. Evidently, she was spending all of her time and expertise going through Mosaic information Ian had found in fucking Wyoming.

That was fine. I didn't need one of Zodiac's top minds helping me. All I needed was a warm body who could watch video footage and let me know when Bronwyn arrived at Kerpar's room.

I'd show up, not stop her from stealing whatever it was she wanted, and conveniently place the tracker on her. Hopefully, not getting any more ribs broken in the process.

I didn't need one of Zodiac's top minds helping me, but I had one anyway, just a different kind of brilliant. "You got anything for me, Outlaw? She's got to be making her move soon."

Mark Outlawson was in the Denver office. "Nothing so far, except me being about to stab a pencil through my eye because this is so boring."

I knew the feeling. "Yeah, I don't envy you."

"I feel kind of like this is somehow my fault," he said. "I should have noticed something was wrong in Marrakesh."

"I don't think when you saw her in Marrakesh there was any problem. I think it happened afterward." If there had been something Mark could see, he would've seen it. He was one of the best contractors Zodiac had.

"Either way, I'm glad I can help you get her back. Even if it's desk duty."

"I'd rather have you than some of the nerds. You at least know what I'm looking for."

I heard him pop his gum—the guy truly hated being behind a desk—and that was one of his coping mechanisms. "Some of them aren't so bad. Jenna, for instance. I can't understand why she's working in this department at all. She's sharp enough to be at any Zodiac office in the world."

"She has her reasons. Believe me. The Linear Tactical team helped get her out of a pretty bad hostage situation a while ago, but I don't have many details, and I don't want to press her if she doesn't want to talk about it."

"Yeah. I worked security for Cade Conner who is friends with those guys."

"The singer?"

"Yeah. So I've spent some time in Oak Creek, but I didn't know Jenna then. You're right, though, I'm sure she has her reasons for never leaving her house."

Outlaw didn't say anything else, and neither did I. We both knew what it was like to not share reasons publicly. Jenna could tell hers if she wanted to.

Twenty minutes went by without any sign of Bronwyn

"Where is she?" I muttered. "She's going to lose her window."

I couldn't stand the thought that she'd aborted her mission and I'd lost the opportunity to get this tracker on her.

"Yeah, it won't be long before Kerpar is back to the hotel. Maybe she couldn't find a way to get another room key—oh shit."

"What?"

"We've got a potential problem down in the garage. I've picked up Kerpar and his men coming in down there, and Bronwyn is there too. It looks like she's moving in for some sort of attack."

Shit. She wasn't trying to steal something from Kerpar's room; she was going to rob him in person.

There were so many problems with this plan I couldn't think of them all as I bolted out of the room and ran down the same stairway Bronwyn and I had fought in yesterday.

Kerpar had armed guards—four of them. They wouldn't hesitate to kill her. Plus, she wasn't trying to keep her identity a secret at all.

"Shit," Outlaw confirmed. "I think she is going to try to take them out herself. She's lying in wait."

I sped down the stairwell, taking the steps two at a time, ignoring the pain from my fight with Bronwyn. "I need you to kill the cameras down there. Whatever's about to happen, I don't want there to be any record of it."

I didn't want Kerpar's counterparts or law enforcement to be able to find her. Both would be looking.

"Roger that, boss."

"And don't let any 9-1-1 calls out of the garage either. Nothing unless you hear from me."

"You better be careful, Virgo," Outlaw said. "This has ugly written all over it."

"I know it does. It has from the beginning."

I didn't slow down until I hit the door for the garage. That I took quietly and was careful not to let it slam behind me. I ducked behind cars and made my way down to the VIP parking lot.

Kerpar, that cheap bastard, should've coughed up the fifty dollars to pay for valet. He could've avoided this.

I heard the noise before I actually saw them, but it didn't take long before I caught a glimpse of what was going on.

Bronwyn was fighting, once again not pulling any punches, and this time, she had a knife.

I stayed low but moved quickly. I could hear faint

moans as she got in blow after blow. I didn't know if she took any hits. I heard the sound of something metal hitting the ground and saw a gun skid across the pavement.

One man was lying unconscious or dead near a parked car. Bronwyn was fighting two others. It looked like the guards had stashed Kerpar in his own vehicle. Where was the fourth man? In with Kerpar?

I was about to intervene when Bronwyn used her knife to take down one of the guards with a stab to the neck. He wouldn't be getting back up.

She was fighting with the remaining bodyguard when I saw the fourth start to crawl out of the car, gun raised. I ran and dove for him just as he got his shot off. I didn't look to see if it had hit Bronwyn.

I ignored the pain in my ribs, landing against the man, throwing him the rest of the way out of the vehicle and onto the ground. I grabbed the gun from his hand and swung it around, clocking him in the head. He wasn't dead, but he wouldn't be waking up for a while.

Kerpar was huddled in the back seat as I climbed in. "You don't know who you're messing with. I have money. I can give you whatever you want. But if you kill me, I have people who are going to come after you."

"Shut the fuck up." I looked away from him to see if Bronwyn was still standing.

It wasn't me he needed to worry about. It was the five-foot-three brunette weighing hardly a hundred pounds currently kicking the ass of all his men who should be scaring him.

"You need to stay down," I told him. I didn't have any lost love for this man whatsoever, but I wasn't going to let Bronwyn take his life if I could stop it.

Before he could get another word out, the door on the other side jerked open.

Bronwyn. Once again not looking anything like the woman I knew.

"Room key." She held out her hand, voice dead. Completely emotionless.

"I'm going to fucking kill you, bitch. Do you know who I am?" Kerpar sputtered.

Faster than either of us could think she would move, she was inside the car and had slit Kerpar on his face with her knife.

"Room key now." She didn't even look at me.

Kerpar put a hand up to his bleeding face. "You cut me."

"I will continue to cut you every five seconds until you give me your room key."

Kerpar was at least smart enough to realize she meant what she said. He got the room key out of his pocket and held it out toward her. "Hey, you're the bitch from the bar, the one with the eyes."

She was going to kill him. I didn't know how he couldn't see it, but I sure as hell could. I dove across the car to stop her, catching her wrist midair, the knife pointing down at Kerpar's chest.

"I can't let you do that, Pony Girl. You're going to regret it someday."

Her eyes stayed glued on Kerpar. "I must complete my mission."

She still wasn't looking at me, but at least she wasn't fighting. Not the way I knew she could.

I didn't want to fight her while she had hold of that knife. The only way for me to stop that before it got out of hand would be to break her wrist—and at this angle, it would cause damage for the rest of her life.

We held our position with the knife over Kerpar, who

thankfully remained quiet. "Don't do this, Pony Girl. Stop now."

She bit her lip until it bled, but she still didn't look at me and didn't ease up. "I must complete my mission."

This was an internal struggle. She was fighting it as best she could.

If I wanted to get this knife out of her hand without hurting her, I needed to fight this battle within the parameters as they'd been set up.

"Does your mission require that you kill him?"

"No," she said without hesitation.

"Then let him go. Go complete your mission."

Her face contorted, and I knew she was fighting whatever was controlling her. I wanted to help her, to get her out now. But I had to play the long game with the tracker. It was the best way to keep her safe even if it meant letting her go now.

Increasing pressure on the knife to keep it out of Kerpar's chest, I grabbed the tiny tracker with my other hand. I reached up and cupped her neck, above that damned choker necklace, forcing her to look at me. "Complete the mission without killing him."

She jerked away, but I'd gotten the tracker on her where her neck met her shoulder. It was small and clear; she wouldn't notice it unless she did a full-body check specifically for trackers.

"You're both dead." Kerpar was still trapped beneath us on the seat. "I don't know who you think you are, but…"

I spun, hoping I wasn't making a huge mistake, and clocked him with my elbow, letting go of Bronwyn. He fell back unconscious against the door. She didn't look at me, but she didn't try to kill him again.

I eased back. "You're clear."

She got out of the car, and I climbed out after her. She still wasn't looking at me. But maybe that was better. I needed to let her go. I heard Kerpar groan behind me and turned back to him to give him one more solid punch on the jaw before she could decide killing him was the way to go.

"Virgo, watch your six. You've got—"

I spun, knowing I'd made a rookie mistake by turning my back on my current enemy—Bronwyn. I expected to feel the slice of a blade. I was looking low, ready to defend from the knife, not expecting the jumping roundhouse kick that caught me square on the temple.

I slid back against the car then down on my ass. I could hear Outlaw screeching in my ear.

She crouched down beside me, but she didn't have her knife out. She cupped the back of my neck.

"No trackers," she whispered.

Shit, she'd already found it. I had to get up. I had to stop her. Without the tracker, I wouldn't know where she was going.

"If you follow me now, we both die."

Her sharp chop to the carotid artery at the side of my neck and my entire world turned gray. The last thing I saw was her walking away before black took over.

Chapter 12

Sarge

I sat looking out at the view of the Rockies from my back porch. My house was relatively small and plain, but the view of the Front Range had made its high price totally worth it. Way too many times in the Navy, I'd wished I'd had some place I could be by myself with nothing around me but wide-open spaces.

Today, I was here less to enjoy the view and more because I was otherwise pretty useless thanks to Bronwyn's gifts from three days ago that kept on giving. A cracked rib and broken nose from our fight in the stairwell, a concussion from that roundhouse kick to the head. Dozens of bruises from head to toe.

And absolutely nothing to show for getting my ass handed to me by someone barely over five feet tall. She'd put that tracker back on my neck like I'd put it on hers. By the time I'd regained consciousness, Outlaw still screeching in my ear, she'd been gone. She'd gotten what she'd needed from Kerpar and disappeared.

When my phone rang, I wanted to ignore it, but I couldn't. Ian and Landon were still in Wyoming tracking down leads on Erick Huen and the rest of Mosaic. They had somebody they were hoping to send in undercover who could report back on Mosaic's inner workings.

I looked at the unknown number with a Seattle area code on my phone. Seeing that it was a video call made me want to throw the fucking thing across the yard, but I refrained. When the call connected, the screen was still dark. Maybe it wasn't a video call after all.

"This is Harrison McEwan." My voice was gruff, but I didn't give a shit. I didn't have time to play around. I needed to get back to solemnly staring at the mountains and feeling sorry for myself.

More silence, no picture. I heard breathing. Great, just what I needed, somebody butt-dialing me and not hanging up.

"Hey, did you dial the wrong number?" I asked. "Hello?"

I was a second from hanging up when I heard her voice. "Sarge?"

Bronwyn.

I dragged my feet down from the side table where they'd been resting, sat up straight in my rocking chair, and winced at the sharp pain in my ribs.

"Pony Girl?" I brought the phone closer.

She shifted a little so that light partially hit her across her face and I could see those eyes. She looked tired, in pain.

"Where are you?" I asked her.

"West. I don't know."

"Seattle? The number is a Seattle area code."

She looked around like she truly didn't know quite where she was. "Yes, Seattle maybe."

I stood up. "Can you stay there? I'll send someone for you. I'll come and get you myself."

She shook her head, her brown hair falling over her face. It looked unkempt, unwashed. "No, I don't have much time."

I kept the phone close to my face as I walked inside toward my computer. I needed to get the nerds tracing this number right fucking now. I was sending someone after Bronwyn whether she wanted me to or not.

"I have to go," she whispered. "I have a mission."

"No. Don't you hang up on me. Stay with me, Pony Girl." I didn't know how she was having this clarity now—able to recognize me and be the Bronwyn I knew, but I didn't want to lose it.

Her fingers came to the screen and touched it, as if she were trying to stroke my face. "I hurt you, didn't I? That was real. We fought."

"I'm okay. I can take a beating."

"You could have hurt me, but you didn't," she whispered. "I remember that. But I hurt you. I'm sorry. I should go. You probably don't want to talk to me anyway."

"Bronwyn, I do." I reached up and touched the screen, mirroring what she had done. "I do want to talk to you. Always."

"Why would you after what I did?" Her voice was hoarse, strained.

"You weren't fighting me because you wanted to. You were fighting me because you were somehow compelled to do it. I could tell something was wrong." I sat down at my desk and opened my laptop with one hand, keeping my eyes pinned to her on the phone.

"So you didn't fight back."

"I wanted to see if I could take you out without hurting you." I smiled, even though I knew it was tight. "Spoiler alert: I couldn't. You were too good."

Her smile was so grim it couldn't be called a smile at all. "I'm sorry. Don't come after me anymore."

"I will come after you. Every single time until you're safe."

I shot out an email to Jenna, giving her this phone number, typing with one hand, not looking at the words, so that my eyes remained on Bronwyn. I hoped Jenna would be able to understand.

"Can you tell me what's different now, Pony Girl? Why are you able to talk and be okay?"

Those blue eyes stared at me. "I'm getting stronger, but they don't know. They still think it takes the same amount of time, but I've been easing it back."

"Easing what back?"

"The meds. The injections. I fight the pain."

I had no idea what she was talking about, but I didn't want her to hang up. "Let me help you. Let me get you and help you."

She shook her head. "I don't have enough time."

Shit. I was going to lose her. "We know about Mosaic. We know about Erick Huen. We know—"

"Erick Huen," she interrupted me. "Yes, he's one. But there are more, many more." She rubbed her eyes. "I don't remember. I know one, one is…" She trailed off without saying anything else.

"Pony Girl, stay with me."

"I can't. I can't anymore. I have to go. The mission, the mission."

Damn it. She was rocking back and forth, and I had no idea how to help. She was going to hang up any second and be gone again.

"Listen to me, Bronwyn. I want you to stay alive. Do you understand?" I didn't know why I said that to her, but I knew I had to. "You do whatever you need to do to survive. Be smart."

She stopped rocking and brought the phone closer to her face. "Promise me. Promise me you'll see me again."

"Yes, absolutely, I promise you." Easiest promise I ever made. "I'm not leaving you behind. I'll be coming for you, Pony Girl."

Her face grew paler; sweat broke out on her forehead. She started rocking back and forth again, coming in and out of the picture on the screen. Whatever was happening to her was getting worse fast.

My hand balled into a fist. She was in so much pain, and there was nothing I could do about it. "Bronwyn—Pony Girl, hang in there. You're so strong. Such a survivor. I know you can do this. I am going to help you."

She stopped rocking and looked straight at me. "Promise me you'll see me again."

"I swear on my life."

"Good. Next time you see me, I want you to kill me."

The line went dead.

I muttered every foul curse I knew and immediately tried to recall the number, but she didn't pick up. I slammed my fist down on my desk, ignoring the pain it sent echoing through the wounds in my body.

I called Jenna. "Did you get my email?"

"Dude, yes," she said. "It took me a minute to translate that many spelling errors. What the heck?"

"I was trying to type while on a video call with Bronwyn."

"What? Holy shit. We traced the call to Seattle, but then it went dead. I did some preliminary research on the number, and it's from a no-contract phone you can pick up at any drugstore or a supercenter."

A burner phone. I ran a hand across my face and sat back in my chair. "Okay. Have someone on your team dig deeper, and see if you find anything useful. I don't think she's going to be in Seattle for long. I know you have your hands full with the Mosaic intel Landon and Ian brought in."

"I'll make sure someone is on it, Sarge. I promise. We'll search every angle."

I knew the nerds would do their best and their best was impressive, but I also knew that we weren't going to find Bronwyn at the end of that phone.

She was gone again.

"Did Bronwyn say anything to you?" Jenna asked. "If she set up a meeting, you should probably be careful. I hate to say this, but it could be a trap."

"No, she didn't say anything about a meetup. She was upset that she had hurt me."

"Okay, that's good. I mean, good that she was remorseful. We'll keep an open trace on your phone. If she calls again, we'll be able to lock onto it immediately."

I hung up with Jenna without providing much more detail about my conversation with Bronwyn so she could get to her job.

I didn't want to let Jenna or anyone know how bad it was getting. That Bronwyn was becoming desperate—like an animal trapped and trying to claw its way out of an impossible situation.

And how dangerous that made her.

•••

Bronwyn

. . .

I hung up with Sarge and smashed the phone under my heel. I stumbled forward a few steps, grabbing my head in my hands to keep myself from falling over. Fighting through the pain, I sucked in breaths until I was a little steadier.

Calling him had been a mistake, too risky. If they had caught me buying the phone, they would know they didn't have full control over me. They would figure out there were minutes I had pushed into hours when the pain was manageable and I still knew who I was.

But I'd needed to see his face, hear his voice.

I had to know if I had hurt him as badly as my cloudy mind remembered. If my vague recollection of kicking him hard, of trying to kill him, was truth or fiction.

One look at him through the screen, covered in bruises, and I'd had my answer. I'd hurt him. The man who'd done nothing but help me. Been nothing but gentle and supportive.

The man I'd been dreaming of for years. Until lately. Now, there was too much darkness for dreaming. And I didn't want to dream anyway when my waking hours felt like some sort of nightmare. Even life back in Prague had been better than this.

I reached back and picked up a tiny plastic piece of the phone, clutching it in my palm. I would keep this piece of Sarge close to me. No one would know what it meant except me.

He would be with me. I would keep him with me.

I stumbled a few more steps, the pain radiating up my skin. I knew where I needed to go, my body pushing me forward toward my mission. Anchorage, a building with some sort of medical files that I needed to steal from the hospital.

I looked down at the piece of plastic in my hand. It was jumping around due to the tremors I couldn't control. This was the longest Dr. Tippens had left me out of the lab, left me out of the dark. They thought they had better control over me than they did.

I had to keep fighting, keep boosting my resistance. It was my only chance…

I was serious about what I had told Sarge. If he met me again before I had this under control, he had to kill me. Otherwise, I might kill him. I had almost done it already. It had been with only the narrowest of margins I'd been able to walk away from his unconscious body in that garage rather than kill him.

Right now, I had to complete my mission; I didn't have any choice. The overwhelming need to press the side of my necklace ate at me. Once I did, everything would fall into place, and nothing would be difficult. Nothing would hurt.

I stumbled out of the building, bringing my hand up to my neck as I went. I pressed, not fighting it anymore. I felt the sting of the injection then waited. It would only be a few seconds before the…

It was time. The pain was gone. The mission was all that mattered.

The piece of plastic in my hand fell to the ground.

"I exist only to obey orders. My final mission is to go home."

Chapter 13

Sarge

Next time you see me, I want you to kill me.

Bronwyn's words echoed in my mind long after she'd hung up. Long after we weren't able to get any trace on that burner phone.

And for every minute of the four days since, I thought it was hyperbole. Something I would tease her about when I saw her again.

Hyperbole would have been something her mother had taught in her university class on literature. Bronwyn telling me to kill her was an epic example of the literary device.

But this latest footage we'd gotten of Bronwyn made me think perhaps her wish wasn't an exaggeration at all, at least not in her mind.

She'd been caught on an ATM camera across from an alley in Anchorage, Alaska.

I watched as she stabbed a man in the chest—a wound meant to kill. I rewound the footage and watched it again.

Bronwyn was lying in the alley, clearly in pain. She vomited more than once and seemed almost too weak to get up. Some shady guy came over and started patting her down, obviously wanting to take advantage of an easy mark.

She grabbed his wrist and broke it. I had no problem with that. I had actually smiled when I saw it for the first time. Good for her.

It pissed the thug off, and he landed a couple of good kicks in her midsection that had me wanting to hunt him down.

He pulled out a knife and bent down closer to her. He didn't try to stab or slice her, just pointed it in her direction. I couldn't tell what he was saying, but probably something along the lines of wanting her to give him her wallet.

Bronwyn didn't respond verbally. Instead, she spun the knife on him and rammed it straight into his chest then back out, the movement efficient, brutal, deadly. The guy fell over in front of her, blood pouring from his wound.

In any court of law, that would hold up as self-defense. The punk obviously had provoked her, and a lawyer would argue that she'd protected herself as anyone would be expected to do. She'd killed him trying to get the knife away.

But I knew the truth. Everyone at Zodiac Tactical would know the truth—that her training would've allowed her to disarm that guy a dozen ways without killing him.

Bronwyn knew the truth too. The camera caught her expression as his body fell over. Devastation clouded her face as she realized what she'd done.

Then her expression fell blank again.

She was going in and out of her own awareness like she had in New York. A few seconds later, she forced herself off the ground and stumbled out of the alley, leaving the guy there, knife in hand.

I watched the footage again. *Still not going to kill you, Pony Girl. We're going to figure this out.*

There was a tap on my office door, and Landon walked in. "I heard you got some footage of Bronwyn."

"Yeah, it's not good."

He sat down across from me. I spun the laptop so he could watch it.

I knew exactly when she shoved the knife into the guy's chest. Landon flinched. Then he watched it again, ready for the violence this time.

He finished and sat back. "Holy shit. This was obviously self-defense, even if…"

Even if we both knew she could have taken that guy out without killing him. I nodded.

"Where and when was this?" he asked.

"Anchorage," I said. "Yesterday."

"She's certainly getting her frequent flyer mile bonus. London. New York. Now Alaska?"

"Yeah. She's being sent wherever Mosaic wants her."

Landon ran a hand through his light brown hair, standing it on edge. "Now that we've got someone on the inside at Mosaic, hopefully we'll get some data and be able to make a move to get Bronwyn back."

"Tell me about this Silas Varela guy." He was the criminal informant Landon and Ian had gotten out of their trip to Wyoming last week.

"Guy beat the shit out of an unarmed civilian and then threatened the life of her daughter. So a real charmer."

"Fucker," I muttered under my breath.

"He's lucky he's still breathing. His options are spending the rest of his life in jail, where Mosaic is certain to get to him at any moment, or providing us some intel. If he does, Ian will make sure he's protected while he's in jail for the rest of his life."

"He doesn't sound particularly trustworthy."

Landon shrugged. "If it gets us information on Mosaic, we'll take it."

Anything on Mosaic was going to get us closer to Bronwyn.

I nodded. "Ian needs to make intel on Bronwyn this guy's first priority."

Landon leaned back in the chair, resting his arms loosely on the rests. His light brown hair and surfer good looks tended to put people at ease—both men and women. He used his charm to his advantage, to Zodiac's advantage, as often as he could. He was endearing, friendly, good with people.

Basically, the opposite of me.

"Ian's goal is to bring Mosaic down as a whole," Landon said. "When we do that, we'll get Bronwyn back too."

I mimicked Landon's stance, leaning back in my own chair. He was trying to manage me, to put me at ease so I didn't demand what I knew was best for Bronwyn.

"Ian is not unbiased when it comes to taking down Mosaic. It's personal, and he'll stop at nothing to do it, even if it means sacrificing others." Bronwyn. "I don't know why that's the case. Ian has never shared the specifics with me. But I know you know the backstory."

Landon didn't get ruffled. His posture remained relaxed. "Yeah, I do. He has his reasons for it being personal. What they did to him, nobody should have to live through."

I thought of how Ian had looked when we'd first gotten the London footage and heard the word Mosaic. He'd been spooked.

I'd known Ian for nearly ten years. The man had held my life in his hands multiple times. Ian DeRose did not spook easily.

I leaned forward on my desk, catching sight of the Bronwyn footage that was playing again on the laptop. "Look, I love Ian like a brother. You know that. You too, even though you're a pain in my ass. And I get that Mosaic, whatever version we're dealing with, is bad. They're terrorists—people we need to stop before they get out of control."

"I think we're all in agreement."

"But the fact is one of our own is in trouble, and we need to help her first and foremost."

Landon didn't say anything for a long moment. He leaned his head to the side and studied me. "You want to tell me what really happened in New York?" He pointed at the last of my fading bruises.

I hadn't told anybody what had gone down between Bronwyn and me. "I got in a fight."

"So I read in the medical report. Two cracked ribs, a broken nose, and some kidney damage. Doc said in the report that you were noncommittal about exactly how it had all happened."

"I didn't sit around discussing my feelings. So what?"

"Turns out, I decided to see who was able to get the drop on the famous Harrison McEwan. What would it take to do that sort of damage? Four guys? Five guys?"

I didn't provide any info, so he continued. "I went to look up the footage, and lo and behold, it had somehow been turned off in the garage. How exactly did that happen, Sarge?"

"Happy accident," I muttered. "What's your point?"

"My point is, there's only one other time I recall you getting your ass handed to you this way. Back in Prague a few years ago. And just like now, you were pretty mum about those details too."

Landon knew. I could deny it all I wanted, but he had put the details together and figured out I knew Bronwyn years ago. I wasn't going to insult either of us by lying to him.

"Fine. I knew Bronwyn back when she was in Prague and she was a kid in trouble. I took that beating because if I hadn't, she was going to be the one to pay the price. I met up with her again after Zodiac opened and told her about the Paris office. She was a pickpocket then; she's a pickpocket now."

"You were involved with her back then?" Landon raised his eyebrow, but his tone remained neutral. He was trying his best not to judge.

"She was a fucking teenager," I said. "No, I wasn't involved with her. I was trying to help her out."

Landon blew out a breath. "Fine. You did the right thing. But she's not a teenager anymore. She's an adult making adult choices."

"She needs our help." I wanted to bang my fist against the desk to emphasize the point. "And we need to be putting our resources into doing that."

"Look at that footage." He pointed at the laptop. "She killed that guy when she could have easily disarmed him and walked away. And New York? There's a suspicious lack of bruising on your knuckles for your ass to have been kicked so hard."

We both knew what lack of bruising on my hands meant. I hadn't fought back, at least not to the degree that I should have.

I said nothing.

"She did this to you in New York."

"I know it looks bad. I know that if you study these

pieces separately, it looks like Bronwyn has gone rogue, that she's working for Mosaic. But I'm telling you there's something more to it."

Landon nodded, steepling his fingers once again. He'd always been the peacekeeper of our group even back when we'd been in the SEALs. He had the temperament for it. "Okay, I'm willing to listen. Convince me, and I'll help you convince Ian."

"I don't have the information yet. All I know is that Mosaic is controlling her some way, some sort of drugs and injections that they give her."

"Mind control?" he asked.

I scrubbed a hand down my face, thinking of her blank look when she'd first seen me. "I don't know. Maybe."

We both knew that mind control was sketchy at best and they certainly wouldn't have sent Bronwyn off by herself if they weren't sure that they could control her completely.

"It has something to do with this necklace she has on." I lined up the footage so he could see it. "And there, see how cold her face is when she kills this guy? Almost blank, nothing. But then, look. A few seconds later, she's distraught. It's like she's coming in and out of her own consciousness."

Landon watched two more times. "All right, I'll give you that. Her reaction seems to be on extreme ends of the spectrum."

"She was like that in New York too. Sometimes she didn't recognize me. But then there were times when she called me by name. She's in trouble, Landon."

"I'm going to ask you the same thing Ian would ask you if he were here and if he didn't have a complex relationship with Mosaic. Was she trying to kill you when you fought her in New York?"

I wasn't going to lie to my friend. I may not like the answer, but keeping this truth from him wasn't going to help anybody in the long run.

"Yes. When she had clarity and recognized me, she wasn't trying to, but most of the time, she wasn't clear. She wasn't Bronwyn. In those moments, she wanted to kill me." She almost had.

"Fine. We'll show this footage to Ian. We'll make our case about getting Varela to find out as much as he can about Bronwyn. But I'm going to tell you, Ian is not going to put all his efforts into that. Especially not when she's acting so much like an enemy."

Fuck that. "Bronwyn is one of us."

"Bronwyn is one of us who tried to kill you. Right now, that makes her a partial enemy at best. Or worse, an unpredictable one."

"Ian's only mission is to stop Mosaic. He doesn't care about her."

"It's not that he doesn't care," Landon responded. "But he knows that, ultimately, Mosaic is the bigger problem. Mosaic is back and more well-funded than ever. We know that there are four heads of the organization now rather than one. We know Erick Huen is one of them. We have a little bit of data on two others, but nothing at all on the fourth one. And unknown variables in situations like this are never good."

"If taking down Mosaic is where Ian needs to focus himself, that's fine with me. But Bronwyn is my priority."

Landon let out a sigh. "The two are not mutually exclusive."

They were to me, and to Ian, but I didn't say that. Landon wanted to believe we could do both at the same time, and I wasn't going to argue.

Landon stood. "All right, let's go talk to Ian. He's up in

his penthouse. He'll come around. He's going to want to help you find your woman."

I stood up, following him out. "She's not my woman."

"Yeah, Sarge, keep telling yourself that."

"I'm serious. It's not like that." I forced the thought of the kiss in Paris from my mind. "She's too young. She's been hurt. She's in trouble."

"Yeah. Sounds like she needs somebody who is older, stubborn, patient, and willing to fight for her. Know anybody like that?"

"You're a fucking pain in the neck."

Landon laughed. "Remind me to say I told you so when you ask me to be one of your groomsmen. Now let's go see what we can dig up on the girl who kicked your ass."

Chapter 14

Bronwyn

D*o whatever you need to do to survive.*

I kept Sarge's voice on repeat in my head when the Mosaic soldiers came and got me in Anchorage and Dr. Tippens had me put back in the dark cell.

Stay alive. Whatever you need to do. Survive.

Sarge had said other things to me too. Things about Mosaic and Erick Huen, but that info was too hard for my battered mind to process and remember.

Instead, I focused on the sound of his deep voice telling me I could do this. That I could survive. That he believed in me.

It made the dark more bearable, knowing that he'd said all those things even after I'd hurt him.

Under Sarge's constant tutelage in my mind, survival took on a different meaning.

Whatever you need to do.

Survival didn't have to mean rebellion. Especially when

it started becoming clear that outright rebellion—refusing to give them what they wanted—would make them tighten their fists around me.

So I didn't fight Mosaic anymore. When they told me to say my words, I did it immediately. I started saying them as soon as they opened the slot in the door.

Let them think I was weak. Let them think that they had found the way to control my mind. As long as I was still inside myself, as long as I could remember Sarge and hear his voice, I knew they hadn't won.

I didn't fight my meds. I didn't fight the injections. Instead, I curled inside myself and talked to Sarge. I listened to him as he spoke to me—told me I could do this. I would survive. I'd survived as a child, and I would survive now.

Focusing on him was hard at first, but it became easier. I could hear him more clearly in my mind. I could talk to him more freely in silence. It almost felt like I could reach out and touch his thick, dark hair.

Maybe hallucinating about a man I'd only spent a handful of hours with—many of those encased in violence —shouldn't have made me feel more sane. But it did.

I realized Dr. Tippens was spacing out my medication more. He and his team didn't know they were losing hold of me. They thought being alone in the dark would break me down further into the tool they wanted.

They didn't know I had someone with me. And as long as Sarge was with me, whatever they were attempting to do to my mind and body wasn't working the way they thought.

I wasn't sure how much time had passed in the dark after they'd brought me back from Alaska. Based on my meals and how many times I was taken to the lab, I knew it was weeks.

I hated the lab. I'd rather be left in the dark with Sarge. Under the lab's garish bright lights, holding on to him was harder.

Today especially. Today, instead of being by myself with one or two medical technicians, the lab was full of people.

Dr. Tippens was here with a team of technicians. And there were dozens of others. Others like me, strapped to chairs and beds.

Some were moaning in pain, fighting the straps that bound them to the gurneys. Some were silent. More than one was completely covered by a sheet.

I knew what that meant.

Sarge always stayed and silently held my hand when I was in the lab. We couldn't talk, I knew that, not here.

But today, he slipped away, fading backward.

"Stay," I whispered, so softly that only he could hear me.

He slid his fingers along my lips, stilling them with a touch I couldn't feel.

You have to listen to what's going on around you without letting them know. Concentrate. You can do this, Pony Girl. I'll be back.

I wanted to cry, to beg him to stay, but with a blink of my eyes, he was gone.

Despair threatened to swamp me, but I forced it back. I would do what Sarge said. Listen. Concentrate. Not give myself away.

Dr. Tippens walked around me, looking at a chart. The other man was there too. The one I knew. The one who had come to my hotel room. What was his name?

"She looks like a zombie," the man from my hotel room said. "Like she has that Bell's...whatever disease."

"Bell's palsy." Dr. Tippens didn't look up from his chart. "And it's not a disease, it's a condition. And evidently, it can be a side effect of the genetic modification we're doing."

"We have interested parties who are going to be very upset if her face doesn't work right."

"Her face works fine, Erick. Let me do my job."

Erick Huen. That was his name. I remember Sarge saying something to me about him. I tried to remember the details but decided to let it go, to focus on now.

"Fine." Erick walked around me, studying me with disdain. I forced myself to remain completely blank, allowing my peripheral vision to fill in details. "It's disappointing to see her this comatose. She was so feisty before. Hard to believe that now."

Dr. Tippens shined a light in my eye. "I agree. She responded much more quickly to the genetic modifications than we expected. We were able to reduce her neuroinhibitors and medication. Sometimes things go right. That's one of the joys of science."

"Glad to hear it after all the funding we've put into your research." Erick moved closer to me again, and I could feel his breath on my face. "And she's ready to kill? We have a very special job for her."

Dr. Tippens let out a sigh and moved his arm to push Erick back from me. "She's killed before, as you know, but it goes against her nature. She was struggling against her programming most when she killed that man in Anchorage. You'd be wiser to use some of our other subjects if you have a murder job in mind."

"Murder job?" Erick snickered. "Stick to the medical jargon, doc."

"I would if you'd get out of my lab and let me do my job," he muttered.

"It needs to be Bronwyn." Erick inched closer to me again. "Evidently, Ian DeRose has found himself a little girlfriend, and we want to send a message to him. Her dead body ought to do that nicely. And then finding out it was done by somebody he hired and trained will make it even sweeter."

It took everything I had to keep myself completely still and not show any expression. I didn't want to hurt anybody having to do with Zodiac Tactical. That would hurt Sarge.

I wished he were here. I needed him.

Listen. Concentrate.

I barely avoided a flinch as Erick slid my hair back from my forehead. "You're going to put a bullet right between Wavy Bollinger's eyes."

"Please stop molesting the patients." Dr. Tippens put his arm out to ease Erick back again. "You know what we're doing here is a delicate balance. Your touch could affect the regimen in negative ways."

"Fine." Erick sounded like a pouting child, but he moved away from me. "Make sure she's ready."

I didn't go back to my cell after that. I went from total darkness to total brightness all the time. The brightness was so much worse.

Sometimes I was in the main lab, but most of my time was in what they called the indoctrination room.

I called it hell.

I was strapped to a chair, my eyes taped so I could do nothing but look at what was in front of me. I couldn't blink, much less cry.

I was bombarded with picture after picture of Wavy Bollinger—a kind-looking woman in her early thirties with a big smile and red hair. In some of the photos, Ian DeRose was with her. But never Sarge.

With every picture, I was told Wavy was my enemy as the doctors did something under the skin at the back of my neck. Sharp pricks and slices and burns, always to reinforce the words surrounding me.

"Wavy Bollinger is the enemy." The pinch of a needle prick at the back of my neck.

"Your mission is to kill her for the safety of others." The burn as they injected something. Did something to my body.

"Wavy Bollinger is dangerous, a threat to be eliminated." The burn spreading as I looked at the woman who'd never done anything to hurt me.

I could feel the hatred bubbling through my veins— whether they were my real feelings or what the doctors were doing to me, it didn't matter. The end result was the same. I wanted to kill this woman.

Wavy's not your enemy, Pony Girl. You hold on to that.

I couldn't see Sarge, but I could hear his voice in my ear. He whispered it over and over, combating whatever the doctors were doing to me.

Dr. Tippens was becoming suspicious that something wasn't right. Maybe I was acting too blank. I wasn't sure how I was supposed to act to stop them from strengthening their attempts to control me.

All I knew was that I had to keep Sarge's voice in my head all the time or else I was going to give in to what they were training me to do.

Kill the woman. Kill Wavy Bollinger.

Keeping myself still and curled up around my thoughts of Sarge had been easy in my dark cell. But here, where I was exposed to Dr. Tippens and all his assistants, it was impossibly hard. I was close to cracking, to screaming, to begging them to stop.

But those reactions would show them clearly that their reduced regimen wasn't working. Then they would fix it. They would up the medications and gene editing and neuroinhibitors—all words I didn't understand but knew were my downfall.

Sarge would be gone for good. Once he was out of my head, I wouldn't be able to hold on. They'd turn me into whatever they wanted me to be.

A killer.

"Her blood pressure and heart rate should not be spiking like this," Dr. Tippens said to one of his assistants, "What has changed?"

"Nothing, sir," the woman said. "We've been giving her the prescribed regimen every day as scheduled, applied during the indoctrination."

The doctor stood behind me. I couldn't see him, even with my eyes peeled open.

"Notify Erick Huen that I need to see him. She's not ready. If we send her out like this, she's going to snap. I don't want to waste the data we've gotten from her. Stop all indoctrination for right now."

I swallowed my sobs of relief as my bed was lowered to a resting position and my eyes were released from the torturous tape. Wavy's pictures faded from my sight.

I was able to turn my head, and I saw Sarge standing there, arms crossed over his big chest, smiling at me with pride in his eyes. I'd made it. At least for now. My eyes drifted closed.

When I became conscious of my surroundings again, Erick Huen was there, standing over me where Sarge had been. I had no idea how long he'd been there. Once again, I barely controlled my actions before they gave me away.

"Tippens, you're disappointing me. What happened to sometimes things go right—the joy of science?" Erick flipped a hand around his head in a grand gesture.

"We are working in uncharted territory. It's hard to know what can cause drastic changes. We need more time to see what's happening with Bronwyn. See what can be done to make the process less of a shock for her system."

"I don't care about her system, and you shouldn't either. Mosaic doesn't tolerate failure, not when we're putting out the amount of funding we are to support your research. My partners are starting to question your results. We don't want that, do we, Tippens?"

Dr. Tippens's voice was hoarse. "I need more time."

Erick walked around to my other side. "Fortunately, I don't need sweet Bronwyn here to kill Wavy Bollinger any longer. I've decided to handle that myself. Plans have changed."

"Changed to what?"

"It ends up that we have a mole in our organization. And I'd like your little weapon here to neutralize him. The name is Silas Varela."

Dr. Tippens let out a sigh. "I would strongly suggest one of our other subjects. There are a number who will do a more efficient job than Bronwyn."

"No, I want her."

"You might be doing permanent damage to her psyche, not to mention our research."

"I'm pretty sure what's going to happen to her at the end of her usefulness will be damaging enough to her psyche. Maybe I'll be doing her a favor if her brain explodes now." He poked Dr. Tippens in the chest. "Get her prepped and ready for the mission. She leaves in two days."

"Erick, I—"

"Two days. She kills Silas Varela and plants evidence at his house that makes it look like a robbery."

I flinched, but neither of them saw me.

"I don't think she's ready."

"Then she will have reached the end of her usefulness, and perhaps you will have too. Get her ready."

Chapter 15

Bronwyn

The walls were closing in on me. I drove my nails into my head as I huddled in the closet in Silas Varela's apartment.

For the past three days, I'd been trying to hold on to the last bit of my sanity. To the last bits of myself that made me who I was. My mind felt like it had been split open and all the pieces of me were oozing out and fading into nothing.

And now I was here, in this apartment, to kill a man.

I'd vomited half a dozen times already until there was nothing left in my system. My nose had been bleeding almost nonstop for the hours I'd been here.

The only thing that made any of it go away was to stop fighting the urge to kill Varela.

Even Sarge's voice wasn't helping me.

You're not a killer, Pony Girl.

Survive.

Right now, those two statements were at odds with each other.

The more I tried to fight the indoctrination I'd gone through in the past forty-eight hours, the worse the pain got. So I gave myself respite by mentally agreeing to kill Varela when he got home.

If I did that, I would survive. But it would prove Mosaic had made me into a killer.

You're not a killer, Pony Girl.

Survive.

I had to choose between the two statements Sarge kept saying to me.

To make it worse, it was getting close to time for me to press the button on my necklace that provided my normal regimen. If I didn't do that, the withdrawal pain would start. I didn't know if I had the strength to combat that on top of the agony in my mind. Especially knowing the regimen would help make all the pain go away.

All of it. No more battles, no more worrying about becoming a killer. Just blessed nothingness.

Make killing Varela as easy as it was supposed to be.

But no. If I kill him, then I won't be able to—

A searing pain shot through my head, stealing my breath, doubling me over.

I had to kill Varela.

I had to kill Varela.

I had to kill Varela.

I kept that other tiny nugget of a thought buried deep inside. The thing I wouldn't be able to do if I killed Varela. I gave it to Sarge to hold for me. He would give it back to me at the right time.

"Thank you," I whispered.

You can do this, Pony Girl.

"I have to kill Varela."

Then that's what you have to do. Rest now.

I leaned my head against the cool closet wall and waited, not fighting it anymore. Sarge understood. It was enough. Sarge would protect me.

I finally heard Varela inside his apartment. I'd already planted all the evidence Erick had demanded, not that it was going to fool anyone for long. I got up, less shaky now that I wasn't fighting the urge to complete my mission.

Sarge would help me when the time came.

I'll help you do what you need to do. We'll get through this together.

I nodded. I trusted him.

Varela wasn't expecting anything. There were way too many locks on his door for him to think that someone could have gotten in through them.

That wasn't how I'd gotten in. I'd come in through the basement window that should've been too small for any human to fit through. I had bruises along my shoulders and my hips because I'd been too big for it, too, but I'd made it.

Varela was whistling and getting sandwich makings out of his refrigerator. I stepped silently behind him into the kitchen and raised my weapon.

Not yet, Pony Girl. Sarge's whispered voice filled my ears.

Right. Not yet. It had to look like an accident.

Not yet. Not yet.

I would kill him, but I was waiting for the right moment. I held my gun in a steady position. I stood there silently until he turned around. He jerked backward.

"What the hell are you doing in here, bitch?"

Still not yet.

What was Sarge waiting for?

Trust me. Not yet.

I didn't say anything to Varela. It was taking everything I had to not pull the trigger.

"You picked the wrong house to rob, lady." He eyed my gun as if he couldn't decide whether to try to take me or not. "Besides, I don't have anything in here worth stealing. I doubt you could carry out a TV on your own."

My gun began to shake. "Please," I whispered. Not to Varela, to Sarge. My nose started bleeding again. I needed to kill the man in front of me.

Varela's eyes narrowed. "Look, I work for some important people, and if you hurt me, they're going to come after you."

Tell him the truth.

"Those important people are the ones who want you dead," I said. "They know you're betraying them."

The mustard he'd taken out of the refrigerator fell from his fingers to the floor, splattering all over his shoes.

"Oh God." He was taking me a lot more seriously now. "Look, whatever they think they know, it's not the truth."

Tell him more.

Why? Why couldn't I kill Varela? But I did what Sarge said.

"Mosaic knows you're working for Ian DeRose and Zodiac Tactical," I continued. "My job is to come here, kill you, and make it look like a burglary gone wrong."

The other part of that job was to make sure I walked by the security camera that was across the street, knowing that Zodiac Tactical would eventually get the footage and put two and two together.

"Look." Varela held out his hands in supplication. "Whatever they're paying you, I can pay you more. Maybe not right away, but if you're willing to give me a chance…"

"Now?" I asked Sarge. "Please?"

Hold on a few more seconds, Pony Girl. You can do it.

I felt another drop of blood fall from my face onto the floor. My stomach cramped; the colors faded from the room. I couldn't seem to get enough air.

"Are you all right, lady?" Varela asked.

Take a breath, Bronwyn. Force yourself to get in air. You can't pass out. You're going to need it for what you have to do.

I opened my mouth, forcing oxygen to my starved lungs. The colors came back, and the room stopped spinning.

That's right, gather your strength.

Sarge was helping me. I was going to make it through this.

Take a step closer and get ready. Then say exactly what I tell you, no matter how much it hurts.

Killing Varela wouldn't hurt, didn't Sarge understand? But I nodded.

No matter what, you do what I tell you.

"Okay."

"Okay what?" Varela asked.

It's going to hurt. You gave it to me, but I have to give it back now. Be strong, Pony Girl.

"Are you crazy or something?"

Ask him if Ian DeRose will listen to him.

What? "Why?"

Sarge's voice roared in my ears. *Do it! You don't have much time.*

"Will Ian DeRose listen to you if you have information?"

"Yeah, I mean, I've been working for him, so yeah."

You know the rest. Say it. Hurry, Pony Girl. You're running out of time.

"Go to Ian. Tell him that Wavy Bollinger is in danger. That Mosaic is going to kill her. Tell him he has to protect her. Tell him to hide you, to get you as far away from here as possible. If anyone from Mosaic sees you again, they won't hesitate to kill you."

This was what I'd given to Sarge to hide for me. If I'd allowed myself to consciously think of letting Varela go, I would've collapsed.

This was the only way to help Wavy.

Wavy was in danger. I had to help her. This was the only way.

I felt as if someone was hitting me with a hammer. Blood gushed out of my nose, and the world spun. I had to drop my gun to catch myself on the kitchen counter to stay upright.

"Go now!" I screamed at him. If I fell and got my gun while he was still in my sights, I wouldn't have the strength not to finish my mission.

He had the good sense to run out the door. I prayed it would be enough.

My vision narrowed. If I'd had anything left in my system to vomit, it would've come back up. I felt some sort of sting in my eye as something happened.

Send the report, Pony Girl. You wrote it while you were waiting. Send it now.

I hit send on my phone, telling Mosaic Varela was dead. I dropped to my knees, falling against the cabinets. Everything was turning black now.

I was going to die.

You did it, beautiful. Rest. You're not dying.

I wasn't so sure.

When you wake up, you're going to forget a lot. That's okay. It's okay to forget. It's your mind's way of protecting you. But there's something very important you're going to remember.

"What?"

You'll remember when you wake up.

~

My eyes blinked open slowly. Where was I? I had no idea. I was in some sort of kitchen, but not mine. My flat in Paris had a kitchen barely half this size.

Paris? No, I hadn't been to Paris in months. I'd been in the dark cell and in the medical chair but…

I couldn't remember.

There was mustard on the floor—and blood. A gun lying next to me.

I'd been here to do something, but I didn't know what.

And I wasn't sure I wanted to know.

You're not going to have much time. If you're going to do this, you're going to have to move quickly.

I looked over and saw Sarge standing in the doorway.

"I don't remember why I'm here," I whispered.

A smile from him. *It's okay to forget that part.*

"But there's something I needed to remember." My skin started to itch. I had the urge to inject my regimen by touching my necklace. Right now, the compulsion wasn't hard to resist, but that would change.

Does your head hurt anymore?

Had it been hurting before? "No. A little, but not bad."

Good. Then it's time to go, if you're going to do it.

"Going to do what?"

He walked over and crouched down beside me. *I can't get you away from Mosaic for good, Pony Girl, but maybe I can give you a reprieve. You need to figure out where you are.*

I looked around. Nothing seemed familiar to me. Not this apartment, not the city.

They underestimated you and overestimated themselves. It will be their downfall.

I slipped my phone out of my pocket. I had no idea

where I was. I opened my maps app. "I'm in Pueblo, Colorado."

That's right. If you move fast, you've got enough time. Not much, but enough.

He disappeared right in front of my eyes.

"Wait, come back! Enough time to do what?"

You know, Pony Girl. Sarge's voice came to me. *They didn't take everything from your mind. You know.*

And then it came to me.

Colorado.

I did know.

I jumped up and ran for the door.

Chapter 16

Sarge

The view of the Rockies I had from my back deck calmed me in a way not much did. But for the past month, even the grandeur of the mountains hadn't done much to help my mind.

I hadn't seen or heard from Bronwyn in almost four weeks. By the time I'd gotten to Anchorage after the footage we'd found of her, she'd been gone. Stopping in Seattle where her video call had originated had led to nothing but a few pieces of crushed phone plastic inside an abandoned building.

I'd made a huge mistake in New York letting Bronwyn go. I wasn't sure if I was ever going to see her again. After the footage from Anchorage, I wasn't sure she was still alive.

And all that kept coming back to me was that if I had just left well enough alone all those years ago—never walked over to stop Nikolai from pushing her around that day she was reading in the windowsill—maybe she would've been better off.

"Sarge."

I had the handgun I kept under my porch banister in my hand a second later. Because that voice could not be who my brain wanted to think it was.

And if it was, it had to be some sort of a trap.

Bronwyn stayed where I could see her with her hands held out to the sides so I knew she didn't have any weapons. At least not one that she planned to kill me with in the next half second.

She looked like hell, but she was alive.

And she was here.

"I don't have much time," she said.

I brought the Glock up higher as she reached her hand up to her head to hold it as if she was dizzy. Although I didn't know why I did. Would I actually be able to shoot her if she pulled her own gun on me? I honestly didn't know.

"Last time I talked to you, you were trying to get me to promise to kill you if I saw you again."

She flinched. "I—I don't remember that."

I wasn't sure whether to believe her or not. "What are you doing here, Pony Girl?"

Another flinch. "You sent me here."

I raised an eyebrow. "I sent you? I'm pretty sure that's not the case."

If I could've sent her here, she would've been here long before now, and definitely not to get me to kill her.

"No, not you. The other you." She shrugged the slightest bit. "The window is narrow when I have control. I spent a lot of it getting here. I can leave if you want."

Her voice was stilted, the words jarring, as if she was having to focus on each one to figure out what to say.

Was this a trap? Yet another thing I didn't know when it came to her. It could be. But if she had wanted to kill me, she could have done it back in New York. She could've taken me out today without making her presence known.

I kept the Glock in my hand, got up, and walked toward her.

"How did you know where I live?"

She swept her hands up and down her arms as if she was cold and she needed to rub her skin to warm herself. The closer I got, the worse she looked. Dried blood was smeared on her face like she'd wiped it. And there was something wrong with one of her eyes—the blood vessels had burst in it. Not a good sign.

"I remembered it when I woke up. I don't remember the rest, but I remembered that you were nearby." She rubbed her arms harder. "I got your address…before. Because I was going to mail you the money if you wouldn't take it from me."

It took me a second. "You mean that eight hundred dollars you insisted you owed me?"

She nodded. "Then today, once I knew where I was, I remembered."

It was feasible. My address was in the Zodiac computer system. I didn't try to hide it from my fellow employees and friends. I stepped a little closer.

"Why are you here, Bronwyn? What's happening to you?"

The collar of her shirt shifted, and I could see that she still wore that necklace. Her fingers crept up toward it. I pointed to it.

"That necklace, what does it do? It injects you with something."

"I don't have much time," she said. "It hurts."

"What hurts? The injection? What they give you? Tell me what's happening. Tell me how I can help you."

"If I press it, it won't hurt anymore, but then I'll be gone."

She held her hand up toward her head.

"Please help me, Sarge."

A single tear spilled from one of those blue eyes. I tucked my Glock into the back waistband of my jeans. If she were here to kill me, she would have already done it, and I wouldn't have stopped her. She needed my help.

I walked toward her, unsure if she would try to run or not. She didn't—just the opposite. She crumpled toward the ground.

Fuck.

I leaped forward and caught her as she fell. I scooped her up into my arms. "Pony Girl, talk to me."

There was no response. I laid my cheek against her forehead. It was hot as if she had a fever. She moved, groaning, like she was in pain and being unconscious wasn't taking it all away.

She was lighter than she'd been. She'd definitely lost weight since I'd seen her in New York, and she hadn't had much weight to lose then. I hurried back toward the house. She was waking up, rubbing her arms again. Her breath hitched.

"It hurts."

"Should I take you to a doctor? A hospital?"

"No," she responded immediately. "No, I can't. A bath. Water helps."

Her breathing grew more erratic and the rubbing more intense. Something was hurting her skin. There wasn't time to draw a bath, so I decided to go straight to the hot tub next to my back porch. Without setting her down, I threw open the top and then stepped us both inside fully clothed, pausing only to take my Glock out and rest it on the edge.

Still in my arms, I brought her down until we were covered up to our necks in water. Almost immediately, she began to relax. Her head fell against my shoulder.

I had so many questions I wanted to ask I could barely keep them all straight in my mind. But for this moment, all I could do was hold her.

"Pressure and movement against my skin make the pain stop for a little while. I discovered it by accident."

I could feel her relaxing more against me. I knew her body's natural state would be to want to rest and sleep now that the pain had stopped, but I needed answers.

"How did you get here, Pony Girl? It's been a month since I saw you in New York. Where have you been?" I didn't want to bring up that I'd seen what had happened in Anchorage.

"My cell. Doctor. Erick. I say the words. I survive. Like you told me to."

Most of this didn't make any sense, but the word Erick definitely did.

"Erick Huen? Do you know where he is? Can you take me to him?"

"No, I can't remember. There were things I had to forget to get here to you."

She shifted in discomfort, so I began rubbing any part of her skin I could reach. She immediately settled back down into my arms. Whatever was going on in her body, touch and stimulation helped control it.

What the hell was going on inside her?

I kept continuous contact with her body, rubbing her back, arms, legs, as I asked her questions. "Tell me about the necklace."

"I press it, and it gives me the regimen. The regimen stops the pain."

"Do you want to press it now?" I couldn't stand the thought of her being in so much pain.

"No." Her head came off my shoulder. "If I do, I go away. The pain stops, but I go away."

Her breathing got choppy, her muscles tightened with tension, her agitation clear.

"Okay. Don't press it. I'll keep rubbing, okay?"

"Take my clothes off, please. I want to touch your skin." She grimaced as her eyes met mine, full clarity there for the first time. "I don't mean... I know you don't want to... I just..."

I kissed her forehead.

"I understand. Let's get your clothes off."

I reached down and pulled the shoes off her feet under the water, setting them on the edge of the hot tub. Her pants weren't as easy in the water, but I rubbed against her legs as I trailed them down and off. I slipped her shirt over her head, careful not to touch the necklace in any way.

I wasn't saint enough to be unaffected by the sight of her naked flesh, but sex was the last thing on my mind. I continued to rub as much of her skin as I could reach.

I caught sight of the scarring along her wrist and held it up. I recognized the markings for what they were. "They restrained you. You fought."

"I can't remember," she said. "I can't remember anything. Not right now."

"You don't have to remember. We're going to help you. All you have to do is survive."

"Yes." Her head fell back against my shoulder once again. "That's what you tell me all the time."

If she'd been hallucinating about me, I was glad I'd said something useful.

The more I rubbed, the more she relaxed. I would sit here and touch her skin for the rest of my fucking life if that would help her.

"I'm sorry I hurt you," she said. "I hurt other people too, I think, but I can't remember."

She didn't need to remember that part. "Tell me more about the necklace. The regimen."

As we talked, her fingers reached for the hem of my T-shirt and pulled it up over my head. "I'm supposed to press the right side every eight hours. But I cheat," she said. "I don't press until I can't stand it anymore."

"How long is that?" I asked her. "Do you know?"

"Almost twenty-four hours. I tricked them. They give me a lower dosage because they think they control me."

I shook my head in wonder. Her body was malnourished and showed signs of abuse, but she'd still had the presence of mind to trick her captors.

I kissed her forehead. "You're amazing, Pony Girl. So strong."

"No. I wanted to kill. I was supposed to—" She sat ramrod straight in my lap. "I can't remember. There was something, I don't know. I can't—"

"Okay." I eased her head back down onto my shoulder and began rubbing her skin again. "Let's keep going. Don't think about it. Tell me more about the necklace."

"I can never touch the left side unless by command. Never."

"A kill switch?" I asked her.

"Yes. It's their way of making sure I don't go offline."

"Are they listening in?"

She shook her head. "No. They know that can be traced."

I bit back a curse. That's exactly what I'd been hoping to do. "Okay, then we'll think of something else."

I needed to get inside, call the office, get some sort of plan working, but I was afraid to leave Bronwyn out here alone. I had to figure out how to help her long-term.

Her pain was ratcheting up again; she pressed herself harder against my hands. Then she rubbed her hands against my chest, both sexual in nature and not. I was thankful wet jeans were pretty damned uncomfortable and kept my body in check.

That wasn't what Bronwyn wanted. She didn't mean for her movements to be sexual. She was trying to find pain relief.

Then she shifted, hooking a leg over my lap so her breasts were crushed up against my chest. "Sarge, I want you."

Maybe that was how she meant it.

Chapter 17

Bronwyn

All I wanted to do was crawl inside Sarge's body to get as close to him as possible. I knew where I was. I knew who I was. I knew who I was with.

It was more than I'd had at one time in what seemed like forever, and I never wanted it to end.

Everything I couldn't remember, all the pieces that didn't fit together, didn't matter when I was this close to him. I pressed down against him, barely swallowing a groan at how good it felt.

This was Sarge. He was really here with me. Big, strong, protective.

I could still feel the pain under my skin, but I could tamp it down. I had time before I was overwhelmed with the need to press the regimen into my skin to stop the pain. And lose myself.

I knew there were things I needed to remember. Why

was I here to begin with? Things I needed to tell Sarge. But if I remembered, it would hurt. Rip my mind apart.

So I wouldn't remember. I would be with Sarge for however long I had before the pain overwhelmed me.

As close to him as possible. I rubbed up against his chest.

"Pony Girl." His voice was so much deeper, sexier than it had been in my head.

It was also tinged with restraint.

"I know," I responded. "I know I hurt you in New York. I know you can't trust me. I know you don't want me."

He cupped my head with his big palms. "It's not that I don't want you. It's about what you need right now, and sex is not it."

I didn't know how to form the words to explain it to him. It wasn't so much that I wanted sex, although I wouldn't mind that at all. I wanted to be close to him, closer than we were right now.

I needed him.

I couldn't stop the tears that leaked out of my eyes. "I want to be able to feel you. I want to be able to know that you're with me when the darkness comes back."

I knew it was coming. Worse than before. Whatever it was that I'd forgotten would drag the darkness back with it.

He wiped my tears away with his thumbs. "I want to help you, Pony Girl, so there isn't any more darkness. Let me take you to the Zodiac office."

He rested his forehead against mine, and I breathed him in. I wanted that so bad—to let him take over the fight for me. The burning pain was already starting to ramp back up.

I was running out of time.

"I won't make it. By the time anyone figures out what to do or how to get the necklace off me, it will be too late."

He growled, obviously torn. "Okay. I don't like it, but okay. But let me get my phone so I can record as much detail as possible about that damned necklace. Zodiac's tech team will study it, figure something out for next time."

"Okay," I whispered. But I didn't know if there was going to be a next time. I rubbed against him more. The pain was getting harder to ignore.

He shifted away from me. "Which will be better for you, for me to leave you alone in the water or for me to take you with me and keep touching you?"

"Please don't leave me alone," I said. The water helped, but without him touching me, I was going to succumb to the pain too quickly.

He nodded. "Hang on to me. I'm going to carry you inside. We'll put you in the shower."

"Okay." I forced the word out. Water wasn't going to help for much longer.

He brushed a strand of my hair back from my face. Somehow, he knew it was getting worse. "You hold on."

I didn't know if he meant literally or figuratively, so I did both. I wrapped my arms and legs around him as he got up out of the hot tub and walked toward his house.

I buried my face in his neck, breathing in his scent. This was better. So much better. My tongue darted out and licked his skin. I heard him groan, but I was so fascinated by the way he tasted that I couldn't stop.

Yes, his taste overwhelmed my senses and helped dull the pain. He had one arm hooked under my hips to carry my weight, his other hand rubbing as much skin as he could reach. I was wrapped around him like an octopus, but I couldn't get enough of how his neck tasted.

He carried me into his bedroom, not caring that we

were dripping all over the place, and laid me on the bed. The second I wasn't in contact with him anymore, the pain ratcheted up to an almost unbearable level.

I let out a groan, my fingers inching toward the necklace. That was what I'd been trained to do. When the pain started, I was to press the right side. Now I was fighting the pain and my training—it felt impossibly hard.

He grabbed my hand, gently pulling it back down from my neck. "No, not yet. You fight for me a few more minutes. Okay?"

I nodded, and he trailed his hand along my arm, rubbing up and down my shoulder as he grabbed his phone off the nightstand and began recording my necklace.

I tried to hold still as he spoke into the recording, noting things about the type of metal the necklace was and the wounds in my neck. But the pain was becoming too much. I needed something to distract me from it.

I took his hand that was stroking along my collarbone and pulled it down until it covered my breast. His fingers slid under my bra and began teasing my nipple, squeezing to the point of pain and then letting it go and rubbing gently.

I relaxed into the bed. Yes.

He was still talking into the recording, but I didn't care. The pleasure from his fingers was enough to ease the pain. He never stopped talking as his hand switched to the other breast, and I arched up into him.

I couldn't stop my moan.

He finally set his phone down. "I think I got everything I ne—"

I pulled him to me for a kiss, cutting him off in the middle of his sentence. I needed his mouth.

I yanked him on top of me, thankful when he didn't

resist and he kissed me back, when he seemed to want me as much as I wanted him. This wasn't only about keeping the pain at bay; this was about Sarge.

His big body covered mine, surrounding me. I pressed up against him and could feel him hard against me. He wanted me, at least on a physical level. Fingers came up and threaded into my hair, holding me still so he could kiss me more deeply.

I groaned into his mouth. Yes, this was what I needed. I needed Sarge. His tongue invaded my mouth, and I reveled in it, meeting it with my own.

I would've kissed him like that forever. I wanted more of him. I wanted to feel him inside me, to be as close as we possibly could be.

But it was too late.

The pain was gaining strength, radiating out from my core once again. Burning me from the inside out. The compulsion to hit the side of my necklace almost more than I could bear.

I had to leave. It would only get worse from here, and nothing he could do would stop it at this point.

I broke my mouth away from his, breathing heavily, and not just because of his kisses. "I have to go. It's too late. It's too much. If I don't leave now, I'll hurt you again like I did in New York. I can't control it."

Those deep brown eyes looked into mine. "I don't want to let you go. I don't want you to be alone in this anymore."

I tried to swallow my terror. I didn't want him to let me go either. "I'll survive."

He slid off me quickly—way too quickly—and I wanted to pull him back. But I couldn't. I arched off the bed as a spike of agony drove down my spine; the room spun. I rubbed my arms again.

Before I could say or do anything, Sarge picked me up and carried me into his office and set me down on his desk. He reached over with both hands and cupped my breasts, teasing my nipples to hardness.

"Stay with me," he said. "A few more minutes."

I moaned, falling back onto my elbows, the pain retreating under the onslaught of his fingers. One hand slipped down my stomach and into the waistband of my panties, not stopping until I felt his finger slide inside me. "Stay with me, Pony Girl. Concentrate on this."

His touch was enough to beat back the pain. I couldn't stop myself from grinding up against his hand. It felt so good.

He grabbed something from one of the drawers. "Bronwyn, this is a micro transmitter." He held some tiny thing in front of my face, but I was too busy focusing on what his fingers were doing inside my body, milking every second of enjoyment to pay much attention.

"It doesn't send your location. It's not a tracker," he continued. "It records your words, activates when you speak, sends it to a voice mailbox. You can talk to me using this. Okay? I won't be able to talk back to you, but you can know that I hear you. You're not alone. I promise."

Another finger slid inside me, and I gasped as he twisted and moved them in a way that tightened something deep inside me. I grabbed his wrist, making sure he wouldn't take his hand away. I needed whatever it was that he was doing.

"I'm putting it in your necklace," he said. "It's tiny, and they're least likely to search for it there. And if I'm right, they make you keep it on all the time."

"Yes," I said. I didn't know if I was answering his statement or responding to the movements of his hand. I felt the necklace shift slightly, but I didn't care. All I cared about was what he was doing to me. He cupped the back of my head as his fingers began moving more quickly.

"Next time I see you, I'm going to be more ready to help you. More ready than this."

"I—I—" I couldn't get a coherent sentence out. My legs dropped open. All my weight from the upper half of my body fell back onto his hand, but he didn't have any problem carrying my weight.

"Come for me, Pony Girl. If this gives you a reprieve, then it's worth it."

His fingers moved faster, harder, hitting that spot that wound the coil in me until it finally snapped. His name came out of my lips in a moan while I shattered with pleasure.

I lay limp on his desk for a long moment, eyes closed. When I finally opened them, there was nothing but him and me. Just us, together.

"I didn't know… I didn't know it could be like that."

"It will always be like that between you and me," he said. "We're going to get you out of this, and I'm going to prove it to you."

I barely had my breath back before the pain started again. This time, I knew I wouldn't be able to control it. It was already worse than before he'd laid me on the desk.

"I have to go," I whispered. "I can't wait any longer."

"Where are you supposed to be?"

I didn't have to concentrate to know my answer. All I needed to do was not fight it and the answer came to me. "The airport. The final part of the mission was to get myself to the airport."

He nodded. "I'll drive you."

He helped me get back into my still-damp clothes and put me into his car. He used one hand to drive, the other hand rubbing my skin as I rubbed the rest. I only had minutes left now.

"The micro transmitter, don't forget it. You can talk to me anytime. I'll be listening, I promise."

He kept repeating it over and over. He'd be with me. He'd be listening. His words faded away as I fought the pain, fought the compulsion to press the compartment on my necklace.

We were a couple of miles from the airport when I knew I'd reached my breaking point. "Here. Stop now." I barely got the words out.

He stopped without arguing. "I'm with you, Pony Girl. Remember that. I'm with you."

I tried to say thank you. I tried to tell him how much he meant to me, how he'd given me the only good things in my life, but I couldn't say any words. All I could do was open the car door and stumble out.

As soon as I closed the door behind me, he drove away. The last feeling I had was thankfulness that he'd understood before my fingers slammed the side of my necklace.

Relief. It was almost instantaneous. The agonizing fires began to be extinguished.

And then there was nothing.

Chapter 18

Bronwyn

I could feel Sarge's hands on me everywhere.

His lips on my shoulder, my neck. Kissing me with feather-like gentleness, then harder as he moved down my chest to my breasts, then lower still in between my legs.

All I wanted to do was lie here and feel. Feel him, knowing as long as he was with me I would be okay. Sarge would keep me safe.

He protected me from the pain. Stood guard against it like my own personal warrior.

But the pain was there, lurking below the surface, surrounding me from all sides. I wouldn't be able to ignore it for much longer, even with Sarge.

I wanted to stay with him forever—just the two of us. I wanted to read books with him and talk with him, travel places with him…

But mostly, I wanted to stay in his bed with him. Let

him touch me, let him do things to me—with me—I'd never wanted from another man.

"You're beautiful," Sarge whispered, voice clear and deep in my ear. "You're strong. So much stronger than you give yourself credit for."

I couldn't stop my sigh.

"Be strong for me, Pony Girl. Remember, you can talk to me at any time."

Wait. He'd said that to me before, right? When?

"Talk to me. I'll be listening."

I didn't want to talk. I wanted to kiss more. I wanted to feel his hands on me again, but he pulled back. I tried to reach out to grab him and keep him next to me, but my arms wouldn't move.

"She's waking up."

That voice wasn't Sarge's. Sarge wasn't here.

I shook my head. I didn't want anyone else. "No. Sarge."

"Did she say the word sergeant?" That was a different voice.

Where was I? I tried to gather my thoughts, but now that Sarge was gone, the pain ate at me. A groan escaped. I needed to be quiet. I pulled at my hands again, but they were restrained.

I cracked my eyes the slightest bit, taking in my surroundings. I was back in the medical chair. I hadn't been restrained in the medical chair since the beginning. They hadn't known there was any reason to restrain me.

They did now.

"Is she awake?" That was Erick Huen, his voice almost in my ear.

Fire burned under my skin, forcing me to swallow a whimper. I couldn't curl into a ball, couldn't do anything to ease the pain.

I gritted my teeth and tried to think. I reached for the things I knew I needed to remember, but my mind wouldn't grasp them. All I could remember were Sarge's kisses. But those weren't going to help me now.

"Yes, she's awake. I'm monitoring brain activity now that I know what's going on." Dr. Tippens's voice was tight, cold.

"Her eyes are still closed."

"She's fooled us before, but not this time. Open your eyes, Bronwyn."

I did as he asked. I wasn't going to be able to stay still or silent much longer anyway. The two men loomed over me.

Dr. Tippens shook his head like I'd personally disappointed him. "Your regimen hasn't been working, and you didn't let us know." He pried one of my eyes farther open and shined a small light then did the same with the other.

I didn't say anything. There was nothing I could say that was going to help me out of this situation. What had I done that had given me away? I'd been given a mission.

I'd failed at the mission. I'd failed on purpose. But why?

"Want to know how we know?" Erick moved to the side so I could see him better and clapped his hands in glee. "We found Silas Varela attempting to make personal contact with Ian DeRose right after you reported that he was dead."

Silas Varela. The failed mission.

I hadn't killed him. I'd let him go because of...some important reason. But I couldn't follow along the thread of memory to grasp what that had been.

"I've got to hand it to you." Erick dropped something wrapped in plastic onto my chest. "You helped us make much more of a statement with Varela."

I looked down at the plastic on my chest.

There was a human hand inside it.

Erick laughed. "See what I did there? Hand it to you."

Oh God. I began thrashing against my restraints in an attempt to get the dead man's body part off me, but all it did was slide farther down my body.

"Don't worry," Erick continued. "You only get the one piece. The rest of Varela was chopped up and sent so Ian DeRose and Zodiac Tactical were sure to find them."

He leaned down and whispered in my ear. "Varela died screaming, begging for his life. You would've done him a much bigger favor if you had killed him like you were told."

Varela. I remembered it all and suddenly couldn't get enough air into my lungs. I'd not only failed, I'd made the situation worse. I'd let him go so he could warn Ian DeRose about the danger to Wavy.

If they'd caught Varela on his way to see Ian, nobody knew about the danger to Wavy. The heart rate monitor beeped frantically as I tried to suck in enough oxygen to survive.

"Wavy," I whispered through parched lips. Was she already dead? Why hadn't I fought harder to remember while I was with Sarge? I'd only been thinking about myself.

"Oh, don't worry, I have something very special planned for Miss Bollinger. She'll be joining us soon. You've been ever so helpful in the formulation of my plans."

I thrashed against my restraints, wheezing as pain radiated throughout my body. I'd failed on every level. Varela was dead. Wavy would be soon—or worse. And Dr. Tippens now knew his regimen hadn't worked correctly on me.

And Sarge wasn't here. He'd never been here. I wasn't

sure that I'd been at his house. If every time he spoke to me, it was only in my mind, how could I trust anything about him was real?

How could I trust anything about my mind at all?

I let the pain take over, not fighting it anymore. I deserved it.

I couldn't hold back my sobs. I knew they'd turn into screams soon. I needed to press the regimen on my necklace, but my hands were restrained.

The necklace. Hadn't Sarge said something about turning it on and talking to him.

Had that been real?

I had no idea. I bit down sobs as Dr. Tippens talked to Erick around me. The fire burning through my skin became stronger. I wouldn't survive.

"Please," I begged. "Please, kill me."

That would be best for everyone. Especially me. My heart clenched at the thought of never seeing Sarge again. Of never feeling his kisses again.

But had I really felt his kisses at all?

"Oh, I don't think so." Erick got near my ear again so I could hear him over the beeps of the machinery and my own sobs. "You've been promised for something else."

I didn't know what he was talking about and didn't care. My breaths tore in and out of my chest until I was sure my ribs would crack.

"Enough, Erick." Dr. Tippens shot out an arm so Erick had to step back. "She's not a toy. We need to see what data we can get from her to figure out where her programming broke down."

"If she can't do what she is trained to do, we might as well get rid of her now."

"No, we need the data. Plus, she shouldn't be written

off yet. We have more extreme methods. She may still be a viable candidate."

"Fine. I have more interesting playthings coming." Erick walked away—tossing Varela's hand up in the air then catching it, like it was a ball—leaving me with Dr. Tippens.

Dr. Tippens looked down at me over his chart, then turned down the monitors so they no longer announced my racing pulse so loudly. "Yes, I think you're still a viable candidate. But I'm afraid this is going to be very painful before it gets any better."

Chapter 19

Sarge

I punched the bag, ignoring the pain in my knuckles that were already ripped open from the eighteen straight days of the abuse I'd already given them.

Eighteen days since I'd let Bronwyn out of my car and watched in the mirror as she'd touched that fucking device disguised as a necklace, and the woman I knew disappeared in front of my eyes.

Part of me had been happy to see the pain that had racked her body the entire time she'd been at my house finally gone. But she'd walked by my car, looked right at me, and there hadn't been an ounce of recognition in her gaze.

Bronwyn's body had been there, but her mind, her essence, had been totally gone. It was as if the time in the hot tub, in my bed, on my desk, had never existed.

I was going to remember those minutes for the rest of my fucking life, but they were totally gone from hers.

Just like in New York, I never should've let her go. If I had known—

"You need to take that fucking thing out of your ear. Jenna told me what you're doing with it."

I didn't turn from the punching bag at Landon's words. I hadn't expected to see him here, or I wouldn't have come at all. The Zodiac complex, including my current location in the basement gym, was like a ghost town. Every able-bodied person employed by Ian DeRose had been put on one distinct mission.

Recovering Wavy Bollinger from the hands of Mosaic. Specifically, the hands of Erick Huen.

She'd been kidnapped a few days after Bronwyn had stopped by my house, not long after Silas Varela had shown up in pieces.

I punched the bag again, harder this time.

I couldn't deny that it hadn't taken long after Bronwyn's appearance for the shit to well and truly hit the fan. I knew she was connected to it all, although not at fault. Ian had enough on his mind—I recognized the haunted look in his eyes every time I glanced in the mirror—so I hadn't filled him in on the details of Bronwyn's visit.

"Are you going to ignore me?" Landon grabbed the punching bag. "Take the damned receiver out of your ear."

"Fuck off, Libra." Landon was one of my best friends in the world, even though we constantly bickered and couldn't be more different in temperament. I wasn't looking for anyone to cheer me up, and I damned well wasn't taking the receiver out of my ear.

It was my only link to Bronwyn.

So when he reached over and pulled it out of my ear himself, I turned around swinging. He ducked and jumped back on the mat.

"You're going to give me that back right fucking now, or we're both going to end up bloody."

He held up the small monitor between two fingers. "What good does this do you?"

"It keeps me motivated."

"I'm not going to let you do this to yourself. Listening to Bronwyn suffer isn't going to motivate you any more than you're already motivated. You're ready to grind the world into dust to get her back. I'd say that's the height of motivation."

"I want to be able to hear if she attempts to communicate."

Landon shook his head. "That, I can understand. But Jenna told me what you're doing. That the nerds modified the device for you so you can replay what's been transmitted over and over."

I had days' worth of recordings of Bronwyn's suffering. Days when she'd gone from weeping to screaming to silent.

The screams had been enough to give me nightmares, but the silence… The silence was going to drive me absolutely insane.

She had been silent for days now. So yeah, I'd forced myself to listen to her suffering.

It reminded me that her pain was my fault. I never should've let her go that day. I should've found another way.

I deserved to break out into a sweat every time I heard her screams. I deserved to have my heart fracture when I heard her whisper my name like she needed to say it to survive.

And I wasn't able to do a damned thing about it.

I narrowed my eyes at Landon. "Give me the receiver right now, or you and I are going to fight."

Landon wasn't deterred. "Then you and I are going to

fight because all you're doing is torturing yourself. And it's not helping her for a goddamned second."

I lunged for him, but the bastard was quick. He always had been. We were pretty well matched in the sparring ring. I was stronger, bigger, but he was faster. I expected him to take another quick step backward, but instead, his fist flew out and connected with my jaw with enough force to send me back a step or two.

Landon wasn't playing.

Neither was I.

He tossed the receiver to the side and put his hands up in a fighting stance. I did the same. We weren't in a sparring ring and didn't have on protective equipment, but the gym at least had a padded floor.

I attacked with a kick-punch combination, pushing him back slightly. But then he ducked under my punch and flew at me in a midsection tackle.

We both fell hard onto the mat. I quickly twisted out of Landon's grasp before I found myself in a choke hold. He grunted as my elbow caught him in the ribs. He let me go. We both jumped up onto our feet. I barely got my arms up to block a series of kicks he threw at me before I attacked with two jabs that Landon dodged.

He caught me with a knee to the midsection, and my breath whooshed out of me. He had me doubled over. I waited for another blow.

Wanted another blow.

But it didn't come. I looked up as Landon stepped back.

"We need you, Sarge. Ian is out of his damned mind over Wavy, just like you are over Bronwyn."

"There hasn't been anything from Bronwyn for days," I finally said between breaths. "I know what that probably means. I keep thinking about those two dead bodies we found in the lab."

We'd gotten a lead five days ago that we'd hoped would take us to either Wavy or Bronwyn—a lab distantly connected to Erick Huen. We'd found evidence that Wavy had been held there, but it had been empty by the time we'd arrived.

Except for the two dead female bodies.

I'd approached the discarded corpses slowly, my heart frozen in my chest, sure one of them was Bronwyn's. But neither had been Bronwyn. Or Wavy. Thank God.

Yet now, as the hours had turned into days without a sound from Bronwyn, I felt like I was slowly approaching corpses once again.

And this time, I wouldn't be so lucky.

Landon grabbed me by the collar. "You don't give up hope, you hear me? You or Ian. You be ready so when Bronwyn and Wavy are found, you're there to give them what they need. Torturing yourself by listening to her in pain doesn't do anything but tear you down."

He was right. I nodded. "Yeah. I hear you."

Landon pulled me in for a hug, and I wasn't too macho to know that I needed it.

"She's going to make it, brother," he said near my ear. "Hang on to that."

I wanted to, but I was afraid. Afraid of hope.

We separated, and I grabbed the receiver. I wouldn't listen to the replays, but if Bronwyn said anything else, I wanted to be able to hear it.

"What was the last thing you heard from her?"

I flinched. I couldn't help it. "Them putting her back in the isolation tank. It was…bad."

I'd never be able to get her sobs out of my head. She was so close to breaking. Total darkness, soundproofing, floating, unable to see or hear or feel anything. It had been bad enough when she'd gone in the first time. Knowing what was coming when they'd put her back had been more than she could handle.

Landon scrubbed a hand down his face. "Those fuckers. Torture without leaving any physical marks."

They took her out every few days for tests. That was usually when the screams started again. But last time had been silence.

"They should take her out again in a few hours, right?"

I nodded. "If the pattern holds." I rubbed my eyes. I hadn't gotten more than a couple hours sleep at a time in eighteen days. "She's close to breaking. Permanently, Landon."

"She's strong."

"Even the strongest break eventually."

Chapter 20

Sarge

I'd promised Landon I wouldn't give up hope, but truth was, I wasn't sure I hadn't.

Silence. Nothing from her but silence.

The transmitter only worked if Bronwyn used her voice, so I couldn't tell if Mosaic had taken her out of the isolation tank as scheduled.

Silence was my enemy.

"Talk to me, Pony Girl," I whispered the next day. At this point, they should be putting her back into the tank. Back into her own personal hell. She should be crying, screaming, like she had before. "Don't you give up. I'm going to find you."

Landon had been right. I'd been wasting my time torturing myself. So I'd spent the rest of yesterday and today going back over the data about her necklace the nerds had dug up based on my video. The types of drugs that might make her body react how it had at my house.

Chemical subjugation and genetic manipulation…all the shit Mosaic was into.

It wouldn't help me find her, but it would help me help her when we did.

If we did. I couldn't deny I was giving up more hope every minute.

And then I heard her voice.

"S-Sarge."

I sat ramrod straight in my desk chair, nearly knocking over everything on my desk.

Bronwyn was alive.

"Yes, sweetheart. Talk to me." I knew she couldn't hear me, but it didn't matter.

She sounded so weak, but she was alive.

"W-Wavy. W-Wavy. Wavy." She stuttered the word over and over. That happened when her body first went back into the water of the isolation tank.

"Tip, tip, tip, tip, tip, tip."

What did she mean? Something was tipping over?

"Pens, pens, pens." She repeated over and over.

Then nothing.

I waited for hours, hoping she'd say something else. Praying those nonsensical words weren't the last thing I'd ever hear her say.

Something about Wavy. Something had made her find her voice and talk when she hadn't for days. It couldn't be mindless babbling.

Unless she'd totally cracked. Totally broken beyond repair. And at this point, considering all she'd been through at the hands of Mosaic, and during her short life-time, I couldn't blame her for that.

It took me nearly all night, and hours of listening to her words on repeat, to figure it out.

It wasn't two separate words: tip and pens.

Tippens.

It didn't take me long after that to discover that there was a Dr. Sheldon Tippens, a genetics research specialist in San Diego. There was something about him Bronwyn was trying to tell me.

I wasn't going to be able to handle this on my own. I needed Ian. I needed the team. I was on my way out the door, planning to call as I drove to the office, and almost ran smack into Ian himself just outside my door.

"I need you, man," Ian said.

There'd been a distance between Ian and me for months. He hadn't focused on Bronwyn the way I thought he should have. He'd been too focused on taking down Mosaic as a whole. And then on Wavy.

None of that mattered now.

"I've got a lead." We both said it at the same time and then looked at each other, surprised.

"I think Bronwyn was trying to get a message to me." I spoke first.

Ian gave a short laugh that held no humor whatsoever. "Funny. I think Wavy was trying to do the same thing. Tell me Bronwyn's message first."

"She was saying something about a guy named Tippens."

Ian's eyes got wider. "Sheldon Tippens, the genetic specialist?"

"How the hell do you know that?"

"Wavy was trying to get me info about him too. She left a message for me at the lab."

Holy shit. We ran toward Ian's car.

"If you know about Tippens, why aren't you getting the team together, ready to move?" We climbed in, and he pulled out, tires squealing.

"Because I'm willing to cross lines to get whatever

information I need from this man. If I bring in the team, then we're going to have Callum Webb and Omega Sector breathing down our necks. They don't want anyone else mailed to them in pieces."

Ian had worked with the law enforcement task force to bring down Mosaic the first time. "Can't blame them for that. And Callum's a good man."

"He is. He won't condone what I'm about to do. But Wavy is out of time."

Bronwyn was too, but I didn't bring that up. I knew what line Ian meant he was willing to cross: torturing Dr. Tippens to find out what we needed.

"So you came to me?"

He kept his eyes on the road. "If you're not willing to do this, I completely understand and respect it."

"I'm willing." There wasn't much I wasn't willing to do when it came to helping Bronwyn.

He drove toward the airfield. "You told me you met Bronwyn Rourke for the first time a few months ago. That can't possibly be true if you're willing to go through these measures."

I grimaced. "That's not technically untrue. I did officially meet Bronwyn Rourke in Paris earlier this year."

"But you knew her before, when she was someone else." Ian was too smart not to figure it out.

"Yes. A teenager with a quick mind and nimble fingers. In trouble. I gave her an out."

"Prague." He put more of the puzzle together. "She was the reason you got your ass kicked that one time. I never did understand why you didn't have defensive wounds."

"It was a situation worth taking a beating for."

"I'm sorry I didn't do more for her when we had

Varela undercover. I thought it would blow his cover. Ends up it didn't matter."

"You couldn't have known. Monday morning quarterbacks and all that shit."

He gripped the steering wheel tighter. "At the time, I had no frame of reference for what it felt like to be willing to do anything—any fucking thing—to get someone back. But I do now. Losing Wavy has taught me that. Losing every bit of color in my world has taught me that."

I nodded. "We're going to get them back. Both of them."

His private jet was waiting at the airfield when we arrived, ready to take us to an airport near San Diego. We were in the air minutes after boarding the plane.

We were both focused on the way, talking only about details of grabbing Tippens outside his house as he left for work. From there, we'd move him to a safe house no one else at Zodiac knew about.

Someplace no one could hear his screams.

Neither of us took this lightly. What we were about to do would leave a mark on our souls neither of us would ever escape.

I didn't care. I would give up my soul to get Bronwyn back. Ian felt the same about Wavy.

When we landed, we made our way to Tippens's suburban, upscale neighborhood and waited as the sun came up.

When Tippens pulled out in his BMW an hour later, we made our move. He wasn't all the way out of his driveway when we rammed our vehicle straight into his. It wasn't subtle, but the neighbors were far enough away from one another that by the time someone called the cops, we would already be gone with him.

We wore masks, and our vehicle wasn't registered to anyone. Dr. Tippens got out of his car, at first indignant that someone had hit him. But as soon as he saw us with the masks, he recognized the danger and tried to dive back into his car.

Ian grabbed him and pulled him toward our vehicle. "If you tell me where Wavy Bollinger is right now, you might live to finish this day with all your fingers and toes attached to your body."

Tippens blanched at Ian's harsh words, but I knew they were for the best. With someone like Tippens, unaccustomed to violence, being terrified of us from the beginning would help things go more quickly.

"Wavy Bollinger?" His eyes got big. "No. I swear, I didn't want to—"

Ian headbutted him. "Where is she?"

I wanted to ask about Bronwyn too, but I knew there would be time. I would let Ian have his turn first.

Blood poured out of Tippens's nose. "I swear I didn't want to do it. It wasn't me."

Shit. Did that mean Wavy was already dead? I looked at Ian. I didn't want him to lose his temper if that was the case. Even if Wavy was dead—and I hoped to God she wasn't for Ian's sake—I still needed to find out anything I could about Bron—

Then our plans and having time went to shit. The impossible happened. A shot rang out from down the street. Tippens collapsed into Ian's arms, a red hole forming in his chest as blood spread across his shirt.

I turned away from them and returned fire, even though I knew it was too late. That had been a kill shot. Tippens wasn't going to make it.

Ian yelled at the man dying in his arms, begging for info about Wavy. "Look, you asshole. Tell me where your lab is. You're going to die. If you don't want your wife and kid to find your body lying here, you will damn well tell me where Wavy is."

I fired again as Ian continued to talk to him. Finding Wavy was the best chance to find Bronwyn. A few seconds later, Ian touched my shoulder where I was crouched behind the tire.

"He's dead."

I let out a curse. "Tell me you got something."

"Warehouse. Industrial district in City Heights. I don't know if Wavy's alive or dead, but I'm going there to see."

I nodded and we got into the car, both of us praying like we never had before.

Chapter 21

Sarge

"They killed Tippens rather than let us have him. That means he knows something they were desperate for us not to find out," Ian said.

We sped toward the warehouse district Tippens had mentioned. We'd fled the scene of a murder, an action that might come back and bite us with the cops, but neither of us cared. All we cared about was getting to that building. To Wavy. And if any of my prayers came true, to Bronwyn too.

The Zodiac team was incoming. We weren't keeping anything a secret anymore. We needed backup—people we could trust. They would be here within the hour. Callum Webb and his law enforcement team wouldn't be far behind.

Ian was as frantic as I'd ever seen him. Something Tippens had said had shaken him to the core. I didn't need to ask—I was sure it was about Wavy, and it wasn't good.

I remained icy focused. The part of me I'd had to let loose to be willing to torture a civilian was still in control. We were one step closer to Wavy, which meant one step closer to Bronwyn. She'd been alive when I'd heard her voice hours ago, and I was not stopping today until someone told me where the fuck she was.

We pulled up at the warehouse Tippens had mentioned. Ian parked way too close for any sort of stealth. He wasn't thinking strategically. He wasn't thinking at all.

I muttered a curse as he opened the car door and started running toward the corner warehouse. He wasn't going to succeed at anything but getting himself killed if he didn't start using his brain. I called after him in a low voice, but he didn't stop.

Damn it. I caught him in a flying tackle about twenty yards from the door. We both went down hard.

"I don't know what the fuck you think you're doing, but you need to use your brain." I wouldn't normally talk to Ian that way, but not only did I not want him to get killed, he was currently my only tie to Bronwyn.

We both jumped back up to our feet, and I grabbed him by his shirt and slammed him into the wall before he could run again. "What you're about to do is not only going to get you killed, but possibly her too."

Her could mean Wavy or Bronwyn; take your pick.

"I'm going in." The son of a bitch punched me, and I took it on the jaw without moving. Ian wasn't himself, so I let him have that one.

But when he swung again, I blocked it, then slammed him against the wall, using my size to my advantage.

"If she's in there and she's alive, the guards will have orders to kill if the building is breached. Now use your fucking brain, and let's see if we can get her out alive."

Ian's fists loosened, and I knew the crisis had passed. "I'm sorry."

I let him go. "Don't be sorry. Be smart. We do recon until backup arrives, and then we go in fast and hard."

We nodded at each other, both fully understanding our mission. I went around to the south side of the building as Ian went in through a fire escape. It didn't take us long to know we were definitely in the right place—there were nearly a dozen armed guards.

Ian texted me. ***Ten armed guards mean something important.***

That was for damned sure. ***I concur.***

I got to a vantage point from the side. The guards weren't at high alert, but seemed to be surrounding a crate. They were talking toward it, poking a stick between the slats.

Someone was in there.

Ian realized the same thing. ***Guards interested in large crate in the northwest corner. Taunting. Someone's in there.***

Shit. He was going to make a move.

He needed to wait until backup arrived. Landon had let us know they were a few minutes out.

Stay frosty, boss.

I thought he might actually listen to me, but then all hell broke loose. The guards received a call and went on high alert and pulled out their guns. Most of them turned away from the crate, but two kept their guns aimed right on whoever was inside, obviously prepared to shoot.

Guards on the move. I'm heading toward that crate.

He was going to get himself killed if I didn't intervene. Waiting for backup wasn't an option.

Ian ran toward the guards, eliminating all sense of

stealth, drawing attention toward himself. He took out one guard, and the other fired at him.

I ran in that direction also, firing from my position, even though I was too far to hit anybody. That at least drew some of the attention away from Ian.

But he wasn't going to make it, even with my help. There were too many of them, and too few of us.

Ian was willing to die to keep them from killing whoever was in that crate. Once he went down, I would be the only one to stop them. I ran faster, firing as I went.

My friend was willing to die for the chance to save the woman he loved—not knowing for sure it was her. At one time, I would've called that ridiculous.

But everything about my perspective had changed.

I took down one guard, then another as I ran, but it wasn't going to be enough. I was out of ammo, but I kept running. One guard on the far side of the room had his sights trained on Ian, and I couldn't do anything to stop it.

I expected my friend to fall, but instead, the rest of the Zodiac team burst through the other door, providing the suppression fire Ian needed. One by one, the guards dropped as Landon and the rest of the team took them out.

Ian never stopped running toward the crate, trusting us to cover him.

We did.

I was happy for Ian. I really was. His instincts—his willingness to die—had been spot-on. Wavy had been the one being held prisoner inside that crate. He'd gotten to her in time.

She was in bad shape, but she was alive.

She had Ian. She had her brother, Finn Bollinger, who was also a part of our small rescue team. They had both taken off with her to the hospital where she could be evaluated and get the treatment she needed. They had hope— the start on the road to recovery, both physically and emotionally.

Which was way more than I had for Bronwyn right now. There was not a damned sign of her anywhere around here.

All that was left was the mess Landon and I needed to clean up. Ian had trusted us to deal with the fallout so he could be with Wavy.

There were two guards still alive, eight dead, and I wanted a chance to talk to one of the still-breathing ones before Callum Webb got here with the rest of his law enforcement team.

And by talk, I meant being willing to do what Ian and I had been willing to do to Dr. Tippens to get the information we needed to take down Mosaic and find Bronwyn.

I walked over to the younger guard, maybe in his mid-twenties, grinning at me and full of himself, despite his hands being bound.

"You'll never take down Mosaic, old man. We're smarter than you, more well-funded than you." He jerked his head toward the crate. "What we did to her is nothing compared to what Mosaic will do to you."

I'd only caught a glimpse of Wavy, but I had seen the hell in Ian's eyes.

I didn't wait for another word. I clocked the guy in the chin. I didn't feel bad about hitting a restrained man. I grabbed him by his arm and hoisted him onto his feet.

I looked over at Xander Voyles, one of the men who worked out of Zodiac's Los Angeles office. "The official report is going to say that there was one Mosaic guard arrested and eight dead. This punk is not going on the report at all."

Because whatever knowledge he had about Mosaic, besides singing their praises, he was about to share with me, the easy way or the hard way. It didn't make a difference.

Xander nodded without saying a word.

I dragged the punk to a back room far away from everyone else and locked the door behind me. I untied his wrists, and he immediately tried to attack me, as expected. I responded with a double punch to the gut and then another across the chin. He fell back onto a stack of boxes.

I crouched down next to him. "We can do this all day, and I can guarantee you that I'm going to outmaneuver you every single time, old or not."

He looked dazed. I shut down all my emotions, grabbed his hand, and with one sharp move, dislocated his thumb. "That should stop you from any more punches."

He let out a howl, but I hardened myself against it. "You're going to tell me everything you know about Mosaic, specifically locations. And I want them right damn now." I reached down and broke the pinkie on his other hand.

There was no swagger left in him now. "Dude, I swear to God. I don't know. They didn't tell us anything. We're trying to get in, you know? Work our way up. That's why we were on guard duty here in the middle of nowhere."

That made sense. "Then I'm afraid this is going to be a very painful next few hours for you. You better think of something you can tell me."

There was a knock on the door, but I ignored it. Nothing was going to stop me from getting the answers I needed, even if I knew I was crossing a line. This guy was probably telling the truth and didn't know anything that was going to help me find Bronwyn. But I'd make damned sure of it before I walked out of this room.

"Open it, or I'm knocking it down." I heard Landon's voice from the other side of the door.

Fuck. I walked over and opened it but kept my arm up so he couldn't enter. "You're not going to stop me, Landon. I'm getting the answers I need."

"I'm not here to stop you."

"Then what do you want?"

"I'm not letting you do this alone. If you're going to put this mark on your soul, we'll do it together."

I hesitated for a second then let him in with a nod.

The guy sat up a little straighter on the floor, obviously hoping Landon was going to be the good cop to my bad cop. Landon crouched down before him and gave him one of his infamous smiles.

"Sarge here isn't much of a people person. That's my job. I've got the friendly grin, charming good looks. People like me." He winked at the kid. "It looks like Sarge here has broken a couple of your fingers."

The guy relaxed a little, thinking the danger had passed.

Until Landon continued.

"But you and your friends were taunting a defenseless woman trapped in a box. So as far as I'm concerned, there are at least two hundred and four more bones in your body we can break before we start the legitimate torture."

The guy's eyes grew wide.

"I'm not here to help you, asshole. I'm here to help him." He hooked his thumb back at me. "If he can't get the job done, then you damn well better believe I'll be able to get it done."

I knew Landon was fast, but I couldn't believe how quickly he reached out, grabbed the guy's wrist, and broke it with a simple snap. The man started sobbing before Landon stood back up.

I nodded at my friend in appreciation. I honestly didn't know how far I'd be able to take this. Having him here meant that if I crossed a line, at least I wouldn't be crossing it alone.

"I don't know how much this guy knows. Probably not enough to be useful."

Landon cracked his knuckles and grinned down at the whimpering guard. "Well, I guess we're about to find out."

The guy scampered away as we moved closer.

"I'm telling you the truth." He held out both injured arms. "I swear to God, I don't know anything. I don't know anything except this building. I was paid to come here every day, and a couple of days ago, they brought that girl in. I don't know anything about her, not even her name. I don't know anything about you. And all I wanted to do was become a soldier for Mosaic."

His bravado was completely gone now.

"Maybe you can think of something to tell us. Once we get to the kneecap-breaking part, ideas usually start popping into someone's head."

There was a sick taste in my mouth at the thought, but all it took was remembering Bronwyn's whimpers in that fucking isolation tank to shut that down.

Whatever this guy knew, he was going to tell us.

My phone buzzed in my pocket, and I was tempted to ignore it, not wanting to lose any focus. But when I saw that it was Jenna, I answered. "Now is not a good time."

"I know, I know. I heard that you guys found Wavy. But listen, one of the soldiers there got away."

"It doesn't matter," I told her. "They will be too late to send in reinforcements. We've already gotten Wavy out."

"No, Sarge. What I'm saying is that we caught him

leaving the building not long after Landon's team infil-trated. We were able to track him via different cameras in town. We think he's heading back toward Mosaic, and we still have a track on him."

"What?"

"Virgo, get your ass in gear!" she yelled in my ear. "We have a viable lead, and we can't lose it!"

Landon and I glanced at each other, then we turned and ran.

Chapter 22

Sarge

Jenna led us nearly an hour outside of town as we followed the vehicle. I gripped the steering wheel until my knuckles turned white, hoping we weren't making a mistake. That guard may not have known much, but we had lost our chance to question him now.

Landon gave me a reassuring nod when I glanced over at him as Jenna barked orders at the rest of the nerds not to lose sight of the vehicle. Every time it made a turn, they had to find new cameras to pick it up. Not an easy feat, even for a team as good as Zodiac's. More than once, we'd had to turn around and go in the opposite direction.

My grip got tighter as silence fell over the phone with no direction from Jenna for a few moments. Had they lost the car?

Then finally, she spoke again. "Sarge, we've got him. He stopped. Keep heading east, and we'll send you the exact address. I'm going to see if I can task some satellites to the building."

I put myself on mute and looked over at Landon. "Does Zodiac have satellites we can task?" I wouldn't put it past Ian.

"Not that I know of. I'm pretty sure this is Jenna putting some not-quite-legal practices into play."

I wasn't going to argue—I'd take any help we could get, legal or otherwise. I stomped down harder on the gas as if we weren't already going at a reckless speed.

Taking a two-man team into what could potentially be a Mosaic stronghold wasn't the best of plans. Our only weapons were what we had in the car—a grand total of three clips each for our handguns. That might get us ten feet into one door. If we were lucky.

The address from Jenna came over in text form. It was only fifteen minutes from where we were. Landon and I rode on in silence.

"All right, you guys." Jenna's voice came back on the line. "Looks like we've got a multilevel compound. Large facility. Evidently, they've gotten word there's trouble brewing because there seems to be a mass exodus."

That was both good news and bad news. Good news because Landon and I couldn't take the entire compound ourselves, but bad news because, if they were preparing to exit, they might not leave any prisoners behind.

If Bronwyn was there at all.

"I'm sending the building plans to Landon," Jenna said. "I don't suppose you'd be willing to wait for backup?"

"I can't, Jenna. I can't take that chance. Not if Bronwyn might be in there."

"Okay. But I have to warn you, this building is not pretty when it comes to infiltration. I'll get you as much information as I can—building plans and such." She disconnected the call.

I glanced over at Landon. "You don't need to do this." I was basically leading him on a suicide mission.

"Don't fucking start with me." He rolled his eyes. "There's no way you're going into that building alone. You won't last a minute."

I didn't try to talk him out of it. He was right. My chances of succeeding were basically zero without him, and not much better than that with him.

But if the roles were reversed, I wouldn't let him go in alone either.

"Holy shit." Landon brought up the plans for the building on his tablet. "This place is huge. Multiple levels, looks like it's almost thirty thousand square feet. And there are—wait, let me do the math…carry the seven—*two* of us."

My chuckle held no humor whatsoever. Those were my thoughts exactly.

He let out a sigh. "Please tell me something's funny about this."

"Less than two hours ago, I tackled Ian to the ground because he was about to run inside a building and get himself killed. And now my plan is even worse."

"I'll make sure I'm stretched and ready for tackling before we head in there."

I scrubbed a hand down my face. "They'll kill her. You know they won't leave that facility with loose ends."

"We don't know for sure if she's in there."

I stared straight ahead. "She's in there."

I could feel it in my gut, an instinct I had long since stopped questioning. It was always right.

"Okay." I was thankful Landon didn't argue. "Then we make the most of the chaos. We get in there and stay alive long enough to get her out. I'll try to figure out what our best entrance is."

We were two minutes out from the building when we got another call from Jenna. "I think she's there, Sarge. I think Bronwyn has been in this facility."

"Why?" I would take anything that confirmed what I was already feeling.

"I ran a hunch when I saw that there was an entire subbasement level. Ends up that there were four different isolation tanks delivered to this address over the past year."

I wrapped my hands tighter around the steering wheel. Bronwyn was there. She had to be.

"Okay, that helps," Landon said. "If she's in the subbasement level, we need to go in the southeast entrance that's closest to that area."

That was at least a plan. "With a compound this size, there's no way everyone knows everybody. Hopefully that works to our advantage. We can act like we belong there."

Landon shot me a grin. "We'll kill them with kindness. Or with a gun, whichever is quickest."

We kept our heads tucked down as far as we could as we sped into the compound. Everyone else was heading in the opposite direction. Nobody stopped our car to ask us what we were doing. But if someone did, we were in trouble.

Landon got back on the phone. "Jenna, call all law enforcement that you can. Local, federal, Boy Scout troops…everybody. Let Callum Webb know where we are right now. Mosaic only thinks we're coming. Make sure they know we're coming."

She agreed and he hung up.

I gritted my teeth. "Law enforcement is looking for Bronwyn too. They'll want to take her in."

"We're not going to let that happen. But right now, we need more people, even if it's to cause more chaos."

He was right. Getting Bronwyn out alive was the primary focus. I'd worry about law enforcement afterward.

But they damn well weren't going to get her either.

I pulled up as close to the southeast entrance as I could. Dozens of soldiers were running around everywhere, carrying out weapons and equipment. Information we needed to help take Mosaic down.

I walked past them without a second glance. Taking them down would have to wait for another day.

Our luck held until we came down the stairs toward the subbasement level. A guard was posted outside the door.

"Hey, no one is allowed here. I'm waiting for the word to eliminate the prison—"

He didn't finish his sentence. I clocked him in the jaw, and he fell to the floor. I grabbed him by his shirt and hit him again to make sure he stayed unconscious.

It was all I could do not to put two slugs in his chest. Knowing we might need the ammunition stopped me more than any ethical dilemma.

"Let's hurry up," Landon said. "Between avoiding bad guys and good guys, things could get tricky. Law enforcement is going to be right behind us."

I burst into the room and ran farther down the stairs. The place was like a crypt—complete and utter blackness. I had to use the flashlight on my phone to be able to see even a foot in front of me.

The isolation tanks were through another door. I ran up to it, cursing when I saw the padlock. "We're going to have to shoot it off."

Landon let out a low curse. "That's going to draw some unwanted attention. I'll cover the door."

We didn't have any other option. Once Landon was in place, I shot out the lock, the noise deafening. There was no way that wasn't going to bring reinforcements down this way.

Once again, I didn't care. For the first time in my life, I turned my back to the enemy in a firefight. I couldn't leave Bronwyn in her agony a single minute longer.

Trusting Landon with my life, I lifted the heavy lid that kept all light and sound out and then opened the zipper of what looked almost like a body bag.

Bronwyn was inside, her naked body floating just under the water, arms restrained at her sides. She looked impossibly frail and almost bloodless.

My heart shattered into a million pieces as I let the sight sink in. Her breaths came out in silent sobs; her eyes flinched against the tiny bit of light my phone provided.

"It's me, Pony Girl." I ignored the gunfire behind me as I placed my hand under her head and lifted it so more than her face was out of the water. "Can you hear me, sweetheart? It's Sarge. I'm here."

She didn't respond but kept flinching. I couldn't imagine the stress her body and mind were undergoing—thrust from utter silence and darkness into the deafening noise of gunfire.

"I'm going to release your wrists, okay?"

She was alive; that was the most important thing. Survival was always the most important thing. I knew that, but still…

Seeing her like this made me want to drop to my knees and sob. Made me want to kill every bastard ever associated with Mosaic. Made me understand Ian's single-minded focus.

I unfastened the fetters at her wrists so she could move. She still didn't say a word, didn't open her eyes, didn't try to move away or toward me. I lifted her up into my arms and out of the water. She'd always been on the small side, but now she felt unbearably breakable.

I settled her into my lap then took off my jacket to wrap around her, thankful it was big enough to nearly swallow her.

The shooting behind us stopped. "I got the ones that came down the stairs." Landon turned toward us. "They stopped coming, so I think the cavalry has arrived."

The cavalry was equally dangerous to Bronwyn right now. "I can't let them take her, Landon. She's—"

I wasn't sure what words to use. Broken? Fading? Damaged? Endured more than any one person should have to?

I carried her over so he could see us more clearly in the light from the door.

"Dear Jesus," he whispered. His lips tightened as he met my eyes. "She's alive. That's the important thing."

He pulled out his phone and dialed. "Jenna, can you give us an update? I'm hoping the good guys have arrived."

"Yeah. Callum and his Omega Sector team are on-site. Damn near every cop in California is on their way."

"Good. Thank you. You saved our asses."

"Did you find Bronwyn?"

"Do you want to be responsible for this information?" Landon replied.

"That sentence tells me everything I need to know."

"Jenna," I said. Landon held the phone toward me. "I need everything you can find on the effects of long-term isolation tanks and how I can best help someone who might have been in that situation. I need to know what can be done without someone going into the hospital, if possible."

"Roger that. I'll send whatever I can find." She hung up.

Bronwyn shuddered in my arms, a low moan falling from her throat. I needed to get her out of here. To get her somewhere safe.

Landon squeezed my shoulder. "I'm going to go run interference upstairs. Keep law enforcement off your tail. You need to get her out of here."

I nodded, looking down at her. More than anything, I wanted those blue eyes to open, to look at me. I wanted to know that Bronwyn was still there inside the shell of the woman I was holding.

"I'm not going to take her to a hospital unless I have no other choice. Law enforcement will check there."

"They'll also be looking at your house. Callum knows how close you two are."

"I'm not letting anybody take her. Not now." Not fucking ever. "What she did, the people she killed...it wasn't her fault. She didn't have control over herself."

"We'll work on clearing her name later. Right now, you get her somewhere safe and out of sight."

"I already know where I'm going."

"Where?"

"You sure you want to be responsible for that information?" I shot his words back at him.

"Touché. But you have somewhere to go?"

"I know a place literally built for her."

Chapter 23

Sarge

I an was going to have to bill me again for using his jet. But it was the quickest and safest way to get Bronwyn where we needed to go, and I didn't hesitate for a moment to use it.

Landon had done everything short of a full Broadway show to distract law enforcement so I could get her out. I'd made a beeline for the airstrip where Ian and I had landed this morning. Landon would make sure the flight plan was changed so no one—good guys or bad guys—would be able to follow us. As soon as he saw we were headed toward the mountains of Montana, he'd know where we were going.

Bronwyn still hadn't spoken a word. She'd spent most of the time since I'd gotten her out of that isolation tank curled up in a ball, her head tucked protectively into her own arms.

She'd sat almost completely lifeless as I slipped my shirt over her. Later, she'd been just as sluggish when I'd stopped at a drugstore where I could see the car from inside and found a pair of child-size sweat pants that would actually stay up on her hips.

I'd tried everything to get her to eat, but she hadn't done more than take a couple of nibbles of anything I'd offered. She kept water down a little better, thank goodness. She was so scary thin, I wanted to feed her a three-course meal every two hours.

She'd finally opened her eyes like I wanted, still the gorgeous blue that was burned into my memory. But her stare was so blank, so empty, it was hard to count that as anything near a victory.

She hadn't spoken a word. Hadn't looked at me with any recognition. Hadn't done anything to suggest she was capable of actions beyond basic life functions.

I needed to get her somewhere safe. I was beyond relieved when Lucas Everett met us at the airfield in Missoula, Montana as I requested. I shouldn't have been nervous. I'd known the man for more than a decade, and he'd never once let me down.

I left Bronwyn in her airplane seat in that state of half-sleep, half-wakefulness she'd been in since we'd gotten her out of the tank, and I walked down the steps to shake Lucas's hand.

"Thank you for meeting me."

He smiled. "After the times you've saved my ass, I would meet you anywhere if you called for help." Lucas had been on a different SEAL team, but we'd crossed paths more than once. "But I have to admit, I was surprised to hear you were coming here in the middle of the night."

"I have a friend." I glanced back toward the doorway of the jet. "She needs a place to heal. To lie low."

"That's what the Resting Warrior Ranch is for."

I nodded. Lucas and a few of his SEAL teammates had started Resting Warrior as a place to help people suffering from PTSD. The ranch itself was open for anyone— former military or not—to come get away from the pressures of life for a while. They also trained service and emotional support animals to help people manage their PTSD. Lucas specialized in horses. And alpacas, of all things.

Lucas knew up close and personal what PTSD was and what it could do to someone. I had nothing but respect for a man who took his personal knowledge and applied it to helping others.

And if there was ever a warrior who needed a place to rest, it was Bronwyn.

"You guys are welcome here as long as you like," he continued. "I think the cabin on the north side of the property will be exactly what you're looking for."

"I have to keep this on the down-low, Luc. There may be people coming after her."

That didn't faze Lucas at all. "I haven't mentioned your arrival to anyone else, so you don't have to worry about anything on our end. Does your friend need medical attention?"

"Probably, but a hospital isn't an option right now. I checked her over based on my field med training, and there don't seem to be any immediate physical threats. But…"

She wasn't in immediate physical danger, but God, it was so impossibly hard to talk about what had been done to Bronwyn.

He didn't push for details. "I hear you. Resting Warrior isn't set up as a medical facility. We get people dealing with emotional trauma and mental health issues, but usually they're past most physical concerns."

I scrubbed a hand down my face. "Yeah, if I could take her somewhere, I would."

"We have some basics I'll grab for you so you can keep an eye on her vitals. Oral hydration enhancers, oxygen saturation monitors, blood pressure cuff." He reached over and squeezed my shoulder. "If she needs more than that, we'll find a trustworthy nurse at the local hospital who can come out."

I nodded and went back to get Bronwyn. She didn't say a word as I carried her down from the jet and we got into the truck with Lucas. But for the first time, she was actually alert. Her gaze wasn't the sharp awareness she'd always had, but at least it wasn't completely blank.

Something about Lucas made her wake up slightly.

My jaw clenched as I sat in silence next to her. Maybe me taking care of her wasn't right for her. If she was afraid of me or more comfortable being around other people, I needed to honor that. Even if it gutted me.

Dr. Rayne Westerfield was the full-time psychiatrist at the ranch. I'd been planning on seeking out her expertise once Bronwyn and I'd had a few days on our own, but maybe I needed to do that right away.

Maybe Bronwyn needed to be with someone else. Not me.

It was only when I realized she was sliding closer to me, away from Lucas, that I finally understood. Her defense mechanisms were kicking in, despite being buried under a wall of blankness. She was attempting to protect herself from a possible threat.

I was glad to see it. She may not want to actively engage in any mental way—and nobody could blame her for that—but her instincts were still firing. And her instincts told her I was a safe place.

Bronwyn was in there.

I couldn't deny my relief in knowing that though she may not be interested in seeing me, she at least didn't consider me a threat.

Lucas didn't try to break into Bronwyn's personal space or engage her in any way. He kept his voice low and calm, talking casually to me about things I knew he didn't consider important—weather, happenings in the nearby town of Garnet Bend. His instincts were correct—Bronwyn relaxed more as we drove.

When we got to the main ranch house, he tossed me a set of keys and gestured to a much older truck parked to the side.

"She's pretty old, but she'll get you out to the cabin. It's fully stocked and should have everything you need for at least two or three weeks. If you need something more, you know how to get in touch with me."

I nodded and shook his hand. "Thanks for your help."

I would've liked to have gone in to say hello to Harlan Young and some of the other guys, but now was not the time. I scooped Bronwyn up and transferred her to the truck. She didn't say anything or look me in the eye, but she didn't make any of those terrified noises like she had when I'd first gotten her out of the isolation tank.

As we drove the fifteen minutes to the far cabin, I tried to tell her as much as I could in case she was interested in knowing.

"We're at a place called the Resting Warrior Ranch. I know the guys who started it—they're former SEALs like me. They do a lot of work with support and emotional service animals now—horses, dogs, and some less traditional ones like alpacas, guinea pigs, and rabbits."

I told her how big and remote RWR was and where we were in Montana. I wasn't sure how much was sinking in with her, but I wanted her to know that this was a safe place, that she had options, that she wasn't alone and helpless anymore.

She didn't say anything or acknowledge my words, but at least she was here, she was awake, and she was alive. And wasn't running from me. Or trying to shoot me.

I didn't get any real reaction from her at all until we entered the cabin and I carried her inside and sat her at the table. Lucas had left the lights on. I was afraid they might hurt her eyes, so I turned off the overhead light, leaving only the dim stove light on.

"No."

It was the first word she had said. I spun to look at her.

"You want the lights on?"

She nodded.

Okay, this was something. She was communicating. She was understanding. I turned on every damn light in the cabin. The place wasn't big, two bedrooms, a small living room, and a kitchen with an eat-in dining section. When I came back, she was still sitting at the table where I'd left her.

"Okay, lights are on and will stay that way unless you decide to turn any of them off. Now, how about some soup?"

She didn't respond. I hadn't expected her to. I opened a can of chicken noodle because it was what my mom had always given me when I wasn't feeling well, and I warmed it on top of the stove. It wasn't long until I set the bowl of soup down in front of her.

She blinked at me with those crystal-blue eyes that would always strike me in my gut. I kept my voice as gentle as I could. "Do you want me to feed you, or do you want to feed yourself? Either is perfectly fine with me."

She stared at me and then looked at the bowl.

"Are you real?" she finally whispered. "Or are you just in my mind?"

I covered her hand with mine. Hers was so much smaller, so much more fragile. "I'm real, Pony Girl. I'm here."

She didn't pull her hand from mine. "I'm afraid I'm going to open my eyes and be back inside the black. Be back in the nothing where I don't exist."

Her fear of that reality was clear by the terror etched in those blue eyes.

I swallowed back the boiling fury. There would be time to make Mosaic pay for what they had done to her. Right now, the most important thing was being here for whatever she needed.

"Never again," I promised her. "No more darkness. No more black. No more nothing."

I knew my words could only do so much. Only time could truly prove that she wasn't trapped anymore.

"Trust your senses, Pony Girl. Eat some of the soup. Feel how warm it is, taste how salty. Keep hold of my hand. I'm here. I'm here, and I'm not going anywhere unless you want me to leave."

She shook her head. "Don't leave me."

"I won't." I'd let her go twice before, and they had been the biggest mistakes I'd ever made. I wasn't sure I was ever going to be able to leave her again, even if she wanted me to.

She stared down at the soup again without picking up the spoon. "I'm broken. I can feel it inside. I won't ever be the same person I was."

My heart cracked wide open at her words. She was so

young to have been through so much. I wanted to wrap her in my arms and keep anything from ever hurting her again.

But right now, I would feed her soup. I picked up the spoon and brought it gently to her lips.

"Then I look forward to getting to know the person you'll become."

Chapter 24

Bronwyn

I came back from the nowhere place to the sound of Sarge reading *The Outsiders* to me. When I blinked at him, he stopped reading and smiled.

"Hi."

That deep voice had become the very center of my existence for the past few... I wasn't sure exactly how long it had been. Sometimes, it felt like hours since he'd gotten me out of that isolation tank, away from the pain and darkness.

But I knew it had been much longer—days. More.

"I slipped," I said.

He knew that meant I had gone to the place where my brain shut off. Usually, it happened when I got scared—something triggered a memory or frightened me in some way.

But sometimes, it happened for no reason at all, like now, and that was the scariest thing. Curled up in my favorite overstuffed chair, wrapped in a blanket looking out into the Montana sky through the window while he read to me—that shouldn't make my mind shut down.

But it had. I had no idea how long I'd been totally unaware of what was going on around me. Sometimes, it was seconds—sometimes, it was hours.

Sarge was always here when I came back out of it.

He set the book next to him on the table. "Remember what Dr. Rayne said? It's your mind's way of protecting itself, and if it needs to go to that place, you have to let it."

I made a face. "Sometimes I think Dr. Rayne says whatever it is I need to hear."

He chuckled. "If I'm not mistaken, that's the point of time with a psychiatrist. Talking through the things you need to hear."

Dr. Rayne Westerfield, the psychiatrist here at Resting Warrior Ranch, had been my other lifeline besides Sarge. I'd seen her three times a week since I'd arrived.

Three times a week. That meant...

I sat up straighter. "How long have we been here?"

He leaned back in his chair and crossed his arms over his chest. "You tell me. How long do you think we've been here?"

Grrr. He did that a lot. Made me think about things; made me use my head to figure out the answers.

I stuck out my tongue at him. "It's easier to ask you since I know you know the answer."

He laughed. The sound was beautiful. There was so much wrong in my life, in my head, in my body. But the sound of Sarge's laugh seemed to push it away. Made me feel as if there was a chance everything would be okay.

A chance. A small one.

I looked over at the kitchen counter. There were rows of medicines, vitamins, and supplements that I took every day. A few of them I took three or four times a day.

Some of it was to help my body restrengthen after months of being malnourished and without proper sunlight. Most were to combat what Mosaic had done to me to control my mind. To fight the effects of the neuroinhibitors. Gene editing. Chemical subjugation. A cocktail of drugs developed from Jenna's research with the assistance of the genetics specialist Ian DeRose had hired to help Wavy.

A number of the medications could've been more easily injected into my body, but Sarge had refused unless there was no other way. My neck still bore the marks of injections—the severely damaged skin and tissue would probably be noticeable for years—and he was adamant about not adding to that process.

So I took the pills every day. Some of them I'd probably be taking for the rest of my life.

They didn't always help with the pain. The agony of withdrawal still itched over my skin at times, but I tried not to make it too noticeable when I could.

Although Sarge noticed. He noticed everything.

He saw where I was looking now, and his laughter faded, although his gaze remained gentle on me. He was tired. He didn't think I noticed, and probably a lot of times I didn't, but right now, I could see the exhaustion etching his brown eyes.

How could he not be exhausted after having to put up with me all the time?

I woke up screaming three or four times a night. I sobbed uncontrollably randomly during the day. I had to eat every two hours since my stomach couldn't handle full meals after how I had been starved in the isolation tank. I could barely walk more than twenty yards because my muscles were so weak. I couldn't take a bath without completely freaking out. Even a shower was iffy.

And my hands shook all the time. I looked at them now. I was warm and calm and safe, but the slight tremor was still visible.

My hands had been why I'd gotten hired at Zodiac Tactical in the first place. My ability to move quickly, to take things without others noticing. Now I could hardly hold a utensil without it clanging against the plate.

I had to be wrapped in a blanket almost all the damn time because now not only was I cold despite the mild weather, my brain was paranoid from lack of stimulation.

We called it the nothingness.

Dr. Rayne and I had talked about it at length. My body and mind had spent too many hours with no sensory stimulation made worse by the drugs and experiments Dr. Tippens had done.

I was now in a near-constant state of desperation for physical contact. I found myself rubbing my skin like I had before, or wrapping myself tightly in a blanket, but not to stop pain this time. Now it was because I loved the feeling, loved to be surrounded, loved touch.

It was basically the only way I could function. Too long without it, and my mind started to panic.

I'd been careful not to tell Sarge, and I'd made Dr. Rayne promise not to either. She'd been offended that I'd felt compelled to ask, but she agreed.

I wasn't going to put that on him. He was already doing so much for me; I wasn't going to make him feel like he had to touch me too.

He studied me now, and I tried to remember what we were talking about. Oh yeah, how long we'd been here in the cabin.

"You've got multiple ways of figuring it out. Pick

one," Sarge said as if I hadn't completely zoned out in the middle of our conversation. He must be used to it by now.

I smiled. "The alpacas."

He rolled his eyes. "You and your alpacas. Fine. We've gone twice a week to see them."

I loved all the service animals here at Resting Warrior Ranch. The horses, the dogs, the rabbits, but mostly, I loved the alpacas and the one little sheep that thought he was an alpaca. The main alpaca he followed around was named Mac, so everyone called the sheep Cheese. Mac and Cheese were inseparable—mostly because Mac couldn't get any distance from his little stalker.

Each time we'd gone to visit the section of the ranch that held the alpacas, I'd learned the name of a new one. I'd met six, so...

"Three weeks. We've been here three weeks."

He smiled as if I'd solved some complex math equation. "Good. What are some of the other ways you could've figured it out?"

I made another grumpy face at the mental work. "The books you've read to me, the number of times I've gone to see Dr. Rayne, the horses I've ridden."

We kept to a routine, so remembering and counting them gave me structure to pull from.

He grinned. "Exactly. There's your brain working."

I rolled my eyes. "Yeah, I should definitely get a prize for being able to do something the average five-year-old can do."

"You've got to give it more time, Pony Girl. We're barely past measuring your release in days. And healing isn't always a straight line. Give it more time."

"Time," I muttered.

How long did we really have? How long could we stay

here? How long could I continue to suck the life out of Sarge?

He got up and walked over to me, picked me up out of my chair, and sat down. He resettled me in his lap and wrapped his arms around me.

This. This was what I loved. The feel of him surrounding me. His smell. The sound of his heartbeat under my ear. I'd spent so much time in that tank alone, unable to tether myself to anything, that being in his arms soothed my soul.

I wanted more from him, and it had nothing to do with combating what Mosaic had done to me.

I wanted Sarge.

I wanted what he had done to my body at his house. Not because of my mind's need for physical touch, but because it was him. Because he'd been the one constant light through this hell. Because he was the only man I'd ever wanted for myself.

Because he was Sarge—big and protective and sexy as hell.

But holding me in his lap or wrapping me in his arms while I cried was the most he'd ever done. No more kisses. Definitely no more touches on my breasts or between my legs.

Maybe those things had never happened. So much of everything was confused in my mind. Maybe I'd imagined his house and what we'd done. My mind had given me something I needed—a fantasy.

I knew that kiss in Paris had been real, but now the attraction between us, at least on Sarge's part, had passed.

How could I blame him? Who would want to physically connect themselves to someone as broken as me? I let out a small sigh.

"Hey." He tipped my chin up with a finger, forcing me to meet his eyes. "Why so sad?"

Because I want you to have sex with me, but I'm pretty sure that's never going to happen.

"We can't stay here forever," I said instead. "Eventually, we have to get back to real life."

"We can stay here as long as we need to."

I wanted to argue, but I was already so tired. I snuggled back into his platonic arms and tried to convince myself that everything would be all right.

Chapter 25

Sarge

"Bronwyn is looking better," Lucas said to me.

I leaned up against the fence rail next to him. "Yeah, I guess a month of getting sunshine, regular meals, and not being tortured does a body good."

But my friend was right; Bronwyn did look better. I knew there would be times when recovery would seem to go backward rather than forward. That was how healing worked. It was hardly ever a linear process.

The nightmares that gripped her sometimes were agonizing—so much more than merely fear. Shudders racked her small body until I was afraid they would snap her bones. And all I could do was hold her and help her live through it.

But right now, in this minute, watching the big grin on her face as she trotted along on an old pony, riding for the first time…it was enough.

More than enough.

So much more than I thought I would get a few weeks ago.

Every smile, every word, every grumpy huff I got from her when progress got hard? Each was a tiny miracle of its own, and I treasured them all.

"She's a natural with animals," Lucas said, "or at least she truly enjoys them."

"Have you seen her with the alpacas yet?" I rolled my eyes.

He grinned. "A lot of people love alpacas. Those things can be contrary as hell but are so freaking adorable to look at. She's welcome to hang with them anytime she wants to."

I chuckled. "Don't tell her that, or I'll never get her back to the cabin."

Which wouldn't bother me at all. The more she wanted to stay outside, the better. It was good for her.

She didn't have any memories at all of the first week we'd been here. No memory of all the blood we'd drawn and tissue samples we'd collected for tests to understand what had been done to her. No recollection of the conversations between Jenna, Dr. Rayne, and me as we attempted to get the chemicals out of her system and figure out what she needed to survive.

She didn't remember me getting that fucking necklace off her and smashing it into pieces. Her throat had been covered with trauma marks from where she'd been injected so many times.

Each mark on her damaged skin was a reminder of exactly how badly I'd failed her. It was a miracle she didn't hate me. A miracle she wanted me around at all.

Bronwyn's laugh rang out as she picked up a little speed on the pony led by Liam Anderson, the ranch's resident jokester and also a former SEAL. Lucas and I smiled. How could anybody not smile at the sound of her laugh?

"You got the message from Landon?" Lucas's smile faded as they trotted by. "Sounds like law enforcement is looking for your girl."

"Well, they can wait. She is not giving any statements to the press right now. Until we have more on Mosaic and are able to clear her name, I'm not letting anybody near her, good guys or bad guys."

"Fair enough." Neither Lucas nor any of the people who worked here would give out info about us to anyone, including law enforcement, especially not on someone like Bronwyn who wasn't dangerous.

The men who had created Resting Warrior knew what it was like to need privacy. Law enforcement might have good intentions, but they may not understand the nuances needed for dealing with someone suffering from PTSD. They may cause more harm than good. I wasn't taking that chance with Bronwyn.

But Lucas had other responsibilities. "You need us to go?"

"No, but there were a lot of dead bodies involved with Zodiac rescuing Bronwyn and Wavy. Landon says Callum Webb is getting some heavy pressure from his superiors to get answers."

I crossed my arms over my chest and hiked my foot up onto the fence railing behind me. "They won't be getting them from Bronwyn, at least not for the foreseeable future."

Lucas shrugged. "They suspect she's with you, but they don't know where. And now that Ian is stalling all their attempts to talk to Wavy—I'm sure for similar protective reasons—they're going to want to find Bronwyn even more."

"I'm sure they are." It didn't matter. They couldn't have her.

"Landon says it's not quite as cut-and-dried with Bronwyn as it is with Wavy."

"That's true, at least in the eyes of the law." I scrubbed a hand down my face, remembering the footage from Anchorage and what she'd done in that New York parking garage. "But anything she did wasn't her. Or at least wasn't something she could control."

"But it was bad?"

"Yeah. Bad enough."

So far, she hadn't had any recollection of the people she'd killed, and I hadn't brought it up. Dr. Rayne felt reasonably certain Bronwyn would eventually remember what she'd done, but we would cross that bridge when we came to it. Right now, Bronwyn's sole focus needed to be on recovering her strength, both in her body and her mind.

Talking to law enforcement wasn't going to help with that goal, so I had no plans to let them find us. I would hide her forever if I had to, especially right now when she needed as much time as possible to heal.

We watched her ride for another few minutes. Neither of us wanted to stop her when she was having so much fun. Eventually, she got off and wandered over. She walked right up next to me and put her small hand on my arm. "Can we go see Mac and Cheese before we go back to the cabin?"

"Sure. Always."

She squeezed my arm. "Okay. Liam is going to show me how to take the saddle off the pony, and then we can go. I'll be right back." She gave me a smile and turned and walked toward the barn. At one time, she would've run, her natural energy driving her forward at a faster pace. But she was walking and smiling, and for right now, that was enough.

I looked away from her to find Lucas staring at me. "What?"

"How are things going with your and Bronwyn's relationship?"

"There is no relationship. Not in the way you're suggesting."

"I see. Has anybody told her that?"

"What the hell are you talking about, Lucas?" I asked.

"The way she looks at you. The way she touches you."

I shook my head. "It's not like that. This is about her recovery, nothing else."

He leaned back against the railing and narrowed his eyes at me. "You do know that because someone suffers from PTSD doesn't mean every single other part of their life shuts down."

"I wouldn't do that to her."

"Wouldn't do what to her, Sarge? Consensual sex between two adults is not a bad thing."

"It would be taking advantage of her."

"Would it? Would it be taking advantage of her if that's what she wanted? I've seen the way you look at her." He held out a hand to stop me before I could make an argument. "And it's exactly the way she looks at you."

"Like what, *exactly*?"

"Like she wants more. Like you want more."

I did want more. I wasn't going to deny it, at least not to myself. Under other circumstances, things would be different, but they weren't. So it didn't really matter what I wanted.

I turned to face him. I knew how to shut him down. "I look at Bronwyn kind of the way you at Evelyn, right?"

The pretty, young woman was new to the area and

living temporarily at one of the Resting Warrior cabins. She and Bronwyn sometimes talked. Evelyn's eyes had that same terrified look I wanted to keep out of Bronwyn's. Lucas's eyes got soft every time he looked at Evelyn, which was often.

His jaw got hard. "I do not look at Evelyn that way. It's not like that."

"Whatever you say."

Evelyn had demons in her eyes as much as Bronwyn did, although I had no idea what was behind hers. I wasn't sure anyone did.

But if anyone was going to discover Evelyn's demons and help her fight them, it was Lucas.

Lucas crossed his arms over his chest and grinned at me. "How about I agree to stay out of your love life and you agree to stay out of mine?"

"Deal."

It was a deal I was happy to make because I couldn't allow myself to think of Bronwyn in a romantic or sexual way. It had been cringe-worthy enough when I'd "only" been a decade and a half older than her. Now thinking of us that way would be so much worse.

Bronwyn didn't want sex; she wanted comfort. I could provide that—was happy to provide that.

But the rest? No. That was off the table, no matter how much I might want it.

I wasn't sure she and I had ever had a window of opportunity for a romantic relationship. But if we had, it was well and truly closed now.

No matter how I might wish otherwise.

Chapter 26

Bronwyn

Sarge and I spent a lot of our evenings reading or watching the small television in the corner by the couch. Most days, I was tired after the physical exertion of merely living and didn't make it very long past sunset before I crawled into bed.

I never knew when Sarge came into bed after me. A lot of times, I would fall asleep to the sound of him doing a workout at the other side of the cabin. Push-ups, sit-ups, and other exercises to keep his body in fighting shape.

He was always in bed with me when I woke up with a nightmare. I could reach for him, and he would be there. But besides that, he was careful to stay on his half of the big bed.

I peered at him now over the top of my paperback, the second of the *Twilight* series, and wondered what he would do if I slid over to his side of the bed tonight.

Wondered what he would do if I kissed him.

Wondered if he knew how much I wanted to.

Wondered if the memories I had of him touching my body at his house were real or a fantasy.

As embarrassing as it was to talk about, I'd mentioned it to Dr. Rayne earlier today during our session. I'd asked her if there was any way to know if a memory was real or not.

I'd felt like a perv telling her what I thought I remembered, but she hadn't batted an eye. True to form, after listening to everything I had to say, Rayne tapped her pen against her lips and made a simple statement.

"I think the real question isn't whether it really happened but whether you wanted it to have really happened. Can you answer that question easily?"

Yes, I could.

And, yes, I did want it to be real. Desperately.

But… "If it did happen, I don't think Sarge feels the same way anymore. He makes sure his touch is never more than friendly, platonic. He always gives me comfort, helps me, is willing to do anything I need. But beyond that…nothing."

Rayne tilted her head to the side. "And why do you think that is?"

"Because I'm broken. Because why would he want to get involved with someone as damaged as I am? I can't force myself to turn off the lights at night."

"I agree Sarge probably won't ever make an advance toward you. But not because he thinks you're broken, Bronwyn, but because he is."

"What?" That didn't make any sense. "Sarge is the strongest person I've ever known."

She tapped the pen against her lips again. "Sarge is the one who got you the job that eventually led to your

JANIE CROUCH

captivity and torture. Sarge was the one who stood by helpless, knowing what was happening to you."

"But it wasn't his fault," I whispered.

"I don't think he sees it that way. And for a warrior, watching someone he cares about—someone he would die to protect—suffer is basically the definition of hell. So I don't know that this is about Sarge not being attracted to you. It's more about forgiveness."

"There's nothing I need to forgive him for. I don't blame him for anything!"

Rayne gave me a gentle smile. "Not you. He has to forgive himself. And, like your healing and recovery, that's going to take time."

"So you think I should leave it alone. Not push for a physical relationship at all."

She broke out into a grin. "Actually, the opposite. You're going to have to be the one to take the lead this time."

"How's your book?"

His question pulled me out of the conversation playing in my head. "I've always loved this series. Have you read it?"

He shrugged. "Yeah, a few years ago to see what all the hysteria was about. I liked it okay."

I had to respect a man who could admit he'd read a sparkly vampire series without embarrassment.

I put the book to the side then scooted a little closer to him on the couch. He gave me a tight smile then stood.

"I think I'm going to do my workout a little early tonight. Are you tired after the horse riding excitement?"

Before today's conversation with Rayne, I would've taken his actions as yet another sign he wasn't interested in being near me. But maybe she was right, and this wasn't about me at all.

"Not too tired. Can I ask you a question before you start? I have a memory that I'm not sure is true or not."

It was the first time I'd asked about something like this. Except for this one memory, I'd been pretty happy to let the missing ones stay missing.

He sat back down next to me. "Of course. If I can help, I'm happy to. Ask me."

It was now or never. I decided to jump straight into the deep end.

"Did I have an orgasm on your desk at your house?"

I'd caught him off guard. He hid it well, only a slight muscle twitching in his cheek giving away that my statement had surprised him. "Pony Girl…"

"I did, right? That's not a fantasy I made up in my mind? You kissed me on your bed, and then we did…more on your desk."

"I…" He shrugged, face tight. "You were in pain. Your skin was…"

"You were helping me combat the effects of the regimen."

"Yes." He rubbed his eyes. "I should've found another way. I shouldn't have—"

"No. I liked it. I wanted it." I reached over and touched his arm. "I want it again. I want that and more."

He closed his eyes, his jaw tight. "Bronwyn…"

It took all my courage to keep going. "I know the situation between us is complicated. I know you must look at me and see someone too broken for repair."

His eyes popped open. "No. Not at all. I think you're strong and resilient."

"But you're not attracted to me? Not interested in me in that way?"

"No. I mean, yes, I am. But I don't want to take advantage of you." He rubbed his hand over his face.

I leaned away from him. "Then we're back to you thinking I'm broken. Or at the very least, you thinking I'm not like other women—normal women."

He shook his head almost frantically. "No, that's not what I mean at all. You're amazing. But you've been through so much…"

Dr. Rayne had been both right and wrong. Right that Sarge blamed himself but wrong in that I wasn't sure he was aware of it.

This was so hard. The biggest part of me wanted to leave it alone, to go back to my little bubble that was full of alpacas and books and nothing that forced me to move forward.

But if I wanted Sarge, if I wanted our relationship to ever be more than mentor and mentee, I had to make a stand here. I had to move us both forward.

"What happened to me was not your fault."

He shot up from the couch and began pacing, not looking at me. When he didn't speak after a long minute, I stood and stopped his movements with a touch of my hand on his arm. But he still refused to meet my eyes.

"Harrison, look at me." When he still didn't do it, I cupped his cheek with my hand. "I'm here, alive, because of you."

Finally, those brown eyes met mine, and it broke my heart to see them brimming with tears. "What you went through…"

"Was not your fault. None of it. You made the best choices you could based on the intel you had. It wasn't your fault."

"But…"

I brought my other hand up so I was cupping both cheeks. "Even more important, it can't be changed. What happened, happened, and all we can do is move forward from here. Both of us."

He turned his head to the side and kissed one of my palms. "You're right."

"You told me you looked forward to getting to know the person I've become." When he nodded against my hand, I continued. "That person wants you. If you want her too."

His eyes closed again. "I do. But I don't want to take advantage of the situation. Or of her. Of you, Bronwyn."

This conversation would become circular if I didn't move it forward. I took my hands from his cheeks and pushed one finger against his chest until he took a step backward, then another, until the backs of his knees hit the couch.

I pressed harder with that finger until he lowered himself to sit and I was standing between his legs. "You're the most honorable and courageous man I've ever known. You won't be taking advantage of me."

I moved closer, setting my knees on the couch so I straddled him. I'd sat in his lap untold number of times, but never like this.

Moving us forward.

I lowered myself until I was fully on top of him, wrapped my arms around his neck, and put my face right next to his. "How about if I take advantage of you?"

A soft growl left his throat as I pressed my lips to his. "Yes, please."

And just like that, all my concerns about if he really wanted me melted away. He did. I smiled against him as he wrapped his arms around my hips and pulled me closer.

I used my teeth to gently bite his bottom lip and slipped my tongue inside to play with his when his lips opened. I pressed down against him and was left with no doubt that he definitely wanted me.

Heat swamped me when he trailed his hands up my back to cup my shoulders and push me harder down against him. We both groaned. He traced my lips with his tongue.

"I have only one thing to ask of you," he whispered.

I drew back so I could see his face. "Tell me."

"We take this minute by minute together. If something doesn't feel right to you, if you need to slow down or stop completely, you tell me. For any reason. Not just now, but always."

It had not occurred to me to ask for reassurances that he would stop.

It was Sarge; he would stop in a heartbeat if I asked. I knew that throughout my very soul.

But he needed to know I knew it. Needed to know that he wasn't ever going to be one of the people who had taken my choices away from me. "I promise. But I need you to trust me too."

"How so?"

I cupped those granite cheeks with my hands again. "Trust that I will do what I've promised. Trust that you don't have to stand guard and hold back. Because I promise I will tell you if I'm not okay. Trust that I'm strong enough to know what I want or don't want."

His rugged face lit up into the most genuine of smiles; it was beautiful to behold. "I can definitely do that."

His lips met mine again, his arms wrapped around my hips, and as if I weighed nothing at all, he stood with me in his arms. I locked my legs around his hips as he walked us to the bed.

He lowered me onto it then slid off his clothes before slowly peeling away mine, studying me with sheer appreciation in his eyes. "I'm glad to have the lights on at the moment, that's for sure."

I was too. I wanted to spend hours getting to know his body.

But he had other plans for right now.

His lips met mine again then moved over my jaw and down my neck to my shoulders. Kissing down and up my torso and arms.

All I could do was take it all in.

I loved the way his body felt over mine, loved all the sensations—not just his lips, but his weight on me, the hair on his legs slightly prickly against mine.

I loved the way he smelled—the scent from his shower gel mixed with a male who spent his time outdoors. A mix uniquely Sarge's.

I loved the few freckles on his shoulders that I could see now that we were this close and naked, and the feel of his scalp against my fingers when I cupped the back of his head to pull his lips to my breast.

All the things that made up Sarge surrounded me, sensation after sensation crashing over me in beautiful symphony—chasing away the nothingness until it disappeared into my mind. I wanted to melt into the sensations. Melt into him.

When his lips became too soft against my skin, I kept my promise and asked for what I needed.

"Harder," I moaned as he took my nipple into his mouth. "Please."

He gave a growl of approval before sucking hard on the flesh. I arched into him as he pinched the other nipple not quite hard enough to hurt, but hard enough to drive me crazy.

I wanted him inside me. I shifted my legs, opening myself so we were lined up perfectly against each other. I slid my hand between our bodies and wrapped my fingers around his hard length.

I loved that he let out a shuddery breath as his head came up from my breast and his eyes met mine. "I wanted to make this last a long time for you, Pony Girl. But I don't think I'll be able to at this rate."

"Longer next time. Right now, I want you inside me." I needed it. I didn't know how to explain that I needed to feel him from the inside out.

"We need protection."

I shook my head. "No. I had an IUD placed before I went on active duty. So as long as that's enough for you…"

He broke out into a grin. "More than enough."

He trailed his hand down and worked his fingers inside me like he had on his desk, slowly at first then faster and deeper when I demanded more.

Then that wasn't enough.

I wanted Sarge over me, surrounding me, inside me. I couldn't get the words out, so I clutched at him. He understood and shifted his weight, his big hands holding my thighs open as he buried himself inside me.

He moved slowly at first, allowing me to adjust to him, but then his movements became hard, long thrusts that brought his body fully up against mine. I wrapped my arms and legs around him, burrowing my face into his chest, breathing in his scent.

I sobbed his name as pleasure crashed over me. He kept me clutched to him as he continued thrusting, then called my name almost as a prayer when he found his release.

He slowed then gathered me closer, still inside me. We held each other, neither of us wanting to move.

The nothingness had never been further away.

Chapter 27

Bronwyn

A week later, Sarge and I were lying in bed. Long gone were the days when he stuck to his side. His big body was wrapped around me, one arm hooked over my waist, the other snaked under my neck and back up around my shoulders, his leg thrown over both of mine.

We discovered that we both slept better this way. With him fully touching me, surrounding me, pressed together almost completely.

At first, I'd been embarrassed about it. We already spent almost all our time together—more so now that we could hardly manage to get out of bed. It seemed selfish to want him so close even when we were sleeping.

But whenever I tried to scoot away to give him his space, he immediately pulled my body back to his.

"Stay."

Even when he wasn't fully awake, he would say the

words and tuck me back under him. Since this was where I wanted to be, I wouldn't get offended that it sounded as if he were training one of the Resting Warrior's service dogs.

His body surrounding mine helped chase away the nightmares.

That, and being so completely exhausted from our lovemaking.

"Evelyn and I are going to go into town to have coffee. It's her day off."

"I think that's a great idea." His voice was a low, sleepy rumble in my ear. I burrowed back into him, which, in turn, produced a little growl from his throat.

I loved that sound, loved that he seemed to want me as much as I wanted him.

I brought his hand up from my belly and kissed his palm. "I like Evelyn, and I like Lena at the coffee shop too."

"Yeah, Lena is something else," he murmured. "Definitely different from you and Evelyn."

Lena was loud and fun, laughed a lot, and had fire-engine–red streaks through her hair. Definitely different from Evelyn or me. "That's why I like her."

"I think coffee with your friends is a good idea."

I relaxed a little. I hadn't been asking his permission exactly, but if he hadn't wanted me to go, I probably wouldn't.

Hell, knowing he wanted me to, it was still going to be hard. But I knew I needed to.

We had to establish some sort of new normal if I was ever going to leave this place and get back to real life. And despite what he'd said about not being in any hurry, I knew we couldn't stay here forever.

Over the past week, Sarge had been getting more phone calls. Or maybe he'd always been getting a lot of phone calls and I'd finally started paying attention. Mostly, they'd been Landon and Jenna. I'd actually talked to Jenna a couple times—it had been good to hear her voice. To thank her and let her know I was doing better.

But whatever phone conversations Sarge was having made his lips pull down and brows furrow. Especially when he didn't think that I was watching.

He never told me what they said, but I knew it wasn't good. What I didn't know was if it was about me. And I was too much of a coward to ask.

I did ask about Wavy. Dr. Rayne had gone to Denver to work with her, and I was glad to hear Wavy was doing better than she had been. But the other... Unless Sarge brought it up, I wasn't going to ask.

"There's some money on the table you can use while you're in town."

I stiffened in his arms. I didn't want to take his money, but what choice did I have?

"What?" he whispered before gently biting my ear.

"I don't like to take money from you." He'd already given me way too much of everything. Money felt over the top. "And don't distract me."

I could feel his lips move into a smile against my skin. "It's not my money. That's your bonus money as a Zodiac Tactical employee who was injured while on a mission. It's a stipend provided to any employee during their recovery."

I turned to face him, mostly to get away from those lips that kept nibbling on my ear and his hand that was rubbing soft circles on my stomach that would distract me way too easily. "Are you making that up?"

"No." He kissed my nose. "It's in your contract."

"Even though I'm probably never going to be an active agent for Zodiac again?"

He pulled me closer. "You haven't given yourself

enough time to know whether that's the case or not, but yes, it doesn't matter if you aren't an active agent, it still applies."

Even if I could somehow get my hands to stop shaking and my nightmares under control, I wasn't sure that I ever wanted to go back to what I'd been doing for Zodiac. But what were my other options? I didn't have any other real skills, and I definitely didn't have any schooling. I wasn't a United States citizen, so I couldn't stay here. I would have to go back to the Czech Republic.

Everything in me rebelled at the thought of being back in the same country as Nikolai. He hadn't forgotten what I'd done—every time he looked in the mirror would be a reminder. If he caught so much as a whisper that I'd come back, he would find me and kill me. I wasn't going back there ever, even if it meant finding a way to be an active Zodiac agent again.

Sarge dipped a finger under my chin to force me to look at him. "What? What are you thinking about right now?"

Now it was my turn to try to distract him. I didn't want to talk to him about my past. The vision of Nikolai's men beating Sarge so badly still haunted my dreams. Sarge wouldn't have forgotten it either.

"I'm a little nervous about my first trip out on my own." I slid my hand between our bodies, down his stomach, and wrapped it around his length. I loved the hiss that escaped his lips. "I'll miss being in bed with you."

He tangled his fingers into my hair and pulled my lips to his. "Then I'll have to give you plenty of reasons to make sure you want to come back as soon as possible."

~

I was almost late for my coffee date.

Sarge had very thoroughly reminded me of what I would be missing and why I should come back to him as soon as possible. I was a little bit sore as he drove me to the main Resting Warrior Ranch house.

And I loved every bit of it.

I loved it when he wasn't gentle and didn't worry about whether I was breakable. Loved to feel him lose control just a little bit. Loved he knew I could handle it.

I waved to Evelyn and got into her car. She kept her distance from Sarge and, as always, pretended she wasn't looking at Lucas. I wanted to ask her about them. Whether they had ever been a couple or whether she wanted them to be a couple, but I wasn't sure if those types of questions were appropriate. I'd never had much experience with girl talk.

But I would try. Because that was why I was doing this, right? Trying to work my way into some sort of normal. "Do you like the ranch? I do. I like the animals, especially the alpacas. Mac and Cheese are my favorites."

Great, now I was rambling.

Evelyn nodded. "Yes, I like it."

"Have you lived here a long time?"

"No, not long. Lucas offered me one of the guest cabins, and I took him up on it when I first arrived in the area."

"Oh. I hadn't realized. Where were you before here?"

Her hands tightened on the steering wheel. "Around."

I stopped asking questions. I understood not wanting to talk about the past. We spent the rest of the ride into town talking about the animals. Saying goodbye to them was going to be the hardest part of eventually leaving.

That and having to share Sarge with the rest of the world.

We made it to Deja Brew, the coffee house where Evelyn worked, timing it so that we would hit between rushes and the owner, Lena, could join us rather than be working.

"There they are!" Lena rushed by us over to the window as we came in. "Did you guys drive yourself, or did Bronwyn's sexy man drive?"

"We drove ourselves." Evelyn hugged her boss as she turned from the window. "So no need to start drooling."

Lena turned to me, fanning herself. "Speaking of drooling, look at that smile Bronwyn has. That is the smile of a woman who has gotten something good. And very recently too."

I could feel the heat crawl up my cheeks, but I couldn't deny it. I didn't want to deny it.

Sarge was my man. I didn't know for how long or what it would ultimately mean. But right now, yes, he most definitely was. And hell yeah, I had gotten something good.

Evelyn smacked her friend lightly. "Stop. You're making her blush."

Lena turned to Evelyn. "When are you and that Lucas going to do something worthy of me teasing you into blushing?"

Evelyn looked away. "It's not like that between him and me."

Lena patted her on the shoulder. "You keep telling yourself that, sweetheart. I've seen the way he looks at you."

Lena kept talking, thankfully moving on from blush-worthy topics, as she grabbed us all some coffee. I'd never known a woman like her, so boisterous and funny, so sure of herself. She'd been out to the ranch a few times, and everyone liked her.

As she put the coffee on the counter, I pulled out my money. "How much?"

She shooed me away. "This is on the house. That's the benefit of owning your own coffee shop."

"Oh." I put my money back in my pocket.

"You look disappointed."

"Not really. I actually have more money than I expected."

She winked at me. "That's a good problem to have."

When Sarge had said there was money for me on the table, I hadn't expected it to be more than a thousand dollars. He'd dragged me over to his computer before I could freak out and showed me my contract. The money really was mine.

I didn't bring it all with me for coffee, of course, but it felt weird knowing I had so much. Enough to take care of myself for a while. At least until I figured out a plan.

My hands weren't quite as shaky as I reached for the mug Lena handed me.

I was thoroughly enjoying hanging out with these women, even if I wasn't talking very much, as one cup of coffee turned into two. I was mid-sip when a cat jumped across the couch out of nowhere. More surprised than afraid, I jerked out of its path and dumped the remains of my cup onto my shirt.

"Holy hell, Bronwyn, are you okay?" Lena jumped off and shooed the cat away. "That thing is a stray, and I haven't been able to get rid of it. Did you burn yourself?"

"No, it wasn't very hot." I wiped at my shirt with a napkin. It didn't hurt, but my cream-colored shirt wasn't hiding the stain very well.

"Are you sure you're not hurt?" Evelyn had lost all color in her cheeks.

"Yeah, fine, promise." I rubbed at my shirt some more, but it wasn't helping.

"Hey, Evie, look at her. She's all right." Lena put an arm around Evelyn.

Something about the hot drink spilling had triggered Evelyn. I didn't ask for details. Triggers were vicious beasts and often struck without warning.

"Yeah, I promise, I'm fine. Just a mess."

"Let me see if I have something in the back you can change into," Lena said.

"Actually." I dropped the napkin onto the coffee table next to my empty mug. "If it's okay with you guys, I'm going to run into the clothing store across the street and buy something for myself."

Lena looked relieved. She obviously wanted to make sure Evelyn was okay. "There you go. Spend some of that money burning a hole in your pocket. I'll bet that's what Sarge would want you to do."

Lena was still soothing Evelyn as I dashed to the small boutique. The teenage girl working the counter barely looked up from her phone when I came in. There was no one else around, so I wandered. I'd never been shopping in the United States before. It was new. And weird.

And wonderful.

I wasn't sure my exact size. The teenager decided to get off her phone and help me, gathering a few items I never would have chosen, and guiding me toward the dressing room in the back.

"You should start with this sweater crop top. It shows off the midriff. It doesn't work on a lot of people." She hung multiple shirts on a hook by the door. "But you've got a tiny little figure, so you can pull it off."

Probably would be best not to explain that I got my tiny little figure from being imprisoned and starved for months.

"Okay, thanks."

"I'll go see if there's anything else. You don't need cream or white. That washes you out. You need color..." She was still muttering to herself as she walked back into the main section of the store.

I tried on the crop top first, but it was way too short, whether I had the figure for it or not. I grabbed the next one, a pink sweater. I brought it up to my cheek and rubbed against its softness.

Yes, this one. I was already in love with it. I pulled it over my head and looked in the mirror.

I looked different.

There were a couple small mirrors in the cabin, but I hadn't really paid much attention to them except when brushing my teeth. But here, with the full-length mirror taking up half the dressing room wall, I couldn't escape myself.

I was definitely skinnier than I'd ever been in my life. But there was a color to my cheeks, a smile pulling at my lips that a few weeks ago I hadn't been sure I'd ever see again.

The pink sweater was soft and feminine with my jeans. And all I wanted to do was show it to Sarge. He would understand why I liked it so much.

Right before he took it off me and threw it on the floor.

I didn't need the teenager to bring me anything else. This was the one. I ran my hand down the soft material again then turned and opened the changing room door.

A man I didn't recognize stood there. "Hello, Bronwyn."

Before I could say anything, I felt a prick on the side of my neck. I turned and found a second man standing silently by the door that led out the back of the shop.

Then everything faded to black.

Chapter 28

Sarge

I hoisted the bag of feed off my shoulder and into the barn with more force than necessary. Bronwyn and I were going to have to leave Resting Warrior Ranch. There didn't seem to be any way around it.

I looked over at Lucas. "I can't bring law enforcement down on you guys. What will happen if you get arrested for obstruction of justice? The work you do here is too important."

While Bronwyn was gone on her coffee date, I was helping Lucas in the barn. I'd been interrupted by yet another message on my phone from Landon. Law enforcement from multiple agencies—particularly Callum Webb with Omega Sector—were starting to get very hard up to talk to Bronwyn.

"We can always tell them we didn't know you were around." Lucas poured feed into a trough. "That you took up residence in the cabin, and we didn't know you were there."

"That's not going to hold much water since they know our military connection."

Callum didn't know Bronwyn and I were here, but it wouldn't be long before he sent someone to ask Lucas what he knew. I didn't want to put my friend in a position where the ranch would be at risk.

Lucas finished pouring the bag and looked over at me. "Do you have somewhere else to go? A safe house?"

I hefted another bag onto my shoulder. The physical work felt good, but it wasn't enough to eliminate the frustration clawing at me. "Yeah, but a safe house isn't what Bronwyn needs."

She needed space where she could be outside. She was starting to turn corners for the better. I didn't want to put her somewhere that limited her activities and forced her to stay inside and hide, slowing her progress or maybe halting it altogether.

But what was the alternative?

"I'll find something," I continued. "She wouldn't want to take a chance on anything happening here because of her."

Lucas nodded. "Why don't we have a meeting and come up with the various safe houses and potential hideout locations among all of us? I know some of the guys have places no one has ever used, even cabins more remote than—"

He cut off as Evelyn walked into the barn. His face all but lit up. Normally, a smile didn't come naturally for Lucas, but it did for Evelyn. "Hey, you. How was coffee?"

She didn't smile back. Didn't move from the doorway. Her hands were clenched together, thumbs rubbing over her fingers nervously. I looked over her shoulder for Bronwyn, but I didn't see her.

"Everything okay?" Lucas asked.

"Where's Bronwyn?" I asked. "Is she here?"

Evelyn bit her lip. "I was hoping maybe she came back here or you knew where she was."

I dropped the feed bag where I stood. "Why would she be back here? You were her ride. What happened?"

"She spilled some coffee on her shirt then went to the store across the street to replace it. She never came back."

Every instinct in my body went on high alert. "How long ago did this happen?"

Evelyn shrank back. I knew I was scaring her, but damn it, I was scared. "How long, Evelyn?"

"I don't know. An hour? It took us a while to realize there was a problem, and finally I came back, hoping she was here. She doesn't have a cell phone."

She looked over at Lucas, hands still wringing. "I should have called you. I don't know what I was thinking."

"It's fine. Bronwyn is fine. We're going to find her. Don't worry." Lucas kept his voice soothing, a lot like how he sounded when he was gentling a horse. Evelyn obviously needed it, but I couldn't worry about her right now.

Where the hell was Bronwyn?

"I need to get into town." The thought of her being back at Mosiac's mercy was like acid pooling in my gut. "I shouldn't have let her go alone."

Lucas nodded. "Let's not assume the worst. Maybe she had a panic attack and wandered off. I'll grab a couple of the guys who are good at tracking, and we'll meet you there."

I ran for the truck.

"I'm sorry." I heard Evelyn whisper as I passed by.

I stopped and turned to her. Time was of the essence,

but I knew Bronwyn would want me to reassure Evelyn. "This is not your fault. She was happy to go with you. Happy to have some friends. Thank you for letting us know."

She nodded, and I turned again and sprinted away.

I kept my eyes along the side of the road as I drove, hoping maybe Bronwyn had gotten overwhelmed and decided to walk back to the ranch. A couple of times, I stopped and got out to shout her name. If she was scared, hiding somewhere, maybe my voice would help her.

But nothing.

I drove the rest of the way to town and parked in front of the coffee shop. Lena immediately ran up to me from behind the counter. "Did you find her? Was she back at the ranch?"

"No. Have you seen anything or heard anything else? Tell me what happened."

"She spilled some coffee then decided to go buy a new shirt across the street. Evelyn was upset, and I wanted a chance to talk to her, so I encouraged Bronwyn to go. She said it was what you would want her to do." Tears welled up in her brown eyes. "I'm so sorry, Sarge."

I scrubbed a hand down my face. "No, it's not your fault. That is what I would want her to do. Was she okay when she left? Any signs of panic or anything?"

"No, she was actually a little excited about it, I think. About having money."

That's why I'd given it to her all at once, right? Because I wanted her to have a sense of independence, even if it was small.

I ran across the street to the clothing store, once again looking for anywhere Bronwyn might be hiding. Although it didn't sound as if she had been stressed or panicked.

I never thought that news would make me feel worse instead of better.

There was a teenage girl working the register in the store. She barely looked up from her phone when I entered. "Hey, did you see a lady come in here? Blue eyes, brown hair?"

"Did I see her?" She slammed her phone on the counter. "She's going to get me in so much trouble with my mom. After all I did to help her pick out an outfit, and then she ran off without paying."

"Slow down. What are you talking about?"

"She wanted to buy something, and I was giving her some suggestions, steering her away from the old-lady shirts she wanted. She's too young and hot to be wearing that sort of stuff." The kid let out a dramatic sigh. "Then, as thanks, she shoplifted."

"So she stole a bunch of shirts and walked out the door?" I was trying to wrap my mind around what the girl was saying. Bronwyn had a history with theft, but I had no idea why she'd do something like that when she had plenty of money.

"No, she walked back to the dressing room, and I brought her some stuff. And next thing I knew, she was gone, along with one of the sweaters."

"The dressing room. Where is it?"

The girl rolled her eyes, not budging. "Man, I'm going to be in so much trouble when my mom finds out that somebody shoplifted."

I fought to keep my temper. "How much was it? I'll pay for it."

"$39.99."

I grabbed two twenties out of my wallet and handed them to her. "Show me where the dressing room is."

Now that the kid wasn't going to be in trouble with her

mom, she was more helpful. She showed me the dressing room, and I immediately froze.

I pointed to the door next to the dressing room. "Where does that lead?"

"Out back. That's why I was going to get in trouble. I'm supposed to have the alarm on, but I didn't because my boyfriend was going to come by later."

"So anybody could have come in or out of the door without you knowing."

She gave a one-shouldered shrug. "Yeah."

"Do you have any security cameras or things like that?"

The girl looked down at the floor.

I knew what that meant. "You turned it off because your boyfriend was coming."

"Look, all I wanted was a chance to make out with him. My mom is super strict. She doesn't like Derek."

Now I had no way of knowing if Bronwyn had run out the back or if someone had taken her. Either way, I headed out the door.

"Don't tell my mom, okay?" the girl called as I left. I threw up a hand to show I had heard her. I didn't know who her mom was, and I didn't care what the kid had done. All I wanted was to find Bronwyn.

The alley at the back of the store didn't show much sign of a struggle, but I wasn't sure Bronwyn would put up much of a fight if she was taken.

Physically, she was getting stronger. But mentally, emotionally… Someone taking her against her will might make her shut down completely. Every bit of progress she'd made in the past weeks could be lost in an instant.

"Where are you, Pony Girl?"

~

We searched for Bronwyn the rest of the day and into the night. Lucas had all the Resting Warrior guys helping us. There was no sign of foul play, which led me to believe that something had triggered Bronwyn.

I talked over everything with Lucas, and we'd come to the conclusion that maybe giving her all that money at once had been a bad idea. Maybe she'd decided she'd be better off on her own.

And while I couldn't deny that was a possibility, it didn't feel right to me. Bronwyn wouldn't run like that. Not unless she had reason to.

There were a lot of other options. Residual brain-washing or something having triggered her. Or someone taking her.

But before we started searching farther out, I wanted to eliminate the possibilities closer in. It was her first time away from the ranch since she'd gotten there. Maybe she'd panicked, got scared, and went off by herself.

We concentrated our efforts in town then on the prop-erties surrounding it. Half of Garnet Bend came along to help in the search though they didn't know Bronwyn. They only knew there was a woman who might be in trouble.

But nothing. No sign of foul play, no sign of stolen vehicles she might have used if she'd run, and no sight of Bronwyn.

It was nearly dawn when I headed back to our cabin, praying I'd find her there tucked up in bed. Maybe she'd have no recollection of what happened, and that would be fine. As long as she was safe.

But again, nothing.

And when I saw she had left some of the money in the cabin, I knew it was time to call in the big guns. There may have been no signs of foul play, but that didn't mean someone hadn't taken her. I'd wanted to believe she was making her way back to me, but with each passing hour, it became clearer that wasn't the case.

I needed Zodiac Tactical. I knew Ian hadn't been in the office much—he'd been spending all his time with Wavy, nursing her mental health. He and I hadn't talked to each other at all since that day we'd been prepared to torture information out of Dr. Tippens. I wasn't sure if he knew Bronwyn was with me.

Or that she had been with me. My stomach dropped like a lead anchor. I hadn't let myself think that she was truly gone again.

I needed my team.

As I grabbed my phone to call Ian, it buzzed in my hand. Landon.

"I've got a problem—" I said with no preamble.

He cut me off. "Bronwyn's gone."

My grip tightened around the phone. "How do you know that?"

Another video from Mosaic? I couldn't live through that again.

Or, Jesus…pieces of Bronwyn mailed to law enforcement like Silas Varela had been?

Bile burned up my throat. I felt like all the oxygen had been sucked out of the room.

"It's not the worst, Sarge. I swear to you. It's not Mosaic."

He had to repeat it again before I could hear him through the roaring in my ears. "Then what the fuck is going on?"

"It's Callum Webb. Omega Sector has her."

Shit. That was better than Mosaic but still bad. "They arrested her?"

"Not exactly. It's not her Webb wants. He needs to talk

to Wavy, but Ian has been completely stonewalling him. Webb wants you to convince Ian to let him question Wavy."

I slammed my fist against the wall. "Webb thinks Ian is going to say yes to me if he's saying no to him?"

"Webb thinks Ian might allow it if it means keeping Bronwyn from being arrested. But Ian won't talk to him at all. That's where you come in."

"How?"

"Ian has taken Wavy out on a yacht for some R and R. Webb wants to land his helicopter there, but there's no way in hell Ian is going to allow that. You, on the other hand, Ian will allow on that ship. Webb will just be with you."

I rubbed my fingers over my eyes. It had been a long fucking night. "Ian'll be pissed."

"But he'll forgive you. Especially because Bronwyn's involved. Webb has given his word he'll take you directly to her as soon as he gets to talk to Ian and Wavy."

Callum Webb wasn't a bad guy. Omega Sector as a whole was one of the top law enforcement units I'd ever worked with.

But that didn't mean I wasn't about to kick some serious ass.

"No charges filed against Bronwyn? We're all agreed to work toward taking down Mosaic, not in pinning blame where it doesn't belong?"

"Yes, Webb gives his word."

"Okay." I didn't like the thought of lying to my boss— my friend—and potentially causing some sort of emotional setback for Wavy. But I would do it to get Bronwyn out. "I'll do it."

"I've already sent the plane for you."

Chapter 29

Bronwyn

With every breath, I fought back the panic.

I was okay, I reminded myself over and over. I hadn't been harmed. And most importantly, I hadn't been put back in any sort of isolation pod.

I could breathe.

I could breathe, and I wasn't restrained. There was a window in the room I was in, along with a table with two chairs on either side and a couch where I'd gotten a couple hours of sleep before the sun had come up.

This room was almost like a much plainer version of Dr. Rayne's office. She had more comfortable furniture and paintings on the walls and a set of clocks that showed the time on three different continents.

All in all, this place wasn't terrible. Not like the cell Mosaic had held me in. There was a bottle of water on the table and some snacks. And a clear view to the outside—

although there wasn't much to see besides an empty parking lot.

But the door was locked.

I sucked in a long breath again, doing my best to swallow past my fear.

When I'd awoken from whatever they'd injected me with, I'd been in a car, the two men from the boutique in front of me. I'd immediately reached for the door handle, ready to throw myself out of the speeding vehicle.

Those doors had been locked too.

One of the men was talking on the phone and turned to me. "Yes, sir, she's waking up now." Pause. "Yes, sir."

He handed the phone back to me, which was the last thing I expected. An image of a handsome man with dark skin and light gray eyes appeared on the screen.

"Bronwyn, I'm sorry for all the drama. My name is Callum Webb. I work for a law enforcement task force known as Omega Sector. I want to assure you that we don't mean you any harm."

I'd heard Sarge talk about Omega Sector, so I knew it was a real thing. I vaguely remembered someone named Callum too.

"Where am I? What do you want from me?"

"We're taking you to a holding facility. Not in Montana."

I vaguely remembered a plane, but I didn't know if that had really happened. My pulse skyrocketed. Holding facility sounded an awful lot like cell. I bit my tongue to keep from curling into a ball and wailing.

"Am I under arrest?" I finally got out.

Callum's brows furrowed. "No. That isn't my intent. As a matter of fact, we took you from Garnet Bend to keep you from being arrested. We were not the only law enforcement agency looking for you."

This still didn't tell me if they were friend or foe. "So you kidnapped me."

"I'd prefer not to look at it that way either." He rubbed his hand over the top of his head. "Agents Monboit and Palgrave have strict instructions to make sure your needs are met and keep you out of law enforcement's hands. Hopefully, this will work out well for everyone."

"I don't understand."

"We need intel from Ian DeRose, and I'm hoping you're going to be the key to my getting that."

"I hardly know Ian." Why was everyone always trying to use me to get to Ian DeRose?

Callum let out a sigh. "I know. But he doesn't want you to go to jail."

"Why would I go to jail?"

He was silent for a long minute. "How much do you remember of what happened while you were held by Mosaic?"

I shrank back against the seat. "Bits and pieces. I'm not sure which memories are real and which are made up in my mind."

Those piercing gray eyes pinned me. "I believe you. And it's what I keep trying to convince my bosses. But I've got to give them something, and you're my best chance for that."

"I still don't understand."

He smiled, but it was more sad than anything else. "No, I'm sure you don't. Once again, I'm afraid you're a pawn, Bronwyn. In a chess game I hope doesn't blow up in my face."

He'd ended the call not long after that—with me still as confused as I'd been when it had started—and I'd ridden on with agents Monboit and Palgrave in silence.

We'd ended up here in the holding facility that wasn't a cell but definitely had a locked door.

I took another deep breath.

Was Sarge worried? How would he know what had happened? Did he think I'd run off with the money? It wasn't an unreasonable line of thought. I didn't know how long I'd been here or how long I'd been unconscious before I'd woken up in that car. There'd been no mountains around, so I definitely wasn't close to the Resting Warrior any longer.

I was back to counting meals to figure out how long I'd been here. Four so far. Monboit or Palgrave had come in and taken me to a small bathroom a few times.

I did okay unless I thought about the fact that I was trapped in this room. That, despite it being larger and nicer and having more furniture than where Mosaic had kept me, I was still at the mercy of others.

Others who could decide at any point to take me out of this room and throw me into a box. Make me lose myself again.

I wouldn't survive this time.

When it started to get dark outside, things got worse.

There was plenty of light in the room, but the walls felt as if they were closing in on me. I sat in one of the corners and wrapped my arms around my head, fighting for each breath.

Hey, Pony Girl.

It wasn't Sarge. I knew it wasn't him. But the sound of his voice helped my throat ease enough to allow air into my lungs.

When I looked over to the side, I saw him smiling at me.

"You're not here," I whispered. "I'm crazy."

You're trapped in a room that reminds you of your captivity. It's getting dark outside. You're struggling to handle it. That doesn't make you crazy.

I shook my head. "No, I'm crazy because I'm talking to you and you're not really here."

You've got to do what you've got to do. Survival is always the most important thing.

I let his words sink in. He was right. And he'd said that to me more than once. Survive. I took a moment and focused. The lights were dimmer in the room, but it wasn't dark. And the nearly full moon out the window would provide illumination even if the lights went out. I was okay.

My pulse lowered, my breathing evened, the room opened back up again.

And maybe I'm here because I like your company.

Sarge winked and gave me his rusty smile, looking so exactly like he did in real life that I would've sworn he was sitting here.

"You're not here."

Are you sure? Feels like I am to me.

It did to me too.

I was so tired. I lay out on the floor and could feel Sarge wrap around me like he did when we slept—one arm around my midriff, one around my shoulder, a leg thrown over mine.

I fell asleep in his embrace there on the floor.

$\sim$

"I see you prefer the floor to the comfort of a couch."

I sat straight up from where I'd been sleeping at the sound of a voice inside the room.

It was morning. I'd somehow managed to sleep through the night.

There was no sign of Sarge anywhere around, but that didn't surprise me. I got to my feet.

"Who are you?" This wasn't either Monboit or Palgrave. He was shorter, a little stocky, and had a European accent.

"I'm Agent Theodore Wilson. I'm not with Omega Sector." He said it almost with disdain. "I'm with Europol. The European Union Agency for Law Enforcement Cooperat—"

"I know what Europol is."

He raised his eyebrow and crossed his arms over his chest as he walked closer to me. I forced myself not to move. "Good. Since they've brought you to Europe, I thought I would take a moment to meet you in person."

Europe. I definitely hadn't known that.

But I would have to freak out about that later. Right now, I needed to handle the threat in front of me. Agent Wilson wasn't like Monboit and Palgrave. Not that I had any abiding love for the other agents, but they'd never looked at me the way this guy did. Like I was a criminal.

This was someone who would like to throw me in a cage. A different one than Mosaic, but a cage nonetheless.

"Where are the other agents?"

Agent Wilson gave me a smile that was closer to a sneer. "Palgrave and Monboit received an important summons and had to go handle some things. Seems like Callum Webb didn't have official clearance to keep you here. Working rogue again."

"So you're here to arrest me."

"I'm here to ask you some questions."

"And if I don't want to answer your questions?"

He pulled out a pair of handcuffs and had them snapped on my wrists before I could move. With a jerk, he had me pulled toward the table and seated in one of the chairs. He attached the handcuffs to a bracket locked on the top of the table so I couldn't get back up.

Now his sneer didn't even attempt to be a smile. "People underestimate me all the time. They assume I'm slow since I'm not as tall or fit as your average agent. As you can see, that's not the case. And I know what you can do, so I'm not going to leave you unrestrained."

I was barely listening to his diatribe. The feel of the metal around my wrists threw me right back into my Mosaic captivity. I began to pull, trying to free myself.

I couldn't let him lock me in a cage. I couldn't go back into the dark. I wouldn't survive. I would—

A slamming noise in front of me jerked me back into the present. "Focus, Bronwyn. I have questions for you. If you want your hands unlocked, then you're going to have to answer them."

I blinked at him, trying to get my terror under control. I wasn't back in the isolation tank or the cell or the lab.

Focus. Breathe.

I wasn't sure if it was Sarge's voice in my head or mine.

Wilson slid some pictures across the desk so I could see them. They were grainy, but they were obviously of me.

"These were taken off a window reflection in a garage in a New York hotel from a few months ago. The cameras in the garage amazingly became disabled during this event, so there's no actual footage, just a few shots from a vehicle security device."

The images were blurry, but I could still make out the dead guys lying on the ground. "So?"

He slid another picture across. This one of a woman standing over a dead body. It caught her from the side, so her features weren't clear.

But I knew. That was me.

"Look familiar?" he asked.

I stared at the images. A memory tugged at the back of my mind. A fight in a garage. A mission that had to be completed.

"Sarge?" I whispered. He had been there, right?

"That's right. Harrison 'Sarge' McEwan was in that garage too." He slid over another picture.

The quality of this one was worse. You could barely see Sarge lying on the ground. I still couldn't identify the woman standing over him, but you could definitely see that she was hurting him. She was mid-blow—attacking a man who was already down.

Me. Attacking Sarge.

Wilson made a face and shook his head. "I'll bet that hurt."

I wanted to cover my ears. I didn't want to hear his words or his stupid accent. I didn't want to think about me hurting Sarge. I closed my eyes.

"You're fortunate that there are no clear images of you. Otherwise, you wouldn't be in this comfortable holding room. You'd be in a cell."

I could feel my breathing become harsher at the thought. The walls were closing in on me again. I pulled at my restrained hands. "Let me go."

Wilson sat back in his chair and stared at me, one eyebrow raised. "I don't think so."

Getting enough oxygen was becoming harder. I could see the gray on the edges of my vision.

Bronwyn, stop. Breathe.

I could swear I felt a hand on my shoulder. I looked over to find Sarge standing there.

I was losing my damned mind. Sarge was not here.

Breathe right now, Pony Girl. Figure out the crazy part later.

I shook my head back and forth. I was insane. He squatted down next to me.

Breathe. Damn it, Bronwyn. Breathe!

His roar inside my head startled me into breathing. The gray that had been taking over my vision receded. And with it the full memory of the fight in that garage returned.

"I remember," I whispered.

I remembered it all. The mission to steal from Peter Kerpar. Sarge trying to stop me, trying to place a tracker on me, trying to help me. Me hurting him.

"I'm sorry." Tears dripped down my cheek as I stared at the imaginary Sarge next to me.

"Sorry that you killed these men? Sorry that's you in the photos?"

Quiet now. Sarge's brown eyes stayed locked on mine. *Focus on breathing.*

Wilson kept asking me questions, but I ignored him. I kept my gaze on Sarge. "I'm sorry."

No permanent harm done. Stay gold.

Wilson slammed his hand down on the table, and I looked up. Sarge disappeared. "I won't be ignored, Bronwyn. Answer the question."

I didn't know what the question was. I stared at him without talking.

"Fine," he eventually said when it became obvious I wasn't going to say anything else. I didn't owe him any of the story. I only owed Sarge an apology. The real Sarge, not the one my broken mind had made up.

"Then how about this." This time, Wilson slid a computer tablet in front of me, then pressed play on a video.

There was no doubt the woman in the alley was me this time. I watched as a man tried to take my wallet, kicked me, then I killed him.

The memory of that pressed on my brain also. The

man had hurt me, made an aggressive move with a knife, and I'd killed him without hesitation.

I still didn't say anything. I didn't need Sarge here to tell me to be quiet.

"Nothing to say about that?" Wilson played the footage again. "I suppose someone could argue it was self-defense. And granted, the guy did have a violent record. But you still should've been brought in for questioning."

I blinked at Wilson. I didn't know what he wanted. I didn't know why he didn't arrest me right now if that's what he wanted. There was no one to stop him.

I could breathe right now, and that was all I cared about. I was keeping it together. The walls weren't closing in.

My job was to keep myself alive, not answer any of Wilson's questions. Dealing with the fact that I was a killer would have to come later.

"Okay, so you don't want to talk about this. Fair enough. Can't say I blame you." Wilson pulled the tablet back from my side of the table. "I'll be honest, the people you've hurt—that's no great loss to society. Kerpar's men were criminals, the guy you stabbed was obviously not an upstanding member of society."

I continued to stare without talking.

Wilson picked up his chair and brought it around to sit next to me. He was too close, but I couldn't escape him with my hands shackled.

Breathe, Pony Girl. It's going to be all right.

I couldn't see Sarge anywhere. I continued to stare ahead, ignoring Wilson next to me.

"I don't care about the others. A few thugs being killed is America's problem." He touched my chin to force my eyes over to his. "Do you know why I'm here, Bronwyn?"

I didn't respond. Didn't want him touching me.

"I'm here because of Mosaic. I'm here because, unlike those thugs, Mosaic is not just America's problem—that terrorist group has branched out into Europe, and I'm going to be the one to put them into the ground."

"Good." I didn't like him touching me, but if ending Mosaic was his mission, I was all for it.

"If that's how you really feel, then why don't you help me?"

"How? I don't remember anything."

I tried to look away, but his fingers got firmer on my chin, keeping my face pointed at him. "You don't remember, or you don't want to remember?"

For the near month we'd been at Resting Warrior, I hadn't tried to remember. Even with Dr. Rayne. I wasn't sure what was real and what was in my head. I hadn't wanted to think about it—hadn't wanted to know what truths made up the nightmares that woke me almost every night.

"Both," I whispered. "And what I do remember can't be trusted."

Because ultimately, my mind was broken. That was obvious in so many ways. Sarge standing in the corner, arms crossed over his chest, watching all of this right now being the main one.

Wilson let go of my chin and went back around to the other side of the table, leaning his weight on his arms, looking down at me.

"Ultimately, that's not the root of my questions anyway. What Mosaic did to you while they had you or what you did while under their control is not what I need to know."

Once more, I didn't say anything. He would get to his point. I looked over at Sarge in the corner.

"The real question is, why you?"

Now my eyes found Agent Wilson's. "What?"

"I've looked over all the data pertaining to you and Mosaic. Looked over all the ties between Mosaic in its original form a few years ago and the version of it now. Erick Huen is the main tie between both versions, and his intent is to get revenge on Ian DeRose."

"I know Erick Huen." I could still remember him dropping Silas Varela's hand on my torso when I'd been strapped to that medical chair. I couldn't stop the shudder that racked my body at the memory.

"The question is, why did Erick Huen know you?"

"What?" I said again.

Wilson pushed himself up from the table. "No offense, but you're nobody in Zodiac's ranks. Erick kidnapped you to use against Ian DeRose, but you'd hardly met the man. He cared about you distantly, as an employee, but had no true ties. If Erick Huen wanted to send a message to Ian using one of his employees, why choose one Ian had no ties to?"

"I don't know."

I didn't know anything.

"That's the thing, Bronwyn. I don't believe you. I think the answer is inside your brain, and what we need in this situation is someone not afraid of asking you the hard questions. So I'm going to ask you again."

He leaned down on the table once more, getting closer to my face this time. "Why you?

Chapter 30

Sarge

"You're fucking lucky Ian isn't having me bury your body where no one will ever find it." I looked over at Webb in the car taking us to the building where he was holding Bronwyn.

He'd dragged me halfway across the damned planet and used me as his ticket to get his helicopter onto Ian's yacht. And had eventually gotten what he wanted—a chance to talk to Wavy.

Webb shrugged. "It was a chance I had to take. You and Ian were hiding the only two people who can give us any info on Mosaic. We've got a body count that has to be reconciled."

"Pull something like this again, and I won't wait for Ian's permission to make you disappear, Webb. Leave Bronwyn alone."

We weren't far from where Bronwyn was being held.

Webb was lucky she was on our side of the Atlantic. If not, I would've been pummeling him the entire flight home.

Was she okay? Scared? Panicked? She had so many triggers. What if the men holding her left her in the dark?

Hang on, Pony Girl. I'm coming.

Webb looked over at me. "I know what Mosaic did to Bronwyn. I know that it's worse than what Wavy went through, and that was bad enough. I don't want to hurt her any further. All I want is your word that if she does remember anything or is willing to talk to law enforcement, that you will let us know. We've got to make progress on shutting Mosaic down. You heard about the bombing in Warsaw last week?"

I shrugged. "Vaguely."

"That was Mosaic. So now we've got two wiped-out buildings we know they're responsible for. One in the US, one in Europe. And a lot of dead bodies. We need intel."

"Bronwyn can't give it to you. Use what you got from Wavy."

"But if Bronwyn's willing to talk—"

"I promise you'll be the first person I call. As long as you're not planning to arrest her. The things she did…"

"We're not. We couldn't make a positive ID of her in New York, and that guy she killed in Anchorage was clearly self-defense. Not to mention, we never found a body."

Mosaic had cleaned it up. At least they were good for something.

"Don't ever try to take her like this again, Webb. If she's hurt…"

"She's not. She's with two of my best men. Monboit and Palgrave are trustworthy and see the overall big picture. Their instructions were to make sure she was comfortable. She's not restrained, not in a small room, not in the dark. Like I said, I'm not trying to— "

He cut off when his phone buzzed. "Speak of the devil." He brought the phone to his ear. "Palgrave, we're about eight minutes out."

I couldn't hear what was being said, but Webb's face got tight at whatever was being relayed to him.

I drove faster.

"Get back to the building. We'll already be there." Webb disconnected the call with those words.

"Problem?"

"My men were summoned by Europol. Or at least they thought they were. Ends up a Europol agent by the name of Theodore Wilson wanted a chance to talk to Bronwyn. He's our European counterpart."

"Is he a problem?"

"He wanted to come with us to talk to Ian, but I said no. He's a good agent but definitely an end-justifies-the-means sort of guy. Not great bedside manner."

"Smart not to bring him, then."

"Agreed." Webb glanced over at me. "But turns out that he drew my men out on a false call, and now he's with Bronwyn."

I didn't say anything but drove much faster than was safe in the French Riviera. I didn't ease up until we pulled up to the building where Bronwyn was being held. I rushed inside behind Webb.

Wilson stood over Bronwyn at some desk—his fucking face way too close to hers—asking why Mosaic had chosen her when Webb and I burst into the room.

I might have been able to get myself under control if I hadn't seen that she was handcuffed to the table. She wasn't pulling at them now, but she had. I could see the red marks on her soft skin.

Over the scars of where she'd fought Mosaic's restraints.

I flew across the table and caught Wilson in a tackle. The guy was a shit-ton smaller than me, but I didn't care. I got three good punches into his face, definitely breaking the bastard's nose, before Webb pulled me off him.

I got in a couple punches on Webb for good measure.

"Damn it, Sarge. Stop." Webb spat blood. "Bronwyn needs you."

No other words would've gotten my head out of my ass so quickly. I dropped Webb and turned to Bronwyn.

"Pony Girl?"

I was expecting the worst. Tears. Demons in her eyes. But she was steady, looking more like the woman I'd kissed in Paris than she had in weeks.

She jerked at her handcuffs. "Want to get me out of these things?"

Webb slipped a key into my hand, and I released her. The metal dropped to the table as I swept her off her feet and jerked her against my chest. Cursing myself, I was about to put her down. This wasn't about what I needed; it was about what she needed. And she may not want to be touched right now.

But her arms and legs wrapped around me, keeping me close.

"Are you okay?" I threaded my fingers in her hair, holding her head so I could see her face.

"I'm okay. I've only been restrained the past hour or so while Agent Jackass was here. Otherwise, a little spooked, but…okay."

"Did he hurt you?" Maybe I'd get to hide a body today after all.

"No. He's not my favorite person in the world, but he didn't hurt me. I promise." She tucked her face in my neck.

"He showed me some pictures of things I did. People I killed. People I hurt. You."

I needed to go punch that bastard another dozen times. The things Bronwyn had done while under Mosaic's influence would have to be dealt with eventually, but not while she was still recovering. I couldn't stand the thought of her suffering more. "What he told you might have been worse than what really hap—"

She put a finger over my lips. "I remember. I think the memories have always been in my head, but his actions jarred them out. I remember New York. Anchorage."

"And you're okay?"

She let out a sigh, arms and legs still wrapped around me. "No. I have to process that I'm a killer. But I think I'd rather know and face it than have it sneak up on me unawares."

Maybe I should've told her. Given her a chance to face it head on. "I'm sorry."

She cupped my cheek. "Just take me out of here."

"My pleasure. And I like your sweater."

~

I took her to Èze. If we had both been dragged against our will to the French Riviera, we might as well enjoy the best parts of it.

Our small bed-and-breakfast offered breathtaking views of the Mediterranean from the medieval village perched high on the mountain cliffs that were only accessible by foot.

"I've never seen anything like it," Bronwyn whispered, face pressed against the window. "But I guess that's not saying much given how little I've traveled."

I walked over and stood behind her, looking at the blue

of the water that reminded me so much of her eyes. "It's truly one of the most beautiful places I've ever been, and the Navy took me all over the world."

We'd been here for two days. I would've liked to have spent the time in bed or enjoying the sea so close to us. But instead, we'd spent it looking through all the footage and pictures from New York and Anchorage.

We'd dragged the table over to the window so we could at least enjoy the view while we dug through hell.

She studied the computer screen playing the footage of her stabbing the thug. "Am I a coward for not facing this sooner?"

"No." My answer was immediate and unwavering. As it had been the other times she'd asked a version of the question.

"If I had sorted through these memories earlier, maybe I'd already be remembering something useful about Mosaic."

I reached over and threaded her fingers with mine. "You were healing. You still are. It takes time. Just like with physical recovery, pushing too hard with emotional recovery can cause setbacks."

I wasn't sure if she believed me, but she'd let it go. We'd probed as much as we could into what she did remember. People—Dr. Tippens, who was dead. Erick Huen, for whom Zodiac was actively searching. We also knew there were three other unidentified partners in Mosaic. Nothing she remembered was helping with that. I hated to see her beat herself up over it.

"Agent Wilson was right," she said in front of me at the window.

"I doubt that." I gently circled her wrist with my hand, bringing it up so I could kiss the bruised skin. "Damn near everything he did was wrong."

"But his question was right. Why me? Why did Erick Huen choose me to get Ian's attention? How did I get on Erick's radar to begin with?"

I wrapped an arm around her torso and pulled her back against my chest. "There could be a lot of reasons. You're young and new. You're part of Zodiac, so Ian would care if something happened to you, but weren't so embedded in the team that it would be hard for Erick to get to you."

"Maybe."

"It might not be that complicated. It could've been nothing more than bad luck. You were the lowest-hanging fruit—a Zodiac employee who spent a lot of time alone. He saw an opportunity and went for it."

She lowered her forehead against the glass. "There's something I'm not remembering."

I kissed the top of her head. "You've got to give it more time. The pieces will continue to come together."

"Will they? I'm not sure. I don't know if I can trust my mind."

I turned her to face me. "Why do you say that? For two days, you've been facing what happened to you head on. You haven't flinched from it, haven't shut down."

Her lips pressed together, and she looked away from me. "But I haven't told you everything. I haven't told you the worst."

My stomach clenched at the thought that there could be more she had gone through that I didn't know about. I wasn't sure either of us could handle it. I hadn't told her about the recordings I had of her from the transmitter. There wasn't any point.

But whatever it was she needed to disclose, I would shoulder for her if I could. If she would let me. I pressed a finger under her chin. "Tell me."

She let out a small sigh. "I see things. People. Who aren't there."

That hadn't been what I was expecting at all. I relaxed slightly. "All the time?"

"No. Mostly when I'm freaking out. Panicking. I talk to them, and they talk to me, but they're not really there."

I yanked her against my chest, wrapping my arms around her. "You scared me, Pony Girl. When you said you hadn't told me the worst, I thought…"

I screwed my eyes closed. I couldn't put into words the worst I could think about, but her conversing with imaginary friends wasn't in the top one hundred.

She pushed back from me. "But don't you get it? This means my mind is broken. It happened all the time when Mosaic had me. Then it happened again while I was in that holding room with Agent Wilson."

My relief was so tangible it was hard to take this seriously, but it was important to her so I needed to try. "Tell me details. Walk me through it."

"When things got bad, I would see…you. You would talk to me."

"What would I say?"

She shrugged. "Mostly to survive. That I could make it. To be quiet if I needed to. To focus. Breathe."

I cupped her face. "If I had been there when you needed me most—and I would give everything I own if I could've been—I would've said those exact things to you. That you're strong. Capable. That you can do anything you set your mind to. That survival, no matter how you do it, is always the most important thing."

Those blue eyes blinked up at me. "I know you would've. You've always done whatever you could to protect me. But still, it's a splinter in my psyche I can feel now. I'm crazy. Broken."

This woman.

She was a dichotomy in every way a person could be one.

Fragile but strong. Capable but unsure. Broken but beautiful.

And I was in love with her. I had been since she was a fucking teenager, although I hadn't felt it in the same way I did now.

Now she was a woman, I wanted to worship her in every way one person could worship another.

I slid my hands down her body and slowly lifted her slight weight into my arms. "I am honored and humbled that your mind chose me as the vessel to talk to you."

She shook her head. "You helped me."

"No, you helped you. Whatever you saw when you were at your lowest may have looked and sounded like me, but it was your mind providing you what you needed." I walked us toward the bed. "I don't call that broken, I call it resourceful. Intelligent. Amazing."

"But why couldn't I say those things to myself? Why did I have to imagine you saying them?"

I put my forehead against hers. "Because you trust me. And that is the most profound gift you could ever offer me. I cherish it."

"You don't think I'm weird?"

I laid her on the bed and slowly peeled off her clothes. "I think you are a survivor. I believe you have gone through what would have crushed most people but have come out the other side—if not whole, then at least with big enough pieces to keep glued together. And I believe being here with you is the greatest honor of my life."

"Sarge—"

I loved the heat in her eyes. I stood at the foot of the bed and pulled my clothes off. I didn't want anything between us. I wanted her skin against mine. Her soul against mine.

I crawled back onto the bed, running my lips up her legs. "You're a warrior. A survivor. Beautiful and giving."

I covered her body in kisses as I spoke. Knees, thighs, hips. I wanted to taste every part of her.

She let out a moan as I covered one breast then the other with my mouth before I worked gentle kisses back down and settled between her legs. All the rest of the things I wanted to say would have to wait.

Right now, I would give her what I could: pleasure.

Chapter 31

Bronwyn

Wavy had remembered something about Mosaic. Something important. Something that was going to help law enforcement put Erick Huen away for good.

Which was more than I'd been able to do.

Sun-soaked days in the French Riviera hadn't helped. Going back to the familiarity of the Resting Warrior Ranch hadn't helped. Knowing there was information inside my head that I couldn't get out definitely hadn't helped.

I hid it all from Sarge. He was so excited that I'd been making forward progress—remembering and dealing with some of what had happened—that I didn't have the heart to tell him I'd hit a wall.

As I sat in the kitchen of our tiny cabin and heard him on the phone with Landon, I knew I couldn't continue down the same path we'd been on since he'd carried me out of the Mosaic compound.

Ian and his team were heading to some island where Wavy had been held. That's what she had remembered. They were going to take Mosaic down. Ian wanted Sarge on the team, but he wouldn't go.

Because of me.

Because, if anything, I'd taken steps backward since first remembering some of my captivity with Mosaic. My hands were shaking again. The nightmares were worse. The need to do something was tugging at me all the time.

But I wasn't sure what.

When Sarge had been out, I'd called the genetics specialist who'd been treating me, the same one who'd been helping Wavy, and told Dr. Han we needed to up my medication.

The doctor wasn't surprised and said that was to be expected. The genetic modification and chemical subjugation experimentation that had been performed on me would have long-term effects. She explained my body might be fighting what they did to me for the rest of my life.

I was prepared for that. Even okay with it. But if my life was going to fall apart forever, I wasn't going to take Sarge down with me. I refused to.

The same way he had refused to help his boss—his friend—because of me.

Always for me.

It was time for me to do something for him.

When he came back to our little cabin from helping Lucas with a new horse, I'd been frank with him. "I'm ready to go back to work. It's time for us to go home."

Home. The word tasted weird in my mouth, as if I wasn't pronouncing it correctly. Maybe because I didn't actually have a home.

Sarge kept his poker face, merely raising a single

eyebrow. "There's no need for us to leave here yet. No hurry."

"I'm ready. Staying here doing nothing isn't helping me. Coddling me doesn't get me any further along in the recovery process."

He crossed his arms over his chest. "Pushing yourself doesn't get you any further along either. At least here you're happy."

I had been when I'd been blissfully unaware of what I'd done, of what was still trapped in my brain. But not now. Now I had a responsibility to help clean up the mess I'd made. And to stop dragging Sarge into that mess with me.

"I need to work." Lies. He needed to work, and I wasn't sure I ever wanted to go back to active missions. But I would say whatever was necessary to get him to believe me. "We both need to work."

"Pony Girl…"

He was going to deny my request. He was going to, once again, go against what was best for him in order to do what was best for me.

But this time, unlike all the other times, I wasn't going to allow it.

"You've got to stop treating me like I'm breakable, like I'm going to crumble at the first hard thing that comes my way."

The words felt like acid in my mouth.

Sarge had never treated me that way. He'd gone out of his way to always make me feel stronger and more capable than I probably was.

Hurt burned in those brown eyes before he blinked it away. "That was never my intent."

I wanted to go to him and wrap my arms around him,

tell him I knew that. That he'd never made me feel weaker, only stronger. But if I didn't make a stand now, I was going to keep letting him protect me to his own detriment.

I blew out a silent breath and gathered my strength. "It's time for both of us to get back to work. We can't keep hiding here. We're needed."

That, he couldn't argue with. He studied me for a long minute then nodded. "Let's pack our things."

"I love Montana, but it's good to be home."

I forced a smile as I walked past the door Sarge opened for me at his house in Colorado. Home. The word, whether he said it or I did, still felt weird to me.

This was familiar, but it wasn't home.

Sarge carried both our bags. We hadn't had much with us at Resting Warrior. We'd stopped by the main ranch house to drop off the vehicle and let Lucas know we were leaving. We hadn't gotten to say goodbye to anyone else.

It was probably better that way. Except...

"Hey, you okay?" He cupped the side of my head and ran his thumb down my cheek.

"I'm going to miss my Resting Warrior friends. Evelyn, Lena..."

"Mac and Cheese?"

He knew me so well. I would keep in touch with the human friends I'd made. But the alpaca and sheep that hung with the alpacas all the time thinking he was one? My heart hurt at the thought of not seeing them again.

"Yeah. Stupid, right?"

Sarge kissed my forehead. "You're talking to a man who's well-known for not having any people skills. I grew up on a farm. I know what it's like to love an animal like it's your friend."

I hugged him. "Maybe Evelyn will send me videos. It'll force her to see Lucas more." I leaned back and waggled my eyebrows at him.

"You little matchmaker. Although I've never known people who could use it more than those two."

"Evelyn has been hurt." She hadn't told me that, but I could recognize it in her.

"I know." Sarge pulled me close again. "That's why she and Lucas are perfect for each other. They'll help heal each other."

At least Evelyn could be healed. I wasn't sure I ever could. I pulled away from Sarge and looked around. "Even with what you told me, I wasn't sure my memories of this place were real."

"You were here." He grimaced. "I should've never let you go. I should've whisked you into Zodiac and figured out a way to get that damned necklace off you and combat everything they'd put in your system."

"You did what you thought was best." My memories of this place were so unclear, as if they were surrounded by a dense fog. I only remembered his hands on my body, chasing away the pain.

He wiped a hand down his face, suddenly looking exhausted. "I gave you that transmitter, thinking it would be enough."

"I don't remember a transmitter."

"No, you were trying to fight off the effects of the regimen. Trying not to press the injector on that necklace."

"But you gave me a transmitter?"

"Yes. It was voice activated. I could hear anything you said after that." He stepped away from me, big shoulders hunched.

"What did I say?"

"Not much. Mosaic must have discovered they didn't have as much control over you as they thought. You didn't say very much in the days after you left here."

I walked farther inside the house. "Are you sure the transmitter worked?"

"Yes. Very sure."

"How do you know?"

He shook his head. "It doesn't matter. Let's just get settled in."

I turned back to him. "Sarge, tell me. I want to put the pieces together."

He crossed his arms over his chest. "Maybe some things are better not remembering."

My hands started shaking, but I had to know. I used my faithful emotional club. "Don't treat me like I'm weak."

But I was weak, and he knew it. He knew I was getting worse and not better. But I'd put him in an impossible place, making him think that protecting me was hurting me.

His arms dropped to his sides, defeat evident. "I know the transmitter worked because I could hear you scream, sob, beg for mercy. I could hear your terror when they trapped you in that isolation tank for days at a time. I could hear you call for me, but there wasn't a damned thing I could do to help you."

Each sentence hit me like a blow. I didn't have clear memories of any of those things, but I knew they were true. I knew they were the roots of my nightmares and the reason why my hands shook. I knew they were the explanation for why, more than a month later, I was still physically weak and underweight.

Those were the days that had torn apart my very psyche, and Sarge had been there as a witness.

"How can you even look at me knowing how broken I am?"

"Because against all odds, and with a strength not known to many, you knit those pieces back together. You continue to do it every single day."

"No. I have to tell—"

His phone rang in his pocket, preventing me from telling him the truth. That I was getting worse. That I needed help. That I wanted to do what was right for him, but that I was afraid my pieces were coming unglued.

He looked at the phone, then set it down on the counter without answering. It continued to buzz.

"Who is it?" I asked.

"Mark Outlawson from work. It can wait."

No, for God's sake, I—and the Greek tragedy that was my life—could wait. "Go ahead and get it. I want to look around, see what I remember."

Sarge picked up the phone quickly enough to let me know that's what he'd really wanted to do, although once again, he'd been willing to forgo that desire to protect me.

"Outlaw, talk to me."

I was turning away when Sarge's low curse had me spinning back around.

"I'm putting you on speaker so Bronwyn can hear you too."

"Hey, Bronwyn," Mark said. "We don't know what happened. I'm piecing it together myself. Wavy shot Landon."

"What?" I yelled.

"Evidently, it was some sort of mind control or something, and Mosaic used her as a weapon. The location Ian and the team went to was a trap. It's fucking chaos. Ian is on his way back."

"And Landon?" Sarge asked, knuckles white around his phone.

"Alive. That's all I know. We've got at least two dead on Ian's team. Callum Webb was with them and got injured. Ian's also injured but not too bad."

"Where's Wavy?" I asked.

"We don't know. She shot Landon then walked out of the building and disappeared. We're working on it." Mark let out a sigh. "Sarge, we need you."

He looked over at me. I could tell that, once again, he was about to decline. I shook my head.

"He'll be right in," I answered before Sarge could say anything.

"Good." Mark hung up without another word.

"I don't have to go." Sarge dropped the phone on the counter again. "Zodiac is bigger than any one person, even Ian."

"Yeah, but Ian and Landon both being out? You're needed. Go." I hardened myself. "I don't need a babysitter."

He rubbed his hand down his face. "You know I don't feel that way."

I was such a bitch. I stepped up to him and cupped his cheek. "I know. I'm sorry. There's a list of people who need you right now, and I'm pretty low for once. So go."

His lips pursed, but he nodded. "I'm going to lock this place down. I've got security measures in place—no one will be able to get in. I'll give you the emergency codes in case you need to get out."

I nodded. I wasn't going anywhere, but I wanted him away from me as soon as possible.

In the chaos of the news, Sarge hadn't put together some pretty simple facts.

Wavy had shot Landon.

Mosaic had used her as a human weapon, and they had only held her captive for two weeks.

If she could shoot someone she knew after only being held that short of a time, then how much more of a weapon could I be when they'd had me for months?

Chapter 32

Sarge

I left Bronwyn in my house, more torn than I'd ever been.

I knew she'd been getting worse since France. She'd been trying to hide it, but I'd seen it anyway. I didn't want to leave her now, but what was happening at Zodiac affected her too.

I called and got an update on Landon on my way into the office. He was critical but stable. Given that he'd taken a point-blank shot to the chest from a .22, critical but stable was the best that could be expected.

I immediately made sure we had Zodiac security at the hospital. We weren't giving Mosaic another shot at him.

Ian was barely keeping it together when I saw him. Not only was he injured, his best friend had been shot by the woman he loved, and now she was missing again.

We worked side by side to put the pieces together. To

figure out where Wavy was and what our next move would be.

There was hell burning in Ian's eyes as he turned to me from watching the footage of Wavy leaving the building for the twentieth time.

"She didn't do this of her own accord. They did something to her."

I squeezed my friend's shoulder. "I know, Aries. We all know that."

I did know Wavy wasn't responsible for what had happened, just like Bronwyn hadn't been responsible for the people she'd killed while under Mosaic's control.

As we dug deeper and realized Erick Huen had planted false memories and trigger words in Wavy's psyche, my gut clenched. Those were things Bronwyn was going to have to deal with too. As if she didn't have enough weighing on her already.

Landon was conscious and going to survive, thank God, but everything about this was ugly.

Thirty-six hours after I'd gotten the call that everything had gone to hell, we had figured out where Erick was holding Wavy. Ian was prepping to leave for a compound in the Sierra Nevadas, the same place where he had died—multiple times—fighting the original Mosaic.

If he wasn't careful, he was going to die there again. It was my job to make sure he didn't. Ian was moving in under cover of night to get Wavy out of the compound that was guarded by dozens of Mosaic soldiers.

My team and I were going to provide a big enough distraction to allow them to make it.

Outlaw and I were prepping the gear we needed. We were wheels up in two hours.

"You okay, man?" he asked me as I placed the explosives we'd be using into a backpack with a little less finesse than was probably wise. "I know this mission is a little slack on the actual planning, details, and probable success rate."

That was putting it lightly. We had zero time, very little intel, and stakes that were way too high. Under any other circumstances, Zodiac would never have considered a mission like this.

But Ian was going after Wavy whether we helped him or not, so we were going to do everything we could to get them out alive.

But that wasn't why I was barely keeping my shit together.

"We'll make it work." I rubbed the back of my neck. "I'm worried about Bronwyn."

I hadn't seen her in thirty-six hours, and it was eating at me. We'd texted, but it wasn't enough. If I had known I'd be leaving her alone less than an hour after arriving back in Colorado, I would've left her at Resting Warrior. At least there, she would've had Mac and Cheese nearby, not to mention a group of former SEALs who could protect her.

I was needed for this mission. But she needed me, and I needed her. I wasn't going to be able to function without knowing she was safe.

The people I trusted most to protect her were either out of the state, in the hospital, or going on this mission. I didn't want to put a random security detail on her that might do more harm than good.

"Do you think she's in danger?" Outlaw grimaced and gave an apologetic look. "Or...a danger to others?"

"I don't think she's either. But I don't like leaving her alone right now, and there are not a lot of people I trust with her."

"Do you need someone who can physically protect Bronwyn? Is that what you're worried about?"

I don't need a babysitter.

Her words rang in my ears. She'd said it more than once. I knew I was borderline overprotective, but it wasn't because I thought she was weak.

I couldn't stand the thought of her having to face her nightmares alone. That was something I was going to have to work on.

I wiped a hand down my face. Jesus, I was tired. "No. She'll be fine, but I wish I had someone who could stay with her while I'm not there. PTSD is such a tricky bastard. It can throat punch you when you least expect it."

"If you need someone who has up close and personal experience with PTSD, who definitely won't mind spending time with Bronwyn, I have the perfect person."

"Who? I don't want a stranger."

"You've got to think a little outside the box. Or, as it may be, deep inside the box."

"I'm not tracking."

"Jenna."

•••

Bronwyn

"It's important to me that you don't think of this as babysitting. I swear to you that's not how I mean it."

I grabbed Sarge's hand as we walked up to Jenna's door. "I know. I never should've said that. You've never treated me that way."

He hooked a hand behind my neck and pulled my lips to his. "We're not sure what's happening, and I have to know you're safe. I can't function otherwise."

I kissed him then leaned my forehead against his. "I

know. Jenna is a good choice. And I don't want you worrying about me either—you need to focus on keeping yourself safe and coming back to me." I raised an eyebrow at him. "I can't function otherwise."

His lips found mine again. "Deal."

I wanted to kiss him more, but we couldn't. He was out of time, and every second he stayed, the more likely he was to realize how terrified I was of him going. I liked Jenna, but being without Sarge gnawed at me. I'd barely made it through the past forty hours without him.

Knowing he was about to put himself in danger on a mission that had a lot of potential pitfalls...

We knocked on Jenna's door and could hear the sound of multiple locks being released on the other side. Neither of us said anything as we waited for the door to open. Those locks would be keeping me safe in a few minutes.

Once we were in, Jenna immediately closed the door behind us, her lips tight. Obviously, opening the door wasn't something she liked doing.

"Hi," I said. I'd seen her before on the screen but never in person. She looked different, but still the same.

She gave me a tight smile. "Hi. Welcome."

Sarge put his hand on her shoulder. "Thank you. This means a lot to both of us."

"It's been...a while since I had a girls' weekend. I'm happy for the company. We'll have fun." She was relaxing more now that the door was closed.

"You're not running the mission comms?" I knew she had all the equipment to do that from here since she never left her house.

"No. We've got a team at the office coordinating with the on-site team. There are others better at this sort of thing." She glanced over at Sarge then back at me.

I let out a sigh. "And because I'm here and could possibly be a liability."

He slipped an arm around me. "Pony Girl…"

"It's okay. It's the right thing to do. I want you to be safe." Even from me.

Jenna nodded. "The current configuration gives the mission the greatest chance of success for a lot of reasons."

"Then I'll take it." I pushed at Sarge's chest. "You go. Come back to me soon."

He kissed me hard then ran out the door without another word. Jenna shut it behind him, visibly relaxing as soon as the locks were once again engaged.

I hefted my overnight bag over my shoulder and followed her farther inside. The front of the house seemed pretty normal—kitchen, living room, even the guest bedroom where she had me put my bag. Best of all, windows with lots of light. If I had to stay inside, I was grateful for that.

I wasn't sure what I'd expected for someone who didn't like to go outside, but it wasn't this.

She caught me staring at my surroundings. "Expecting coffins or something?"

I gave a low chuckle. "More like grenade launchers and barred windows."

"The windows are made of bullet-resistant glass. No need to worry about break-ins."

"Good."

She shrugged and walked toward the kitchen. "I don't go out. Everybody knows it. In this day and age, you don't have to anyway. Everything I need I can get delivered here —groceries, medicine, clothes, toilet paper. I like the safety of my house."

She was defensive, but I wasn't about to point that out,

276

especially not when I was so intimately familiar with avoiding the real world.

Jenna wasn't avoiding it; she'd just built her real world in a fashion that worked for her.

I should probably take a few notes from her playbook.

"I like the safety of your house too. I'm not going to try to talk you into a picnic or to go pick flowers. I'm good here." I shrugged. "Although I'm not exactly sure how good I will be at the girls' weekend stuff."

Jenna leaned back against the counter. "That works out well because I've got a much better plan than us painting our nails."

Chapter 33

Bronwyn

"I've been going through everything we have on you, especially after what happened to Wavy," Jenna said. "When Sarge asked if we could hang out, I was going to put it all away, but…"

My eyes flew to hers. "You have it?"

"Got a whole room of it. Want to see?"

"Hell yes, I do."

I followed her into what should have been another bedroom, but instead looked like some sort of shrine. There were photos everywhere. Printouts, timelines, all dealing with Mosaic—specifically Wavy and me. There were pictures of me, Wavy, Erick Huen, Dr. Tippens. I didn't like looking at those, so I turned to the printouts of buildings and locations I didn't recognize.

I walked around, staring in silence for a long time. This was way more information than I knew about the past few months of my own life.

I stopped in front of a picture of a large building. "What's this?"

"That's where you were being held when Sarge and Landon got you out."

I nodded as I turned from the photo and caught Jenna sliding something out of sight.

"What was that?" I asked her.

"Nothing."

"Hey, we're in this now. Don't start pulling your punches."

She slid the paper out so I could see it. It was the specs of the isolation tank I'd been held in. I stared at it for a long moment. Make, model number, size...including a picture.

My throat tightened as I studied the information, making it hard to breathe. My hands shook so hard I stuffed them under my armpits.

I didn't have clear memories of my time in that tank, but they were pressing at the edges of my mind.

That was the problem, wasn't it? If I was going to remember it all—enough to be helpful in taking Mosaic down—then I was going to have to remember it all.

I'd told Jenna not to pull her punches. Was I sure I could handle the blows?

"Are you okay?" she whispered.

My nod was jerky. "Trust me, I like looking at it much better from the outside than I did from the inside."

I turned away from the information, anxious to see anything else. There were all sorts of medical charts everywhere, from both Wavy and me. "Do you understand this stuff?"

She gave an awkward shrug of one shoulder. "Actually, yes. I had a double major in computer science and biomedical engineering. I didn't actually start using the computer science part of my degree until much more recently."

"I had no idea," I said.

"Yeah, most people don't," she said. "It's part of a past I don't talk about."

I walked around the room more, thumbing through images and looking over reports. The data she had was more than complex.

"Did Ian ask you to do this?" I turned to face her. "Or Sarge?"

She shook her head. "No, both of them have been busy." She tucked a strand of her black hair behind her ear. "I've been providing them information if it would help your recovery, but looking at all of this holistically is a little much."

"Then why do you do it?"

She gave another awkward shrug. "I get a little obsessed with things. Maybe it's a by-product of being alone. Most of the time, I get obsessed with stupid stuff like painting a room until it is the exact color I saw in my mind. Or writing a computer program for something nobody needs. In this case, my mind got stuck on figuring out the details of what happened to you and Wavy."

My stomach tightened, and I flinched. Hearing Wavy's name triggered an unpleasant sensation like seeing the pictures of her had.

Jenna noticed it. "What just happened?"

"I don't know. Something about seeing the pictures of Wavy and hearing her name. It makes me angry. That's so unreasonable, but ever since I've been getting my memories back, I have this distinct dislike for her. I didn't realize it until now."

She pulled out a computer tablet and started typing faster than I'd ever seen anyone type. "What do you mean dislike? As in, you don't want to hang out with her? As in, she shot Landon and you're pissed?"

"No." I rubbed a shaky hand down my face. "As in, I feel the need to hurt her."

"That's pretty extreme."

"I don't know. I've never felt like this toward anyone."

She nodded, then showed me another picture. "And Silas Varela? How do you feel about him?"

I studied the picture. That same ugly feeling in my gut. I wanted to rip up the photo. Punch him in the face.

I wanted to kill him.

"The same. Looking at his picture makes me angry. I want to hurt him, or worse, even though I know he is dead." My mouth went dry as I shook my head. "That makes me a pretty shitty person, doesn't it? I know that Erick Huen killed Varela and chopped him into little pieces."

"Not in that order, but yeah, he did," she responded. "Based on what you're telling me and how Erick manipulated Wavy, I think you were probably programmed to kill both of them. You have all the residual signs."

"How do you know that?"

"Because in my other life, when I was a biomedical engineer, I was forced against my will to develop some of the biomedical methods that Dr. Tippens would've used to help foster those behaviors. I assisted in their design of the programming."

"Oh," I whispered. "Will these feelings ever go away?"

She nodded. "Probably, with time, since you're no longer being given the drugs or being subjected to their programming on a daily basis. You and Wavy may never be besties, but you won't want to hurt her."

"That's good." I looked around a little more, dread

pooling in my stomach. "But I'm probably a walking time bomb like her, aren't I?"

Jenna ran a hand down her dark hair. "Based on the medications we found in your body, what Mosaic did to you is not the same as what they did to Wavy."

"But I could still be used as a weapon, couldn't I? I could have some sort of trigger word."

"It's unlikely," she replied. "Yours was more of a chemical subjugation rather than genetic."

"But it's possible?" I asked.

"Yes, it's possible."

"Then I want you to tie me up."

"Why?"

I sat down in the chair in front of the desk. "Because it's time for us to figure out what information is still inside my head that I'm suppressing. I have intel that we need to get to. You have both the knowledge and the skills to get it out."

"Are you sure you want to do this?"

"Yes."

She rubbed her eyes. "Tying you up is probably overkill. And is probably going to be a bitch on your psyche."

"I don't care. If there's something in this that's going to trigger me, I want to make sure that I don't hurt you. We both know that with your computers here, if something triggered me, I could take you out and do all sorts of damage to the mission that Sarge is on. I won't take that chance."

Jenna nodded. "Okay, tie you up it is."

W e went through everything.

Sarge had walked me through a lot of it already, but it didn't take me long to realize he'd been protecting me, sheltering me from a lot of the details.

Or, after listening to the recordings of me trapped in that isolation pod, maybe he'd been sheltering himself. The sound of me on the recording—the screaming, the sobs, the deafening silence—was hard to bear, but I did it without flinching.

Because as hard as it was to listen to, it had been much harder living through it.

I remembered. With each piece of intel Jenna fed me, my mind cracked a little more and let the memories through.

For the first time since I'd been taken, I could piece together a true timeline of what had happened to me. How I'd been taken. Exactly how long I'd been gone. People I'd hurt or killed. Things I'd stolen.

None of it had been of my own free will, but I'd still done it. And it was time to face it, no matter how shaky it made my hands or how many more nightmares I might have.

And I knew there would be many. There was no going back to the cotton wool of selective amnesia.

Jenna and I were both tired. We'd been at it all night, confronting painful detail after painful detail. But neither of us wanted to stop. We were both desperately aware there was something we were missing. But we could see it was coming.

She'd untied me after twelve hours of nothing triggering me, and we'd gotten word that Sarge's mission had been a success. Thanks to the work of Sarge and the team,

Ian had rescued Wavy relatively unharmed. Erick had been arrested in the process of fleeing.

Sarge had to debrief but then would be coming home. I wanted him here with me. It was as if a piece of me was missing every time we weren't near each other. I was tired, cranky, frustrated, and I wanted him home.

Home.

"That phrase." I studied a picture of Peter Kerpar. "I keep coming back to the words they made me say."

I exist only to obey orders. My final mission is to go home.

I didn't like to say it out loud. I could more clearly remember the early days of captivity now—the dark, the cold, those words repeated over and over until I'd finally said them.

Jenna crossed her arms over her chest and leaned back against the desk. "You didn't have any reaction from either saying them or hearing me say them."

We'd tested for all sorts of physiological responses to those words—change in blood pressure, pupil dilation, adrenaline spike—but I hadn't had any.

"I know. But there's something about the word home that keeps scratching at my mind."

"All right." Jenna grabbed her computer tablet and jotted down some notes. She was nothing if not thorough. "That's something to consider. But it's possible that you feel displaced. You're an uprooted orphan. That's why the word home bugs you."

I winced at her almost brutal honesty but couldn't argue with what she said. "That's true. I guess my question is, why would Mosaic have put that in my programming? What is home?"

"For their purposes, it was probably a fail-safe put into your programming so you would always return there."

"So why am I not there now?"

Jenna set her tablet aside. "Genetic reengineering and chemical subjugation aren't exact sciences when it comes to controlling human beings. Maybe something went wrong. Or maybe they didn't get to finish that part of your programming before Sarge got you out. Maybe you were resistant to it, or only triggered by Dr. Tippens saying it. It could be one of a hundred things."

I walked around, looking at all the images and print-outs on the walls without really seeing them. What Jenna said made sense, but…

"I feel like this is the key to something, but I don't know what, and I don't know why."

She grabbed her tablet again. "Okay. If there's one thing I learned during my captiv…" She trailed off and restarted. "If there's one thing I've learned, it's to not fight your gut. So let's discuss home for you."

"Like you said, I don't really have one."

"Where did you live growing up?"

"I was born in Ukraine, but honestly, I don't have much memory of that. We had to relocate to the Czech Republic, and then my parents died, so not much of a home there either."

"Okay, no house that you think of when you say home. It must be code for something, we just don't know what."

I rubbed my eyes. I was tired and trying to force a lead that was going nowhere. "You're probably right. I never really used the word much. The only time I ever heard it used growing up was by Gregory. He was the leader of the family"—I rolled my eyes at the term—"when I lived in Prague."

"I assume that means it wasn't much of a family."

"Not unless you consider stealing, prostitution, and regular beatings as part of being a family."

"Damn," she whispered. "How did you make it out of there at all?"

"Sarge. He met Bronya Roch before she ever became Bronwyn Rourke. He helped me get out."

"Doesn't surprise me at all."

"But no, Prague is not the place I would call home. The only person who would want to call that home for me would be—"

I came to a picture of Erick Huen on the wall, and suddenly everything clicked into place.

"Oh my God."

Jenna rushed over to me. "What?"

"I remember something Erick said to me when he came to my hotel room in Marrakesh. *I was informed you were feisty.*" I shook my head. Everything was now making a sick kind of sense. "That asshole Agent Wilson was right."

"I'm not following. Agent Wilson, the Europol agent?"

"Yes. He said there had to be a reason Erick Huen picked me. It wasn't only because I was part of Zodiac Tactical—it was more personal than that."

"Okay, that would make sense."

"Mosaic has a partner in Europe. And I have a sick feeling I know who that is."

"Who?"

"The only person who would want me to come home. So he could destroy me."

Chapter 34

Sarge

As far as missions went—especially ones where we were shorthanded and going into the situation practically blind—this one had had the best possible outcome.

It almost hadn't ended that way. Ian had nearly died at Erick's hand and was only still alive because Wavy had risked her own life to save his.

Now those two were at the hospital getting their wounds tended to, and that bastard Erick Huen had been arrested.

I'd like ten minutes alone in a room with him. I wouldn't waste time asking him any questions, but I'd damn well make sure he understood what it felt like to be helpless and in agony. Give him a tiny taste—one that would involve multiple broken bones—of what he and Tippens had done to Bronwyn.

Unfortunately, I'd have to settle for him spending the

rest of his life in prison. I almost hoped he would cut a deal and provide info about Mosaic in exchange for his freedom. I was sure it wouldn't take much for me to convince Ian that the world would be a better place without Erick in it.

And if it meant my soul burned in hell for it, I'd consider that a fair trade.

But right now, I had to face my own temporary kind of hell: debriefing. Ian had needed medical attention and refused to leave Wavy's side, and Landon was still in the hospital, although thankfully out of the woods.

That left me as the highest-ranking member of Zodiac who needed to answer for the number of Mosaic bodies littering the wilderness camp in the Sierra Nevadas. Law enforcement was pissed. They'd been left out of the loop again.

There hadn't been time to do this by committee.

I wished I could give a written report and be done with it. Callum Webb owed me after that stunt in the French Riviera. But somehow, I didn't think *bad guys shouldn't mess with us or we'll fuck them up*—which would basically be my report—would fly anyway.

So I was sitting here in this holding room waiting to answer whatever questions I could, when all I really wanted to do was get back to Bronwyn. Talking to her on the phone to let her know the mission was over and everyone was safe wasn't enough.

I needed to hold her. I needed to let her know that we were going to make it through this. That if what had happened to Wavy happened to her, we would figure it out.

That I wasn't going to let anything hurt her.

If we needed to move back to Resting Warrior to keep her away from other people for the rest of her life, I was willing to do that. More than willing. I'd happily do it. I was raised on a farm; I knew animals. And what I didn't know, I would learn. Lucas and the guys would give me a job.

I'd miss active missions; I wasn't going to lie. I may be in my forties, but I still had a lot of good years left to fight bad guys. I'd miss my Zodiac team, my friends.

But I'd walk away from it all if it got Bronwyn what she needed. She'd paid way too high a price for someone so young. Now it was her turn to live a life free of fear and pain. I was damned well going to give it to her.

I would if Callum Webb would get his ass in here so we could get this debrief over with. It had been twenty-four hours since we'd finished the fighting. More than half of that time, I'd spent on-site overseeing the damage and walking the law enforcement agents through what had happened. Then I'd been brought here.

I needed a damned shower. But more, I needed to get to Bronwyn.

But it wasn't Webb who walked into the room a few minutes later. It was Theodore Wilson. Every hackle I had rose at the sight of that asshole.

"Where's Webb?"

Wilson gave me a tight smile. He still had the strip of white medical tape over the bridge of his nose where I'd punched him last week. Good. I hoped it fucking hurt. "Callum Webb has been relieved of duty. He is no longer an active agent for Omega Sector."

"Why?"

Wilson shrugged. "One too many renegade choices, I would assume. Allowing Zodiac Tactical to make move after move unchecked. He's lucky he's not facing criminal charges."

"What are you doing here rather than in Europe?"

Wilson took the seat at the table across from me. "I've

been placed in charge of the interagency task force charged with taking down Mosaic. Believe me, I will not be as lenient as Webb was when it comes to your cowboy shenanigans."

Cowboy shenanigans. I barely refrained from rolling my eyes. I didn't have time for this pissing contest.

"Look, Mosaic brought the fight to us, not the other way around. Zodiac wants to keep its people safe. Erick Huen decided to seek revenge on Ian DeRose and bit off more than he could chew."

"Zodiac can't go around playing vigilantes without repercussions."

I crossed my arms over my chest, more to make sure I didn't punch him in the face again than a show of machismo. "That's bullshit and you know it. Ian DeRose worked for you guys taking down Mosaic the first time. He almost died multiple times doing it. Scratch that, he *did* die when his own brother and Erick buried him and revived him multiple times."

"That was then. Now Mosaic is back and committing acts of terror all over the globe—much worse than their original version. Allow me to show you what happened yesterday in Hamburg, Germany while you were running around the mountains with your friends."

Running around stopping fucking terrorists. I swallowed the comeback. Barely.

And the comeback was completely forgotten as I watched a pretty young woman not much older than Bronwyn walk up to the front of a government building, then proceed to blow it and herself up.

Her face was completely blank as she did it. A blankness I recognized from Bronwyn in New York when she'd had no idea who I was. "Oh shit."

"That was Tenisha Day, American graduate student.

No known ties to any terrorist organizations. She had two loving parents and three younger brothers. She killed twenty-two people yesterday."

He paused for dramatic effect, but I knew there was more.

"Before yesterday, her family hadn't seen her in four months. But we found this." He spun a picture around so I could see it. It was Tenisha Day and Dr. Tippens. "She was one of Mosaic's zombie soldiers. Like Bronwyn was."

I scrubbed a hand down my face. "This is tragic, Wilson, I agree. And hell yeah, it needs to be stopped. But we're all on the same side. Quit acting like you don't know that. All I want to do is give my statement and go home."

"To Bronwyn Rourke."

I sat up straighter in my seat. "You'll leave her out of this if you're wise."

I had to give it to the man; he wasn't intimidated even though I had probably six inches and fifty pounds of muscle on him.

"Bronwyn Rourke knows more than she's telling."

"No, she doesn't. Believe me, she's not hiding things."

Wilson studied me with narrowed eyes. "Maybe that's true. But at the very least, she knows more than she thinks she does. The key to finding out the truth behind Mosaic— and who's in charge—is with her."

"No. Bronwyn has done her part, and she's out of this. You've got Erick Huen in custody. Go question him to get your answers."

Wilson crossed his arms over his chest. "You and I both know Erick Huen isn't going to say a thing that doesn't help him directly. Plus, any information is going to take too much time to get. Bronwyn will be quicker."

I could feel my fists itching for his jaw again. "Bronwyn

is not an option. She doesn't remember anything valuable."

"We can try nontraditional methods. Hypnosis. Chemical assistance. Medical scans. They might be a little invasive, but in the end, if it saves lives, it will be worth it."

I gritted my teeth until my jaw ached. "So you want a woman who has already been subjected to physical and mental torture to waltz in here and let you poke around her brain a little more?"

"It might be uncomfortable for her, but I think we'd all agree it would be worth it if we got any information."

I leaned forward, putting my weight on my elbows on the desk. "Did my fist feel uncomfortable when I broke your nose, Wilson? I can break it again if you need a refresher."

He was wise enough to lean back in his chair. "No need for melodrama, Mr. McEwan."

"You are not going to poke around in Bronwyn's head, further torturing a woman who has damned well been tortured enough, to try to get info that may or may not be there."

"That's not your decision to make."

"I tell you what, if Bronwyn comes to me and asks to use any known methods to retrieve her memories, you'll be the first person I call. Until then, you will not demand anything from her."

Wilson and I stared each other down, but my brain was already jumping into full gear.

Bronwyn and I might have to run for a while. Hide out. That wouldn't be any great hardship. I'd keep her in bed and feed her. That sounded like a perfect way to spend a year. Or a lifetime.

We'd get the hell out of Dodge and let law enforcement

work its magic to figure out how to get intel about Mosaic from Erick. Bronwyn wasn't a pawn for their use.

The sooner the bastard sitting across from me figured that out, the better.

"I'm done here, Wilson. I'll write up my statement, but the questioning is done. Stay away from Bronwyn. You want to threaten someone, go have a power play with Erick Huen. Get intel from him."

Wilson left without another word. I got to work writing out my statement about the events of the past forty-eight hours. I gave them only the details law enforcement needed. In this case, brevity was best for multiple reasons —reducing Zodiac Tactical's liability and because I wanted to get the hell out of there as soon as possible.

Less than an hour later, they let me out of the holding room, and I was heading toward the door. With every step I took, I felt more relief because each step was taking me closer to Bronwyn.

I was almost to the front door when I heard Agent Wilson's voice.

"Mr. McEwan, hold a moment."

I turned. He had a man on either side of him. I shook my head. "I'm done, Wilson. I'm leaving."

"Actually, you're not."

Do not break his nose again. Witnesses present.

"Yeah, I think I am. You have my statement."

He gestured to the two men with him. "No, you're not going to be leaving. You're under arrest."

I knew instantly what the little fucker was doing. "Don't do this, Wilson. Don't use me to get to her. You have Erick; he's your best bet."

"Actually, Erick Huen was killed an hour ago before we could get any information from him. Evidently assassinated by his own lawyer—Mosaic doesn't like to leave loose ends."

"Shit." I scrubbed a hand down my face.

"And now the only loose end we have available is Bronwyn."

Chapter 35

Bronwyn

I needed Sarge.

I was almost numb to what I'd figured out. Although she tried to comprehend, I couldn't explain the full scope of it to Jenna. But Sarge would get it. He'd known me then. Known my situation.

Known the person who had reason to hate me enough to sell me out to Erick Huen.

Nikolai.

Nikolai Novotný was Mosiac's European leader. He was the reason I'd been taken to use against Ian DeRose— not because I was such a great candidate, but because Nikolai wanted revenge for what I'd done to him when I'd escaped Prague.

"Are you okay?" Jenna had sat me down at her kitchen island and started pushing food in front of me. Cheese cubes, chicken salad, chocolate chip cookies…evidently

Jenna wasn't much of a cook. "You look worse than you did before we dove headfirst down the rabbit hole."

I nibbled on a cube of cheese. "The thought of seeing Nikolai again, being anywhere near him at all…" I set the cheese back on my plate. "I can't stomach it. You probably think I'm a coward."

She let out a short bark of humorless laughter. "Honey, you're talking to someone who doesn't leave her house anymore because of her past. Trust me, I don't think you're a coward."

"Jenna, I—"

The loud knock on the door startled us. Every bit of color bled from Jenna's face.

Her phone beeped. She looked down to read the text.

"It's Outlaw. Mark Outlawson. He says he's outside."

A fist slammed against the door again. "Jenna, let me in. Hurry."

Some of the color came back into her face, and we rushed to the door. She looked through the control panel to confirm it was really Mark then unlocked and opened the door. He stepped inside, and she closed it quickly.

"What's going on?"

Mark looked over at me. "I'm here to get you out."

I couldn't stop the terror that climbed up my spine. "Where's Sarge?"

His mouth had a grim twist to it. "There's been a complication."

The terror enveloped me further. "What happened? Is he hurt? Taken by Mosaic?" I looked over at Jenna. "What if—"

Mark shook his head. "No. He's not hurt. But he has been arrested. Law enforcement wants you, Bronwyn. They think you're the key to finding out more about

Mosaic. Sarge got word to me, and I'm supposed to get you out. He doesn't want—"

Another fist slammed on the door; Jenna and I jumped, and Mark muttered a curse under his breath.

"Jenna Franklin, this is the police. Open the door. We have a warrant for the arrest of Bronwyn Rourke, and we know she's in there."

I recognized that voice. Agent Wilson. I turned to Mark. "Wilson is the one who arrested Sarge?"

Mark nodded. "Maybe I can get you out the back."

"Open the door now, Ms. Franklin, and I won't have to arrest you too. I'm only here for Bronwyn. This is your choice."

Jenna's eyes darted around her house, her breaths coming in and out so rapidly it wouldn't be long before she passed out.

I grabbed her by both upper arms. "Breathe, Jenna. I'm going to go out there to surrender myself."

"No," Mark interrupted. "I can get you both out."

"You can't get us both out, Mark." Jenna would be comatose within seconds if he tried. "It's okay. I'll go with Wilson. You stay here with Jenna."

Mark shook his head. "Sarge went to a lot of trouble to get a message to me and—"

Something slammed against the door, and we all jumped back. Jenna hadn't reengaged the locks after Mark had come in. Wilson was using some sort of battering ram. Another slam and the door burst open.

Jenna whimpered, huddling against the wall, arms wrapping around her head protectively. A uniformed officer stepped to the side, and Wilson walked in.

"We meet again, Ms. Rourke. I've gone to a great deal of trouble to find you, including letting Mr. McEwan think he was getting an encoded message to Mr. Outlawson here.

Then it was a simple matter of following him straight to you."

I rolled my eyes. "I'm beginning to think you missed your calling in theater with all the melodrama, Wilson."

He gave me a patronizing smile. "You can come with me now and I'll leave your friends, or all three of you will be cuffed and taken in for interrogation. I don't think Ms. Franklin finds that thought very appealing."

Jenna had crouched down, curled into a ball, arms still around her head. I couldn't stand it.

"Leave them. I'll come with you willingly."

He raised an eyebrow. "And submit to whatever testing we need to do to get the information about Mosaic out of your mind?"

"Bronwyn, Sarge specifically tried to keep this asshole from getting his hands on you." Mark stepped toward me, and the uniformed officer drew his weapon.

I held out an arm to stop him. "Take care of Jenna. Sarge was trying to rescue me like he always does. But this time, I'm going to rescue him."

Outlaw nodded slowly, although he obviously didn't like it. Maybe he realized Jenna needed someone by her side right now more than I did. Either way, I walked away with Wilson and heard the door close behind us.

"So we're clear," Wilson said, "by coming with me, you are agreeing to the utilization of whatever methods are necessary in order to get the information out of your head."

I didn't look at him as I walked to his car. "You won't need to use any of your nefarious tactics. I already have the information you need. I know who the Mosaic leader is in Europe."

"Who?"

Now I looked at him. "I'm not telling you a damned thing until you release Sarge and I see him myself."

~

I got half of what I asked for.

"There he is." Wilson pointed to Sarge on the other side of a two-way mirror. He sat ramrod straight in a chair with his hands cuffed behind his back.

"Let him go." I wanted to go in there, kiss him, make sure he was really all right. He looked exhausted.

"Not going to happen. You said you have a name for me."

My hands shook again, so I clasped them behind my back. I had to stand my ground. Once I told Wilson about Nikolai, I'd lose all leverage.

"You move Sarge to a more comfortable holding room, and you take those cuffs off him. And they stay off. And then you let me in the room with him."

Wilson's eyes narrowed. He didn't like giving up any of his power. "I have you here now. I can run the tests."

I forced myself not to show how much the thought of someone digging around my brain without permission terrified me. I wouldn't survive intact. I already knew it. "You can. But you'd be wasting time fighting against me, especially since I'm willing to give you what you want right now."

"Fine."

I had to give him credit; once Wilson made up his mind to do something, he was quite efficient with his actions. Within fifteen minutes, Sarge was uncuffed and being taken to another room. I had to watch in silence from the other side of the glass as he demanded to know about me—if I was there, if I was okay.

He lunged for Wilson when the man walked through the door, but he was stopped and re-cuffed by two other agents.

"Don't you touch her, Wilson. I will fucking end you."

"Now, now, Mr. McEwan, threatening a law enforcement officer is a crime."

If Sarge could've gotten his hands on Wilson right that second, it would not have ended well for the smaller man. The other agents began leading Sarge out the door.

"Where are you taking me?" Sarge demanded.

"Somewhere more comfortable. Somewhere you don't have to be restrained, if you'll cooperate. Thankfully, some people are more reasonable than you. We're all on the same side, remember?"

"Bronwyn is here, isn't she?" Sarge struggled against the men holding his arms, but there wasn't much he could do. He realized that and stopped walking. "Wilson, listen to me. Don't do this. Bronwyn, she… Don't do this to her. Please. You don't know what she's been through. I'm begging you. I swear I'll quit Zodiac and go full time helping you take down the rest of Mosaic. Just don't do this to her."

I put my hand up against the glass, wishing I could get closer to him.

"Interesting," Wilson murmured. "But I think she's stronger than you know."

"She's stronger than anyone I've ever known, but even the strongest break." Sarge bowed his head. "If you need a fall guy for shit that has gone down with Mosaic so far, I'll take the blame. I'll do time if that's what has to happen. Please, don't do anything to Bronwyn. She's been through too much. Please."

My heart shattered as Sarge's voice cracked on the last

plea. He was willing to give up everything for me. To put his pride aside and beg.

Wilson shook his head. "You two are quite a pair. She came with me willingly if I agreed to release you based on intel she provides."

Sarge closed his eyes and let out a shaky breath. "If you're going to do this, let me stay with her. She'll need me. All the rest of my offer still applies. Just please don't make her do this alone."

Wilson tilted his head to the side. "You broke my nose."

Sarge didn't hesitate. "You can return the favor right now."

I was about to start slamming my hand against the mirror. I didn't know if Sarge could hear me, but I wasn't about to let him take another beating for me.

"That won't be necessary. Follow me." He led Sarge out of the room, and I couldn't see them anymore.

By the time Wilson came back to get me a few minutes later, I was ready to break his nose myself. "Was that really needed? Why didn't you tell him I'd remembered on my own and your invasive methods weren't needed?"

"We'll see if your intel truly provides anything useful. The tests aren't off the table yet." He shrugged. "And besides, he broke my nose."

We walked down the hallway, and he stopped in front of the door. "This gives you both a little bit a comfort, but believe me, it's temporary if what you provide isn't use—"

"Nikolai Novotný." I cut him off. I didn't need more threats. "He's who you're looking for."

Wilson raised one eyebrow. "In Prague. He's been on our active watch list for a while. You're sure?"

"Yes. It's how I got on Mosaic's radar in the first place."

"How do I know you're telling the truth?"

"How long has he been on your watch list?"

"Since his father died and he took over and started quickly growing the family terrorist and racketeering business. Almost three years."

I crossed my arms over my chest, once again to stop my hands from shaking. "Two and a half years ago, Nikolai was attacked and his face was scarred."

"Yeah. I've seen the photos. So?"

"I'm the one who did that to him, to get out from under his power. He sold me out to Mosaic as part of his revenge. Find Nikolai. He's the one you're trying to stop."

Wilson nodded and opened the door. I stepped inside, not caring that the lock clicked behind me as the door closed.

I flew into Sarge's arms.

Chapter 36

Sarge

I caught Bronwyn as she crashed into me. I clutched her against my chest, breathing in her scent. "I'm so sorry, Pony Girl. I didn't want you here. I was hoping Outlaw could get you out."

She shook her head against my chest, arms wrapped around me tight. "No. I wasn't going to leave you here."

"But the things Wilson wants to do to you to get the information…" I closed my eyes. I couldn't bear to think about it. I would give anything if I could go through the anguish rather than her.

All that stuff I'd offered Wilson had been nothing less than the truth. I would do anything to keep Bronwyn out of this situation.

I opened my eyes when her head left my chest.

"None of that will be necessary. Jenna and I worked together while you were gone, and I remembered some things. I know who the European leader of Mosaic is. It's Nikolai. You remember him, right?"

"What?"

She reached up and cupped my face. "Are you okay? You look tired. Let's sit down."

I wasn't going to take my arms from around her even to walk the few steps to the couch. I lowered them to her hips and lifted her up and walked us over there, sitting her in my lap.

"I'm fine. It's been a long few days. But tell me more about Nikolai."

She cuddled into me, and between having her here and knowing she wasn't about to get mentally tortured by the good guys, I could almost relax. I could at least breathe, which was more than I'd been able to do since Wilson had threatened to use Bronwyn to get the info he wanted.

"I remembered something Erick said the night he took me in Marrakesh—that he'd heard I was feisty."

"Shit. Nikolai called you that the day I met you."

She nodded. "He called me that all the time. And it ends up Wilson was right. There was a specific reason why I'd been targeted to be used against Ian DeRose. It wasn't luck or chance—Nikolai pointed me out to Erick. He wanted me to suffer."

"Why? Because you got away from him?"

Her hands shook in her lap, and she gripped my arm to control the movement. "When you came back the second time and told me about the job in Paris, I knew I wanted to go. Almost right away, I went to Gregory, Nikolai's father, to see if I could work out a deal with him. I knew I'd have to pay money to make up for what it would cost him to lose me, but he'd always been reasonable."

"He wouldn't let you go?"

"I think he would've. I hid and heard him and Nikolai

fighting about it. But a few weeks later, Gregory had a heart attack and died. There was no way Nikolai was going to let me go."

"So you lost your way out and your protection against Nikolai all at one time."

"Yes," she whispered.

I held her tighter. "God, Pony Girl. I'm so sorry."

Once again, she'd been alone to face her horrors. Once again, something I could've prevented if I hadn't let her go. I should've taken her with me from day one. Gotten her out of the situation for good.

She burrowed in closer to me. "I didn't fight him. I knew that would make it worse."

I closed my eyes. Fury ran up and down my spine, but that would have to wait. I kept my voice even. "That was smart. You did what you had to do to survive."

"Nikolai got tired of me after a few months. Then he decided to offer me to his men. That's when I knew I had to leave."

"Good."

"He caught me. Hurt me. To escape, I burned him with some boiling soup that was on the stove. He has scars all over his face."

"Good," I said again. "I wish you'd killed him."

"He was already growing in power after his father died. He wanted to do more, control more. I was hoping he would forget about me, but I knew I'd be looking over my shoulder for the rest of my life."

"Instead, he sold you out to Erick Huen."

"He wouldn't want me to have a quick death. He would want me to suffer. I know Erick was reporting back to him, telling him what they were doing to me. My agony probably entertained Nikolai to no end. Everything that was done to me makes more sense now."

There were so many people I wanted to kill for this woman. Everyone who had ever hurt her. I couldn't do that, but I would damn well stand between her and anyone else who would ever try.

"I'm glad you remembered and Wilson didn't have to do whatever god-awful experiments he had planned."

"Me too." She moved, shifting until she straddled my hips rather than lying draped across my legs. Those blue eyes looked more clear and focused than they had since France. "I heard you a few minutes ago. The deals you were prepared to make with Wilson to stop him from performing the tests on me."

I shrugged. "There isn't anything I wouldn't have given him to keep him from hurting you."

"You have to stop rescuing me, Harrison McEwan."

I kissed her nose. "That's Sarge to you, Pony Girl. And I think you were the one who did the rescuing this time. I'm sure Outlaw could've gotten you out, but you came back for me."

"I wasn't going to leave you to pay the price for my freedom."

I cupped her cheeks. "It would've been worth it. Knowing you were safe? Not being hurt? That would be worth any price. And if doing whatever I can to keep you safe is synonymous with rescue, then you can be expecting me to do that for a very, very long time."

Her eyes filled with tears. "I'm still broken. My hands shake all the time. And I'm scared. So scared. Even when I know I'm safe."

I started to interrupt her, but she put a finger over my lips. "I know some of that will get better. But some of it won't. Nobody is ever going to describe me as feisty again."

As if I was ever going to use that particular word to describe her with the connections it had to Nikolai.

I kissed her finger then brought it down from my lips. "You are who you are. I wasn't lying when· I told you I was looking forward to getting to know the new person you rebuilt yourself into. You're lying in ash right now, but the phoenix is going to rise from that. And I want to be there to see it."

"You won't mind my shaky hands? I don't think that's ever going away."

It probably would, but only time could prove that to her, so I wasn't going to argue.

"I won't mind that if you won't mind that I'm almost twenty years older than you, generally cranky, and will probably be yelling at people to get off my lawn sooner rather than later."

She laughed, the sound the most beautiful thing I'd ever heard. "I think I can handle that. I'll just wheel you back inside in your wheelchair."

I brought her lips in to mine. "I love you, Pony Girl. Who you were, who you are, who you'll be."

Her hands, still a little shaky, came up and threaded into my hair. "You're the only person in the world who will ever know all three."

I fell asleep on the couch with Bronwyn in my arms. She hadn't declared her love for me, but I didn't need the words right now. They would come when she was ready.

When I woke up after a couple hours, she was awake next to me, stroking my head with gentle fingers.

"You okay?" I asked her. "Wilson is an asshole, but I'm sure he'll release us soon."

"They're going to have a hard time taking down Niko-lai. He's so much more powerful than before. Wilson showed me footage of the woman who blew up that building in Hamburg. He said Mosaic had programmed her the way they'd programmed me."

"Yeah, he calls them Mosaic's zombie soldiers." I pulled her closer. "Wilson and his team will stop them."

"Wilson thinks Nikolai has a lot more of them—more people under Nikolai's control. And he's right. I know it for a fact because I saw them myself."

"Pony Girl…"

"I remembered more while you were sleeping. They were in the lab with me—dozens of them. All young women."

She shot up from the couch and began pacing. "It's going to take Wilson too long to get to Nikolai. How many more people have to die before Wilson takes Nikolai down? Hundreds? Thousands? Nikolai will use the time to esca-late because it will bring him more power. He'll use those women as his own personal terrorist squad. And I had totally forgotten they existed until now."

I scooted to the edge of the couch. "None of this is your fault, Bronwyn."

She paused her pacing. "You're right. It's not. Nothing of what has happened up until this point is my fault. There was nothing I could have done to stop it."

I knew what she was going to say and wished there were some way I could erase the thought from her mind.

I knew what she wanted to do.

And I knew I wouldn't stop her even though it was going to damned near kill me not to. She was right that I had to stop rescuing her.

This she needed to do to rescue herself.

"Go on," I whispered.

"You know what I'm going to say, don't you?"

"Yes." I caught one of her hands and brought it to my lips. "But say it anyway."

"I can stop Nikolai. I can be used as bait to draw him out. He's not rational when it comes to me, and he will take chances he might not normally take to get me back under his control."

I let go of her hand and stood. "I want to say up front that I don't want you to do this. You've already paid a high enough price. Let somebody else bring Nikolai down. They'll get him eventually."

"I know. But it will come at a much steeper price."

I scrubbed my hand down my face. "Yes. Strategically, using you to flush him out is the best bet."

We stood staring at each other for a long minute before I yanked her into my arms.

"Knowing everything, I still don't want you to do it." I buried my face in her neck and whispered, "We can walk away from this, Pony Girl. Walk away and never look back. Just the two of us. I can make sure no one will ever find us again."

She stepped back and looked up at me. "No. Every time more people died, I would know I could've stopped it. We have to do this. I have to do this."

I'd never had any doubt that would be her stance. I kissed her on the forehead. "Okay, but it's not going to be easy. The Zodiac team is mostly down. We're going to be stuck with Wilson, and, news flash, he's an asshole."

"But a competent asshole. He wants to stop Mosaic and Nikolai."

"Agreed. Jenna and Outlaw will back us up, if Jenna is okay."

"It would have to be a small team anyway if we want to draw him out." She stepped deeper into my arms, and I tightened them around her. "You and I were a good team before I joined Zodiac, and we'll be a good team together again. I need you to believe I'm strong enough to do this."

"Your strength is not in doubt. And there is no one else I'd rather have on my team than you. Always."

Chapter 37

Bronwyn

T welve hours later, we were on a plane back to Prague where everything had started for Sarge and me.

Not surprising to either of us, Wilson had agreed that using me as bait for Nikolai was the best plan. The specifics for how to do that without getting me killed were a little more unclear.

Of course, he hadn't come right out and said it, but my survival was secondary to making sure Nikolai went down. That's why we were moving so quickly without a true plan in place.

Wilson had been working a plan with his team at the back of the plane. He'd informed us that he'd let us know what it was when we needed to know. As if it wasn't my life on the line.

I'd had to stop Sarge from breaking the man's nose again.

So when Wilson walked up with a laptop and placed it

on the table in front of Sarge and me, we were both surprised.

"You've got a video call."

We clicked the open button to find Jenna's face staring at us. As soon as she could see us, she brought her face close to her camera.

"Bronwyn, I'm so sorry. I'm so sorry about what happened at my house. I totally threw you under the bus with this asshole, and it's all my fault you're trapped in this situation now."

I pulled the computer closer to me. "Jenna, stop. It's not your fault. There was no reason for me to run when I already knew Nikolai was behind all this. I'm glad you're okay."

Although, honestly, she didn't look okay. She had dark circles under her eyes, and her jaw was tight. "Still. What I did was—"

"Understandable. It was understandable given the circumstances and threats involved." I turned to glare at Wilson. His flair for melodrama was what had sent Jenna into her panic attack to begin with.

He reached over and turned the computer in his direction. "How were you able to contact us through this computer?"

She let out a snort. "A determined second grader could hack your task force's communication system. And given the fact that your people are gabbing with two different continents on four different phones at this moment, I happen to know you're over the Atlantic right now. I can give you a specific location if you want me to."

Wilson's face tightened. "This conversation is over. Don't hack our system again, or I'll send someone to show up at your house to take you in."

I dug my nails into Sarge's hand. Maybe I was going to break Wilson's nose.

But Jenna took it in stride. "Simmer down there, Special Agent Asshole. I didn't call to chat with my friend. I have information you need if you want to successfully take down Nikolai."

"We don't need your help."

Sarge found it within himself to be reasonable. "Wilson, Jenna is capable of digging up better intel than almost anyone on the planet. Hear her out. We need it."

For a second, I didn't think Wilson would comply, but then he sat down across from us, sliding the computer to the end of the table so we could all see Jenna. "Fine. Go. Although I doubt you've found anything about Nikolai Novotný that's going to prove helpful."

"Nikolai is not where your solution lies, Agent Asshole, so you're right, I won't be providing any intel about him."

Now she had Wilson's full attention. "What are you talking about?"

"Not such a big shot now, are you?"

Sarge twisted the computer so the camera was more focused on us. "Tell us what you discovered, Jenna."

"The key wasn't Nikolai at all—it was in Dr. Tippens's research. I dug into his experiments on you in particular, Bronwyn. It was incomplete data, but I was able to extrapolate his intents. Specifics for what Tippens was programming in you—because of Nikolai. The home stuff."

"My final mission is to go home," I muttered.

"Exactly. They were always planning to turn you over to Nikolai when your usefulness for Erick Huen and Tippens's research came to an end."

"It's why they didn't kill you outright," Sarge muttered against my hair. "I never understood that. I was thankful, but it didn't make sense."

"How does this help us take Nikolai down?" Wilson asked, for once, his tone not combative.

"I know where home is according to Nikolai's and Tippens's plans. I know what Bronwyn would've done once she got there if she were still under the regimen. We can fool Nikolai into thinking you're still under his control."

Wilson's eyes grew larger. "And then you can find out where he's keeping the other people under the regimen. His zombie army."

Jenna nodded. "I can show you how you would've behaved—phrases, actions—if the regimen had worked completely and Nikolai had you under his power. I think we can convince him that he's won."

"Then we move in and take him out." Wilson looked over at me. "But it means you'll have to go in alone at first. Are you up for it?"

"Yes." I kept my answer simple even though I wasn't sure the one word was the truth. But until Nikolai was taken down, I would never be safe. Neither would Sarge, nor would anyone at Zodiac Tactical. Nikolai would continue to come at me any way he could.

If he couldn't hurt me personally, he'd start hurting the people I cared about.

I looked over at Sarge, his face tight. He obviously didn't like this plan. I couldn't blame him. I didn't like a plan that put me back in Nikolai's power even for a short time.

"I'll do it."

Wilson turned to Jenna. "Give them all the data they need to make her interaction with Nikolai believable. I'll go tell the rest of the team the plan."

He got up and headed toward the back of the plane.

"I really do believe this is going to work," Jenna said. "I can leak some data to Nikolai's organization that will give a plausible excuse for where you've been the past few weeks. Then all you have to do is make him think the programming has worked and you got there as soon as you could."

"You're sure you've got enough details for her to be able to do that?" Sarge's hands tightened around mine. "She'll be by herself with him. Her life is at stake."

"Yes. I know what she'll be asked, and I know how she should respond to prove she's under the regimen. We can get her ready. Plus, I have a gift for you guys. It should be there when you land."

I squeezed his hand. "It's better than the wandering-around-Prague plan we had before. It probably wouldn't have worked anyway, just gotten me a bullet in the head."

Of course, there was no guarantee that wouldn't still happen.

"Yeah," Sarge muttered. "But I still don't like it."

We didn't have to like it. We just had to do it.

"Okay." I let out a breath and pulled away from Sarge. "Let's start going over all the details of what I need to do. We don't have much time. And the sooner we get Nikolai, the more lives we'll save."

Including mine.

"I don't like this," Sarge whispered into my hair. "Test your comm unit again."

"I'm going to be okay."

It was both a test of the tiny transmitting device—not unlike the one Sarge had given me when I'd shown up at his house that one time—and a reassurance for both of us.

We were in Prague, and I was about to step out of the safety of his arms and walk to where my programming would've taken me if I were under Nikolai's control.

We'd spent every second until we landed going over the details of how I needed to behave. Answers to trick questions Nikolai would ask as fail-safes.

Jenna had leaked data that I had been held in isolation at a military base in Nevada for the past few weeks. Only recently had I been moved and placed under civilian psychiatric care.

She kept the details loose from there. It was completely feasible that once I was in a mental hospital rather than a military brig, I would be able to escape and do what my programming demanded: return to Prague.

We made sure my entry into the country was known. Now we had to see if Nikolai would take the bait. He wouldn't come pick me up himself unless we got ridiculously lucky, so I would be taken to him, and have to be face-to-face with him alone for at least a little while.

"You don't come for me unless you have to." I hugged him closer. "Let me do some good. Let me get as much info as I can."

We all knew that Nikolai probably had a plan in place to eliminate his zombie army if he was arrested. I needed to find out where they were.

"I'm not letting anything happen to you."

"Get those women out first, then come for me. Wilson is right in wanting to make sure that happens."

He cupped my cheeks and kissed me. "Outlaw and I will be ready, no matter what asinine decisions Wilson makes."

Mark Outlawson had been Jenna's gift for us. He'd shown up not long after we'd landed. At least now I knew someone had Sarge's back while he had mine.

"Let's go." Wilson walked over and tapped me on the shoulder. "If your computer guru is correct, you have to be out on Radlická Street right at noon. That's the first security measure we've got to cross. If we don't get you out there on time, we have to wait twenty-four more hours."

I looked up at Sarge. "I love you." I should've said it earlier, not when we were rushed and Wilson was standing so close I could hear his breathing.

Sarge rubbed his thumb against my lips. "You tell me that again in a day or two when this is over and I have you naked in a bed somewhere."

"Deal."

"I'll see you soon, Pony Girl. Believe it."

I did. I believed it with every fiber of my body. If I didn't, there was no way I'd be able to do this.

I turned and walked out from the back room of a restaurant where we'd been holed up and outside into the dreary Prague weather. I didn't shiver or show any reaction to the cold dampness at all.

Someone under the regimen would not be aware of the discomfort.

I walked straight ahead until I arrived at Radlická where it met a secondary road. Then stood, as directed, near the edge of the street.

People walked around me on either side, not paying me much mind. I felt conspicuous, but to most people rushing along with their own lives in the middle of downtown, I wasn't doing anything except being in their way for a second before they passed.

I stood, completely still, staring straight ahead. That was what my programming would have me do. I had no doubt Nikolai had someone watching this corner at noon every day to see if I arrived.

I kept my hands by my sides, forcing myself not to clench them to stop their shaking. Of everything, my hands were most likely to give me away. Someone under control of the regimen would not have shaky hands.

The longer I stood, the harder it became. For the first time, I wished I could escape my mind and let my body float out of itself.

We're going to get through this, Pony Girl.

Sarge was with me. Both in my mind, where I needed him, and at my back, where I needed him too.

"Yes," I whispered without moving my lips. "We'll make it through this."

I believed it.

Then a car pulled up at the curb, and I was yanked inside, taking me away from my salvation and back to my nightmare.

Chapter 38

Bronwyn

I didn't recognize either of the men in the car. The one who grabbed me used a wand over my torso and limbs to check for weapons or recording devices, but he didn't come near my throat or the tiny, clear transmitter pressing against my vocal cords. He immediately restrained my hands.

"Say your words," he said in English.

I stared straight ahead. "I exist only to obey orders. My final mission is to go home."

"And where is home?"

"At the feet of Nikolai."

Both men snickered, but I carefully kept my face blank. Someone under the regimen would have no reaction to the humiliating phrase.

Sarge had nearly lost his temper when Jenna had told us about the trigger phrase and the corresponding response. She'd found it in Dr. Tippens's notes. He'd argued against it as a response phrase, insisting Nikolai use an alphanumeric code, but Nikolai had refused.

Nikolai's need to lord his power over me had definitely worked in our favor. Jenna would've probably never found some random code in Dr. Tippens's notes, but that phrase had caught her attention.

The men switched to Czech, but I still understood perfectly.

"I can't believe she actually showed up," the driver said. "I'll miss my daily coffee as I wait for someone I never thought would arrive."

"Why do you think Nikolai is so obsessed with her?" The man in the back with me trailed a finger up my arm. I kept my fingers clenched together and showed no response. "She is attractive but not worth so much trouble. Maybe we should find a place to pull over and try her out."

The driver chuckled. "Maybe Nikolai wants someone who doesn't pretend not to see his scars. Look at her, she's a robot."

"She looks close enough to flesh and blood for me." He slid his hand up my thigh.

I grabbed the wandering hand, twisting it to the point of breaking even with the cuffs on. "Nikolai only."

The man howled, and I let go. The driver laughed. "Maybe not completely a robot, Jarek."

I didn't know if my actions would be part of my programming, but it was a risk I was willing to take. I wasn't going to become a plaything for these two on the way to Nikolai.

Jarek huffed back against the seat. "Bitch."

But at least he left me alone.

The roads of Prague were vaguely familiar. I'd mostly walked and stayed in the same two-mile radius growing up.

We weren't going back to the old neighborhood, that was for sure.

We were heading outside of the city, not in the direction that intel put Nikolai's residence.

"North," I muttered softly. I hoped Sarge and the team were following this vehicle closely enough to realize we weren't going in the direction we'd expected. Or that this would at least give them a clue.

"That's right, bitch," Jarek said. "Nikolai is having us take you to the place where no one ever leaves except in a body bag."

Thankfully, he was too busy laughing at his own joke to see my flinch. I had to get my actions under control, or I was going to give myself away. Especially once I was in front of Nikolai.

I wished I could have had Sarge's voice in my ear rather than him only being able to hear me.

You do. I'm here.

Maybe it was my mind projecting his voice, but he was in my heart. It gave me hope. Strength.

But the closer we got to Nikolai, the harder it was to stay calm. By the time we pulled up to the doorway, I didn't think I was going to be able to go through with it.

Do you want a future? Then you have to do this.

This time, it was my own voice inside my head. And it was right. If I wanted a future with Sarge, if I wanted to protect him, then this was where I had to make my stand.

And you're not alone. Sarge.

I probably needed to talk to Dr. Rayne about all the voices in my head.

Jarek yanked me out of the car and pushed me inside the door and down a narrow hallway. I focused on breathing. There were no windows anywhere around me, and the concrete walls and sterile floors reminded me of my personal hell. I wouldn't be able to escape the place on my own.

You're not on your own.

We finally stopped in front of a door, and Jarek knocked. I sucked in a breath, glad my hands were still restrained so I could clench them together to hide their shaking.

The door opened, and Jarek led me inside. I stared straight ahead, but I could count three men out of the corner of my eye. Then the one who was right in front of me, looking out at something through an interior window.

Nikolai.

He turned to face me, and keeping my face neutral was maybe the hardest thing I'd ever done. The burn scars on his cheek and chin were even worse than the pictures I'd seen after I'd escaped.

Scars I'd given him and he'd demand payment for.

"You found her." He walked toward me.

Jarek nodded. "Yes, sir. She was at the location right at the time you said she'd be there."

Nikolai passed out of my vision as he circled around me. I knew a blow could come any minute. A literal knife in the back.

Steady. These are the most important minutes.

That voice was a mixture of mine and Sarge's. But it was right.

"You look different from when I last saw you in person." Nikolai passed back around so I could see him. That made it easier. "Of course, I've seen footage of you with Erick and Dr. Tippens—screaming, crying, begging. That was nice. But not the same as seeing you in person. I wish I could have been there."

He leaned forward so his face was directly in front of

mine, his breath hot against my skin. "I'll look forward to the screaming, begging, and crying in person."

Be strong, Pony Girl.

I remained expressionless. The only thing that gave me away was my hands, but nobody was looking at them.

Nikolai backed away, eyes narrowed, still studying me. "She said everything correctly?"

"Yes." Jarek nodded enthusiastically next to me.

"Say your words," he said to me.

"I exist only to obey orders." Saying these words by rote was easy. I'd had so much practice in the lab. "My final mission is to go home."

"And where is home?"

This was harder. "At the feet of Nikolai."

He broke into a big grin. "Yes, I definitely like the sound of that."

The four other men in the room chuckled.

Nikolai walked slowly around me again. "But look at you, all the feisty is gone with you like this. I want to see Bronya, not this robot." He leaned closer to my ear. "Release code four-two-seven."

I kept myself still. Jenna had gone over a release code number, but that wasn't it.

Did she have it wrong? Had it changed? If I didn't move, would he know the truth?

Jenna hadn't steered me wrong thus far, so I held.

Nikolai stepped back and studied me. "Just checking. One can't be too careful. Release code two-one-two."

That was it, the one Jenna had given me. Two hundred and twelve, the temperature at which water boiled. Since I'd burned him with boiling liquid... Trust Nikolai to have a meaning behind everything.

I allowed my emotional mask to fall away, to let all the

terror I was really feeling show. I unclenched my hands—they were shaking so hard tremors moved up my arms.

I moved away from Nikolai, something I'd wanted to do since I first saw him. Jarek grabbed my arm to keep me in place.

"There she is." Nikolai trailed a finger down my cheek, and I flinched. "There's my little runaway. I've been waiting for this moment a long time."

"Nikolai? What? No. How did you—?" It was easy to inject the terror into my voice.

"You've always been under my power, little Bronya. You just didn't know it." He touched my cheek again, exactly where the scar was on his own face. "So smooth. Maybe not for long."

"Let me go!"

"I don't think so. I think you owe me a little more than one pound of flesh. And I intend to collect however I see fit. You will be under my control until you die." His smile was pure evil. "Which probably won't be too long. I do have other, more important things to do besides toy with you."

The shaking in my hands was starting to cause tremors through my whole body. I prayed Nikolai wouldn't try to apply the regimen on me right now because there was no way I'd be able to go back to being fake robotic.

He laughed. "You're scared. I like that. First fear, then pain, then death. That's what you have to look forward to, Bronya."

I forced my chin up, the way the old Bronya would've done. Hopefully, some of that feisty girl still existed inside me. "Because I made your face hideous?"

I heard the intake of breaths of the men around us. They hadn't known.

His backhand knocked me to the floor. He grabbed me

by my hair and yanked me back up to my feet. "Trying to get me to kill you quickly, Bronya? It won't work."

No, I didn't want him to kill me, but I did want him off-balance enough to keep talking.

"How did I get here?" I brought my tied hands to my stinging cheek, glancing around at his men who were watching the show unfold in front of them. "How did you do this?"

"It was in the works before you left. Before Father died. Mosaic was expanding and needed leadership and manpower in Europe. I had funding for their brain experiments. You allowed me to kill two birds with one stone."

"I don't understand."

"I provided them with subjects for Tippens to experiment on. Including you—although we had special parameters for you. In return, I now have three dozen mindless clones willing to do anything I say. For example, I used one in Hamburg recently."

"That was you?"

"Yes. The perfect vessel for terrorism. All young women, trained and willing to kill without blinking. None of them are on any law enforcement watch list. You all look so young and innocent. Lovely and guileless. Women who can walk into places most people can't." He trailed a finger down my cheek once more. "Of course, you won't be able to do that much longer. Your features will be too distinctive."

I knew that meant I'd have my own scars. I let out a whimper. His men snickered.

"The best part is, I can send you out, and you'll still come back to me. Every single time, you'll come back to the feet of Nikolai, no matter what I do to you."

"No."

"Oh yes. I have to admit, I thought Erick had lost you.

It was part of the reason I didn't show up to help him a few days ago like I was supposed to. Then I had him killed so he couldn't talk. I can't have the police figuring out I'm the head of Mosaic in Europe."

I couldn't do this. I needed to get out of here. The walls were closing in on me. Nikolai and his men filled up my vision.

"Let me go."

"I'll never let you go, little Bronya, my feisty one. My face will be the last thing you see before you die."

Chapter 39

Sarge

Listening to what was happening to Bronwyn was throwing me back into my own personal hell. Granted, this time, I knew where she was, but she still felt too far out of reach.

Nikolai taunted her with the fact that he could have her perform sexual favors with his men then still come crawling back to him.

"She's not going to make it much longer," I muttered to Wilson.

He shook his head. "She's terrified, but that works in her favor right now."

I didn't want her terrified. And I especially didn't want her anywhere near Nikolai Novotný and all his nefarious intents toward her.

We were less than a mile from the compound where Bronwyn was with Nikolai, but we might as well be hours away. He could kill her a hundred times over in the five minutes it would take us to infiltrate the building.

And even if he didn't kill her, the other things he could do…

"We need to go in," I said to Mark in a low voice.

He shook his head. "She wanted this chance. Bronwyn knows more than anyone what Nikolai is capable of. But it's worth facing him to help get those other women released. It's worth facing him so the two of you can have a future together."

Mark was right, but I didn't like it. "I would walk through any hell for her if it meant she wasn't hurt or afraid anymore."

"I hear that."

I got the feeling we weren't talking solely about Bronwyn.

"Why isn't she getting the data we need about the other victims?" Wilson asked.

"Stand down, Wilson." I gritted my teeth. "She's doing the best she can."

"Well, her best might cost a lot of people their lives."

I wanted to punch Wilson in the face—again—but he was telling the truth. Bronwyn might not be able to get the info we need.

"Chances are the other women are in that building," I said. "Look at it. It's a fucking compound. I say we move in now and take our chances."

Move in now, and get Bronwyn out.

"No. We wait and see what information she can get."

A cry from Bronwyn drew our attention back to the speaker where her transmissions were broadcast.

"Goddammit, he hit her again." I stood from my seat in the back of the cargo van. "I'm going in there."

Wilson moved in front of the door. "No, you're not. She knew the risks."

"We thought he'd be taking her to his house. Some-place we could get in quickly. This is not what she signed up for. Get out of my way."

"Don't make me draw my weapon."

"Don't make me break your nose again, Wilson."

"You guys, shut the fuck up and listen!"

Wilson and I both turned back toward Outlaw at his words.

"You can hit me all you want, Nikolai. But I still think you're a liar. You don't have an army. You can barely keep me here, forget anyone else."

"She's baiting him," I muttered. It was dangerous. If it backfired…

Acid burned in my gut when Bronwyn cried out again. I couldn't see what was happening, but I knew it wasn't good. "I'm going to enjoy scarring you the way you scarred me."

I'd heard enough. "Get out of my way. I'm going in, with or without you." I wasn't going to sit here and listen as Bronwyn suffered.

"There." Nikolai's voice came through the speaker. "All of my little slaves, just like you."

"Are those walls…dirt?"

I locked eyes with Mark. If the walls where the other women were being held were dirt, then they weren't in that building with Bronwyn.

"For now. Soon, this building will be ready to house them. Look closer. You know where that is."

A long moment of silence passed before Bronwyn spoke. "Your father's secret wine cellar. Where I hid from you when he died."

"And I found you there, didn't I?"

Bile rose in my gut. I didn't have to guess what had happened in that cellar after Nikolai found her.

I'd never wanted to kill anyone as much as I did this bastard.

Come on, Pony Girl. Get us the info we need so we can get you out of there.

"I can't believe you're keeping that many women hidden in that wine cellar in Havlíčkovy sady. Under the fountain."

She'd done it. She'd gotten the information.

Wilson was immediately on the phone, calling in support. We had the location of the missing women.

Nikolai chuckled over the transmission. "Every time I walk in that park, I think of our time together."

Bronwyn, wisely, didn't respond.

"She did it! Let's go." Wilson was already climbing toward the driver's side. "We've got to move now. Once Nikolai knows we're on to him, he'll have the women moved or killed. We're the closest ones. We can't call Prague police because at least some of them will be on Nikolai's payroll."

"No." I wasn't leaving Bronwyn.

"McEwan, we have to. We'll get the women out then immediately come back for Bronwyn. She's doing okay. She only needs to survive another hour."

That was a fucking eternity.

"No. I'm not leaving her." Not again. Not ever again. This would not be one more time I would look back on and think I shouldn't have left her. "You guys go. I'll get Bronwyn out."

Wilson scrubbed a hand down his face, for once looking sincere. "We don't have the manpower to support infiltration in both places. We have to go with what will

330

benefit the most people. I swear on my life we will immediately come back for Bronwyn."

His life didn't mean anything to me. Only hers. "Take your team and get the women out. I'm going after Bronwyn now."

"You'll die," Wilson said. "Like you keep telling me, we're all on the same side. I don't want to lose someone on my team."

"He's right, Sarge." Mark put his hand on my shoulder. "You won't make it alone."

I didn't care. "I'm not leaving her. If I die, it will be getting her out."

Mark turned to Wilson. "You and your team get to the wine cellar. Sarge will make sure Bronwyn gets out, and I'll make sure he's still alive when he does."

Timing was going to be key to our survival. Nikolai may be a sadistic bastard, but he wasn't an idiot. Once he got word the hidden wine cellar was under attack so soon after sharing the data with Bronwyn, he was going to put two and two together quickly.

And put a bullet in her brain.

I had to be in place before that happened.

Our two-man infiltration team wasn't pretty. There was no finesse whatsoever as we burst through a back door and began moving way too quickly down the main hallway.

"This is going to get us killed," Mark said as we dipped our heads around a corner and saw a few guards at the far end.

"I don't know what else to do. I've got to make it to Bronwyn before Nikolai gets word of what's going on. He'll kill her."

"He'll kill her just as fast if he gets word there's someone in the building shooting his men."

Mark was right, and I had no idea what to do. "Fuck. I need two minutes to get to that southeast office."

He nodded. "I can buy you two minutes. Make them count, brother."

Before I could ask his plan, he'd jogged down the hall toward the guards. "Hey, excuse me," he called out. "Is this the building where we meet up for the Vltava River Cruise? I think I might have come to the wrong address."

The man had guts; I had to hand it to him. It wouldn't fool the guards for long but long enough.

I snuck around behind Nikolai's men as Outlaw continued his role as lost tourist. I was almost to the office when I heard gunfire back from his direction. My jaw hardened as I gave up any pretense of stealth and pushed for full speed. I prayed my friend hadn't lost his life to buy me these seconds.

I got to Nikolai's office and kicked the door in. Time slowed as I evaluated the threats. Nikolai. Three other men. Bronwyn standing to the side, still alive. That was the most important thing.

Time snapped back into place. I didn't hesitate, rushing forward to knock the gun out of the hands of the first man while he was in the process of drawing it. A spinning kick sent another man's gun skidding across the floor. With two steps, I was at Nikolai, knocking his weapon before he could fully aim it.

But I wasn't going to get to the fourth guy in time. I blocked the punch Nikolai threw and waited for a directive to freeze or maybe a bullet straight in the back.

It didn't come.

I spun, kicking out at one of the first two thugs, and saw

that Bronwyn had taken care of the last man's gun. Her hands were still restrained in front of her, but she was holding her own. I gave her a grin and continued my spin to fight the three I was in charge of. She would take care of the one on my six.

But we were only a few more seconds in when Nikolai stepped back and spoke up. "Bronwyn, protocol activated immediately. Say your words."

I blocked another punch, expecting to hear Bronwyn tell Nikolai to go to hell.

"I exist only to obey orders. My final mission is to go home."

My heart sank at her words. I spun to see what was going on and caught a punch in the jaw for my lack of focus.

Bronwyn was still, no longer fighting, her gaze staring out blankly ahead of her.

She was gone. The robot was back in her place. And Nikolai had a gun in his hand once again. I stopped fighting.

Nikolai walked toward me. "You. The American. I remember you from years ago. I remember having my men beat you to the ground to see if I could get a reaction from Bronya."

His hand holding the gun slammed into my midsection. I doubled over, air disappearing and pain exploding through my gut. "If she had begged me not to hurt you, I would've killed you right there. But she didn't seem to care, so I let you live. My mistake."

My eyes were on Bronwyn as I righted myself. She was still staring sightlessly in front of her. The chances of me being able to take the gun from Nikolai, fight off three of his men, then get her out of here if she was resisting were zero to snowball's chance in hell.

I had no idea what I was going to do. Nikolai still had that gun pointed at me and…

Wait.

Had Bronwyn moved the slightest bit closer to Nikolai?

That might not mean anything, but…

She did it again. While he was continuing his monologue about how he never should've let me live the first time and would rectify that mistake.

I looked at Bronwyn's hands clasped in front of her.

They were shaking.

She definitely wasn't under the influence of the regimen like Nikolai thought. She was biding her time.

The best way I could help her get a chance to make a move was to draw attention away from her.

"Has anyone ever told you that you talk too much?" I shook my head at Nikolai. "I meant to say that to you the first day I met you."

That got me a punch in the face from one of his men. I turned to that guy. "Come on, you've got to be thinking it too. Nikolai likes to hear himself talk."

Bronwyn moved another half step closer to Nikolai. She was making her way. I hoped he didn't shoot me first. I was counting on the fact that he would consider a bullet too quick of a death for me.

And God, I hoped Wilson and his team had gotten those women out of that wine cellar or this was all for naught.

"You think I talk too much?"

Nikolai—nothing if not predictable—nodded to his men. Fists flew at me from all directions. I didn't use a tenth of my close-quarter combat skills to stop them. I let them beat me until I was lying on the ground. I'd have a couple cracked ribs and wouldn't be able to see out of one swollen eye in a few minutes, but hopefully it would be worth it.

Nikolai called off his guys. "Seems like my men are always beating you to the ground."

She was almost in position to make her move. She needed a little more time.

I started to laugh.

Nikolai didn't like that at all. "What's so funny? Do you think I'm not going to kill you?" He pointed the gun directly down at me.

"No, I'm sure you plan on it." I shifted my weight, the groan escaping me not fake but definitely meant to make them think I wasn't going to be getting up any time soon.

"Then what is funny?"

I shook my head and continued to chuckle. "Zodiac Tactical made the same mistake you did. We thought that Bronwyn's strength was in her nimble fingers, her ability to steal and pickpocket, to blend. We all missed the obvious."

His eyes narrowed. "And what's that?"

"Her greatest strength is her mind. She's smarter than all of us."

"I'll remember that when she begs for her life and I kill her anyway. I'll remember that she's smarter than me as she falls to the ground. She's mine."

Bronwyn moved faster than I'd ever seen her, even at the top of her game. She chopped Nikolai in the wrist, grabbing the gun from his now-numb fingers. She shot all three of his men before they could get their weapons from the floor.

I'd planned on jumping up to help her, but she hadn't needed my help at all.

"I will never be yours," she spat the words in Nikolai's face then sent him reeling with a sharp punch.

She rushed over to me. "Are you okay? I'm sorry. I was

pretending to be under the regimen, but I wasn't sure if you understood. I needed to—"

I kissed her with lips that were already swollen. "I know, Pony Girl. Once again, you were doing what you had to do to survive. This time, for both of us to survive."

"How?" Nikolai whined, wiping blood from his nose where she'd hit him. "How did you break the regimen?"

Bronwyn didn't look at him as she helped me to my feet. "Because I'm not alone anymore. Because unlike those other women you targeted—unlike the person I was before—I have a team, a family who made sure my mind was clear and my back was covered before coming here. You will never have any control over me again."

Nikolai's face turned nearly purple with rage. He reached down and pulled a knife from his boot and rushed toward us.

His intent was clear. I reached to push her behind my body, but she pulled away. She brought up the gun with both bound hands and shot Nikolai three times in the chest. He fell dead to the floor.

Her hands weren't shaking the slightest little bit.

Chapter 40

Sarge
   Six Months Later

W hen I woke up, Bronwyn wasn't in bed with me.
      It wasn't unusual that she'd woken up early.
Sleeping was still a tricky thing for her. Even with Mosaic
completely gone—Erick and Nikolai dead and the other
two leaders having fallen not long after—it didn't change
what they had done to her.

Twenty-two women had been rescued that day in
Prague. Wilson may have been an asshole, but he'd gotten
them out and taken a bullet while doing it. Many of those
women were way worse off than Bronwyn, but they were
at least all alive and receiving medical help.

Outlaw had been shot, too, once his lost tourist act had
failed. But he'd survived and had taken four men down
with him as he'd bought me the time I'd needed to get to
Bronwyn.

He was now in Wyoming working with the Linear

Tactical guys on a special project centering around Jenna and her past.

Bronwyn was still healing. For the most part, her hands still shook. We were both coming to accept that might permanently be a part of who she was. Even though she'd done an admirable job of stitching her pieces back together, that didn't mean she hadn't been broken.

Her broken pieces were the most beautiful part of my life, and I would treasure each and every one for the rest of my days.

I knew where she was, so I didn't hurry as I rolled out of bed. Although I was surprised that she had gotten away from me without my waking up at all. We still slept like a couple of octopi, entwined as much as two people could be.

We both slept better for it.

I got dressed and padded into the kitchen. The coffee had already been made, so I poured two more mugs and made my way outside.

We'd moved a few months ago about an hour outside of Denver. I'd given up my house with the view of the Front Range—Landon was currently renting it. After he'd gotten out of the hospital, stairs had been a bit much for his body to handle. He'd needed a place all on one level.

I'd needed a place with more land.

The house Bronwyn and I had moved in to didn't have a fabulous view of the Rockies, but it had a few acres. I knew that was where Bronwyn would be now, out in the fenced-in area.

Watching Mac and Cheese.

Once life had settled down after we'd returned from Prague, she'd asked if she could go visit the alpaca and alpaca-at-heart sheep back at Resting Warrior.

It had been Lucas's idea that we find a way to bring the

animals back to Colorado. They weren't trained as service or emotional support animals, but they were both those things to Bronwyn.

So we'd found a place that had acreage and a small barn. A couple months later, Cheese, the sheep, and Mac, along with two other alpacas she'd named Peanut Butter and Jelly—because why not?—had become part of our family at our new home.

Cheese was currently following Jelly around. Mac and Peanut Butter ignored them both, chewing on grass in the gentle light of the dawn.

"Are the four food groups doing okay out here?" I handed her a mug where she sat perched on the fence rails watching the animals.

"Yeah. Cheese won't leave Jelly alone. Mac couldn't care less."

I smiled. "Is Jelly being aggressive toward Cheese?" We'd been a little concerned that the other two alpacas wouldn't be as tolerant of the sheep as Mac had been.

"Nah. Just annoyed."

"Understandable." I rubbed a hand down her back, and she leaned toward me. "And you? You doing okay? It's a big day."

She blew out a breath. "I'm scared."

"Your tutor doesn't think you'll have any problem at all. She said she'd never seen anyone complete the GED work so quickly."

It took most people six months to a year to pass their high school equivalency exam. Bronwyn had aced it in a little over six weeks.

Color me not surprised.

The blue eyes—still taking my breath away as much as they had that very first day—pinned me. "Maybe I should wait. Maybe I shouldn't start a program that's both a bachelor's and master's degree combined. Maybe my professors are going to realize I'm a fraud."

I slipped my hand into her hair and pulled her in for a kiss. "Maybe you're going to complete this program with flying colors, get your PhD. And become a literature professor like your mom."

She hadn't been interested in remaining an active Zodiac employee. Although I hated that she thought it was because she couldn't do that sort of work as well anymore, her being out of danger suited me just fine.

"I'm scared," she whispered again.

"It's okay to be scared." I kissed her again then turned back to the animals. "First days of school are scary. But I know you're still going to go, and I know you'll succeed."

"I will succeed," she muttered.

I grinned without looking at her. "Then one day when you teach your own college literature class, I'll take it. And we'll tell our kids how we were the second generation of literature professor and student."

"Our kids?" she whispered.

"Is that okay? Is it okay that I want to marry you and have kids of the human type running around, not just alpaca kids?"

A smile lit up her face. "I want that too. But not today. Today, I have to get ready for school."

"I love you, Pony Girl."

She took my hand, and we turned from the gold of the dawn to walk back inside. The light wouldn't stay gold; it would change as the sun came up.

It was what Robert Frost had been referring to in that poem quoted in *The Outsiders*. The one Ponyboy recited as he and Johnny watched the dawn.

Nothing gold can stay.

We got to the door, and Bronwyn turned to me. "I used

to dream about what my life would be when I grew up. I never once considered it would be this wonderful or with a man I would love as much as I love you. My own personal cranky hero."

She grinned and bolted inside.

"Don't make me late on my first day," she called over her shoulder, laughing.

Oh, she knew I was going to do my damnedest, even if it meant I had to drive her to campus myself so she made it on time. I dashed inside after her, the sound of her laughter everything that had meaning in my life.

Frost had been wrong.

Our gold would stay.

•••

Acknowledgments

Sarge and Bronwyn were unique characters for me. Outside of the vague details mentioned in Code Name: Aries, I wasn't sure exactly where their story would be going when I first started it.

All I knew was their love had to be fierce in order to overcome such hard things. I ended up with a story I adored and two characters I felt were perfect for each other.

And, you know, alpacas and sheep that think they are alpacas.

(PS—idea shamelessly stolen from the real life of author Jennifer Armentrout. Animals around her house/farm are crazy).

And, shameless plug…if you liked the animals, I truly hope you'll check out the new Resting Warrior Ranch series I've developed with Josie Jade. I'm so stinking proud of that series and I think you'll love it! (Grab Book One HERE)

As always, there are many people I need to thank for

their help with writing a book. *Code Name: VIRGO* is no exception.

I huge thanks to my alpha readers, Chasidy Brooks and Denise Hendrickson, for picking through the book before any editing was done to it to provide feedback on the story itself. Your insight and encouragement were a blessing.

To my editing team, Marci Mathers and Lisa at Silently Correcting Your Grammar: thank you for making my words shine. Sorry I'm such a disaster with commas.

A huge thanks to my proofreaders, Maralize Roos, Tesh Elborn, and Susan Greenbank (as well as the afore-mentioned editors and alpha readers who also doubled as proofreaders) for catching those pesky errors that try their darnedest to make it into print.

And to my readers, thank you for continuing this journey with me. The Zodiac Tactical series continues with Landon's story in Code Name: LIBRA later this year. Plus, I'll be heading back to Oak Creek to give you Outlaw and Jenna's story! I can't wait!! <Rubs hand in glee>

Believe in heroes,

Janie

Also by Janie Crouch

ZODIAC TACTICAL RESCUE UNIT

Code Name: ARIES

Code Name: VIRGO

Code Name: LIBRA

Code Name: PISCES

RESTING WARRIOR RANCH (with Josie Jade)

Montana Sanctuary

Montana Danger

Montana Desire

LINEAR TACTICAL SERIES (series complete)

Cyclone

Eagle

Shamrock

Angel

Ghost

Shadow

Echo

Phoenix

Baby

Storm

Redwood

Scout

Blaze

Forever

INSTINCT SERIES (series complete)

Primal Instinct

Critical Instinct

Survival Instinct

THE RISK SERIES (series complete)

Calculated Risk

Security Risk

Constant Risk

Risk Everything

OMEGA SECTOR SERIES (series complete)

Stealth

Covert

Conceal

Secret

OMEGA SECTOR: CRITICAL RESPONSE (series complete)

Special Forces Savior

Fully Committed

Armored Attraction

Man of Action

Overwhelming Force

Battle Tested

OMEGA SECTOR: UNDER SIEGE (series complete)

Daddy Defender

Protector's Instinct

Cease Fire

Major Crimes

Armed Response

In the Lawman's Protection

About the Author

"Passion that leaps right off the page." - Romantic Times Book Reviews

USA Today and Publishers Weekly bestselling author Janie Crouch writes what she loves to read: passionate romantic suspense featuring protective heroes. Her books have won multiple awards, including the Romance Writers of America's coveted Vivian® Award, the National Readers Choice Award, and the Booksellers' Best.

After a lifetime on the East Coast, and a six-year stint in Germany due to her husband's job as support for the U.S. Military, Janie has settled into her dream home in Front Range of the Colorado Rockies.

When she's not listening to the voices in her head—and even when she is—she enjoys engaging in all sorts of crazy adventures (200-mile relay races; Ironman Triathlons, treks to Mt. Everest Base Camp...), traveling, and hanging out with her four kids.

Her favorite quote: "Life is a daring adventure or nothing."
~ Helen Keller.

facebook.com/janiecrouch

amazon.com/author/janiecrouch

instagram.com/janiecrouch

bookbub.com/authors/janie-crouch

Made in the USA
Monee, IL
07 April 2022

94265256R10208